Praise for *Mary Clay's* *DAFFODILS* Mysteries*

(*Divorced And Finally Free Of Deceitful, Insensitive, Licentious Scum)

"Witty and hilarious..."
Midwest Book Review

" ... a crisp pace with plenty of humor ..."
Romantic Times BookClub

"*The Ya Ya Sisterhood* meets *The First Wives Club.*
A cleverly done light mystery that's a rare find ..."
The Examiner (Beaumont, Texas)

"The Turtle Mound Murder is light and
accentuated with the familiar mannerisms
of Southern women. ... A fun book."
Southern Halifax Magazine

"Bike Week Blues is one of the funniest capers
this reviewer has had the privilege of reading."
Harriet Klausner, #1 Reviewer, Amazon.com

"Sometimes we just need something fun to
read. The DAFFODILS Mysteries fit the bill."
The DeLand-Deltona Beacon

Meet the DAFFODILS*
(*Divorced And Finally Free Of Deceitful, Insensitive, Licentious Scum®)

Leigh Stratton, Ruthie Nichols and Penny Sue Parker are sassy, Southern sorority sisters with very unique views ...

On Each Other:

Penny Sue was an exasperating flake, but a person would be hard-pressed to find a better friend.

* * *

Ruthie hasn't been right since she drove off the bridge and cracked her head.

* * *

"Always thinking, that's why Leigh was president of the sorority," Ruthie said matter-of-factly.

"That's why she's always covered in spots," Penny Sue sniggered, pointing at a splotch on my blouse.

On Men:

"Even straight men act like a pack of dogs, sniffing each other and posturing. All that butt slapping and carrying on, it's in their genes, goes back to ancient Greece where they played sports in the nude."

On Psychologists:

Penny Sue threw back her head and laughed. "Of course, dear, he's a therapist. They're all weird. You teach what you need to learn."

On Fashion:

Penny Sue chose a black leather halter top with a Harley Davidson emblem in the center, below the boobs. She wanted to buy leather shorts to match, but Ruthie convinced her otherwise.

"One continuous yeast infection," Ruthie pronounced quietly.

Those four words eclipsed all my arguments about propriety and image.

A DAFFODILS* MYSTERY

*Divorced And Finally Free Of Deceitful,
Insensitive, Licentious Scum®

Murder in the Stacks

Wishing you prosperity & joy —

Mary Clay

DAFFODILS Mysteries
written as
Mary Clay

The Turtle Mound Murder

Bike Week Blues

Murder is the Pits

Murder in the Stacks

New Age Fiction
written by
Linda Tuck-Jenkins aka Mary Clay

Starpeople: The Sirian Redemption

A DAFFODILS* MYSTERY
**Divorced And Finally Free Of Deceitful,
Insensitive, Licentious Scum®*

Murder in the Stacks

Mary Clay

*An **if** Mystery*
An Imprint of Inspirational Fiction
New Smyrna Beach, Florida

Published by IF Mystery, an imprint of Inspirational Fiction
P. O. Box 2509
New Smyrna Beach, FL 32170-2509
www.inspirationalfiction.com

Cover Design: Peri Poloni-Gabriel, Knockout Design, www.knockoutbooks.com
Back cover beach photograph used with the permission of Debbie Ledbetter.

This is a work of fiction. All places, names, characters and incidents are either invented or used fictitiously. The events described are purely imaginary.

Copyright © 2010 Linda Tuck-Jenkins
ISBN: 978-0-9710429-4-0
Library of Congress Control Number: 2010938059

Printed in the United States of America

For Christa Kelsey,
the woman with the beautiful smile.
We miss you.

As usual, I have benefited from the suggestions and advice of many friends and colleagues. Thank you Adele Aletti, Sheila Brust, Cindy Burkett, Erica Davis, Emily & Dale Ellis, Bonnie Gattanella, Beverly Poitier-Henderson, Deborah Jacklitch, Carla Steele and Martha Swanson.

Special thanks to my husband, Chris Jenkins, and my editor, Mimi Hall, for good humor, infinite patience, and editorial expertise.

Chapter 1

"How was your first day at work?" Ruthie set her book aside and smiled hopefully at Penny Sue, who scuffed down the hall of my condo. I followed, careful to keep my distance. Penny Sue was in a foul mood.

"My feet are killing me!" Penny Sue kicked off her red-soled Christian Louboutin pumps and headed to my refrigerator. "Leigh, do you have any Chardonnay?" she asked, butt up, rummaging through the lower compartment. A moment later she was on her knees, stretching to the back of the bottom shelf.

"No, but there's some Sauvignon Blanc in the door."

Penny Sue swiveled with a loud grunt, grasped the edge of the counter, and hauled herself to her feet, cradling the bottle of wine. Without so much as a "thank you," she pulled the cork out of the bottle with her teeth and filled a juice glass she found in the cabinet. She took a long swig. "Not Chardonnay, but okay," she heaved, finishing the wine and pouring another. "This stuff isn't half bad. Have any more?" Penny Sue asked as she held up the empty bottle.

"Are you willing to share it with Ruthie and me?"

She raised her chin regally. "Of course! I was just a little stressed. Please forgive my rudeness."

"There's a case in the utility room."

Penny Sue's eyes sparkled as she brushed past me to the hall. I could almost hear her thoughts, *"A case! Party hearty!"*

I shook my head. As a proper Southern woman raised in Roswell, Georgia, Penny Sue's mother, bless her heart, was no doubt having a conniption as she stared down from Heaven at her only daughter. I could almost hear her snap, "Penny Sue, I taught you better than that! Only heathens drink straight from a bottle! And where is your napkin?"

Things change, and Momma hadn't been around for a long time to keep an eye on her impetuous daughter. Penny Sue's father, Judge Warren Parker, who we affectionately called "Judge Daddy," thought raising children was a woman's job, so he didn't keep close tabs on his daughter after his dear wife passed away. Basically, the Judge only got involved when Penny Sue did something completely outrageous, which had happened far too frequently in recent years. The downhill slide in Penny Sue's behavior accelerated when her hormones started to go haywire at about age 45. Lord knows what would happen when she turned 50, an age that Ruthie Nichols, Penny Sue Parker and I, Leigh Stratton, were approaching fast.

Sorority sisters at the University of Georgia, we drifted apart after graduation, what with the marriages, children, and divorces, but reunited when I canned my slime ball husband who was having an affair with a stripper our daughter's age. That's when I was initiated into the DAFFODILS (Divorced And Finally Free Of Deceitful, Insensitive, Licentious Scum®), and Penny Sue and Ruthie tried to cheer me up with a vacation in New Smyrna Beach. As the Fates (Ruthie's word) would have it, I stumbled over a dead body, which wasn't particularly cheery but did take my mind off my sorrows.

That initial event set a precedent. Since then, I'd moved to New Smyrna Beach and was living in a condo next door to Judge Parker's unit, but every time Ruthie and Penny Sue came to visit, we invariably encountered one or more dead people. Understand, it was never our fault, but unnerving, to say the least.

Back in college, Penny Sue always said we were women cut from the same cloth. Same cloth, ha! It had to be a patchwork quilt! Although most of my sorority sisters were pampered southern belles, my family was a hundred percent middle class. And our looks were just as diverse. Penny Sue was tall, pudgy, with streaked brown hair and decided kewpie doll tendencies in makeup and dress. Expensive, almost haute couture, yet kewpie doll, nonetheless. In college she had an hourglass figure that attracted men like ants to honey, but she had put on a few pounds over the years so the bottom of the hourglass was now larger than the slightly drooping top.

Ruthie hadn't changed a bit. She was shorter than we were, about five six, and disgustingly slim. A typical strawberry blonde, fair and freckled, she favored clothes with tailored, simple lines— the ones that were so minimal they shouted, "mega-bucks!"

On the other hand I was middle-of-the-road. I was tall like Penny Sue, though a little slimmer, and my shoulder-length brown hair was darker than hers by a couple of shades. I bought my clothes on sale at Dillards and Talbots favoring elastic waists and comfort whenever possible. When I did dress up, I opted for tailored suits and dresses that didn't shout anything. Rather, they spoke in a normal voice.

I glanced at Penny Sue as she popped the cork on the bottle of wine. The way she was slugging down wine, you'd think she'd been through a horrible ordeal. I loved working at the library and was very grateful to land a position there after budget cuts eliminated my job at the Marine Conservation Center. The people were nice, and I would be eligible for health insurance and a retirement plan.

One day volunteering at the library and Penny Sue was already complaining. Heck, she'd spent most of the day in training. Thank the Lord I didn't have to train her. Guthrie Fribble, our neighbor and library volunteer, was given that honor. Being spacey most of the time, Guthrie was probably the only person

on the planet who could stand eight straight hours of Penny Sue.
As a newly hired Library Aid assigned to checkout and shelving
books, I caught sight of them several times during the day. Penny
Sue's expression was extreme boredom; Guthrie's was full of
enthusiasm and glee. Glee for sorting books, you wonder? Well,
you have to know him. An old hippie in his fifties, Guthrie's
sunny disposition could have something to do with overindulg-
ing in herbs and pharmaceuticals in his Woodstock days. Even
his name, Guthrie, was a moniker that stuck from his love for
Arlo Guthrie and the movie *Alice's Restaurant*.

Penny Sue's day actually was a big deal, because it was the
longest she'd ever worked in her life. Until recently she'd been a
very wealthy woman, mostly due to the settlement she received
from Sydney, her second husband, who turned out to be bisexual.
Judge Parker took Sydney's aberrant (the Judge's word) sexual
preference as a personal affront and went for the jugular. Poor
Sydney paid dearly for that parting. Sadly, Penny Sue ignored
her father's investment advice about diversification and not putting all of one's eggs in the same basket. Like other wealthy
people, she fell for the Madoff scam, investing and losing most
of her fortune. She was dumb and trusting, just like I was with
my divorce settlement. My ex-husband, Zack, was a partner at
Parker, Hanson and Swindal, the Judge's prestigious Atlanta law
firm. Swindal, the name fit Zack to a tee. I'd be living in a
tent if Judge Daddy hadn't stepped in to help. And Madoff's
name, pronounced made-off, should have been a clue to that
sleazeball's intentions. Maybe there *was* something to karma,
vibrations, and the Law of Attraction as Ruthie, our New Age
expert, claimed.

Back to Penny Sue's plight. Fed up with her three marriages
and numerous escapades, Judge Parker finally had enough. He
refused to help her unless she sold her stately Roswell, Georgia
home that overlooked a lake, and turned over a new leaf. He
offered to let her live in his New Smyrna Beach condo rent-free,

provided she went to work. Getting a job in the middle of a recession presented a problem for a woman whose only skill was throwing parties, and she had contracted most of those out.

Guthrie and I convinced her to volunteer at the library, with the hope it might work into a paying job with benefits one day. At least it would give her something other than marriages, divorces, and parties to put on her resumé. So, Penny Sue was living in the other half of our beachfront duplex and working with me at the library. Whoopee! Don't get me wrong, I love Penny Sue, but her presence invariably means trouble.

"Who wants wine?" Penny Sue called. "It's warm, so you'll have to use some ice."

Ruthie and I signaled that we did. One more glass of wine would, hopefully, give Penny Sue time to process her day, and she'd go home to her side of the duplex where her houseguest, Cousin Kevin, likely waited.

I pulled out real wine glasses that Penny Sue stuffed with ice. Ruthie sauntered to the counter that partitioned the kitchen off from the dining area and great room. "So you had a bad day?" she asked Penny Sue.

Penny Sue filled her glass, took a sip, then poured ours and passed them around. "Remind me never to wear heels to work again."

I rolled my eyes. "Penny Sue, why would you wear $800 pumps to work? Didn't you know you'd be on your feet all day?"

"I wanted to make a good impression. You know Daddy says I have to get a real job."

I shook my head. "This is the beach; people dress casually. The Dior suit with those fancy shoes made you stick out like a peacock in a flock of crows."

"Hey, there were some other well-dressed women in the library."

"That was the New Smyrna Ladies' Investment Club. They meet at the library every week. They're all skinny and dressed to kill, but you outdid them."

"And I was wearing an old outfit." Penny Sue arched a brow and grinned smugly. "Guthrie loved it."

"Of course," I said. "Guthrie's gay. He appreciates quality and probably wished he had your shoes. I think his feet are about your size." I backed up out of her poke range and did my best to keep a straight face.

"Tacky! You are just tacky. Besides, you know Guthrie prefers jeans and tee shirts." Penny Sue tossed her hair that was down to only two colors now that she was pinching pennies. No more $300 multi-color highlight jobs. "He said I really classed up the place."

I glanced down at my black slacks and tailored cotton shirt. Perhaps I should spiff up a little if I wanted a promotion.

"In fact," Penny Sue went on, "a man reading magazines couldn't take his eyes off me."

"The man with curly brown hair and a navy striped shirt?" I asked.

"Yes." Her bottom lip inched forward, a sure sign Penny Sue was peeved by my question. "Why do you ask? Do you know him?"

"He comes to the library all the time. We suspect he's homeless, a pedophile, or a man on the prowl the way he gawks at the investment club ladies. He was probably surprised to see someone dressed better than the other women. Or, he could have been watching Guthrie."

Penny Sue's eyes narrowed and her lips pursed to a full pout. Thankfully Ruthie, our resident peacemaker, interrupted. "Shouldn't we invite Kevin to join us? He worked all day on his debate and is probably ready for a break. I spoke with him earlier and he seemed upset. Maybe his presentation isn't going well."

"Sure, give him a call." I winked at Penny Sue.

Ruthie had been staying with me for the last several months since her elderly father passed away. He left her millions, not counting the mansion in the elite Buckhead section of Atlanta.

Alone and grieving, Ruthie moved in with me. She was massively depressed for weeks but she perked up with the arrival of Kevin Harrington, Penny Sue's first cousin. Kevin was in town for the New Smyrna Beach Founders' Day celebration, which included a scholarly debate at the library on whether New Smyrna Beach or St. Augustine was the oldest city in North America. In sharp contrast to his rambunctious cousin, Kevin was a soft-spoken, serious historian on sabbatical from Columbia University. He was also exactly the right person to draw Ruthie out of mourning. Penny Sue and I were thrilled to see Ruthie smile after his arrival, a first since her father's death. She'd even begun venturing out of the condo alone.

"They'd be a perfect—" Penny Sue stopped suddenly as Ruthie returned with a wide grin.

"He'll be over directly. Guthrie's with him."

"No-o," Penny Sue moaned as she thunked her forehead on the kitchen cabinet. "How did he get into this? Eight hours of Guthrie is all I can take."

"There was something about a female acquaintance from Kevin's days at Yale—" Ruthie started but didn't have time to finish. Guthrie came barreling down the hall with Kevin trailing behind.

"Man, do we need a drink. Glad you called so we could get rid of her. That lady was a real bitch! Snappy doesn't begin to describe her. Maybe it's because she's quitting smoking; I saw one of those patches on her shoulder. Whatever it was, she makes my crazy Aunt Harriet look good." Guthrie hopped on a stool in his usual place at the corner of the L- shaped counter. "Got a scotch?"

"Sure. What can I get you?" I asked Kevin.

"Man, he probably wants a gun," Guthrie said. "Hide the weapons and ammunition."

Kevin answered quietly, "Wine would be fine."

As I fixed the drinks and pulled out some cheese and crackers, Penny Sue went for the details. "What woman? What's going on?"

"Her name's Abby and she's, like, a witch—"

Ruthie turned on Guthrie with uncharacteristic forcefulness. "Hush! Let Kevin tell the story."

Kevin sighed and took a sip of his drink, eyes downcast. "The woman is Dr. Abigail Johnston. She dropped by to inform me that she's representing St. Augustine in the debate tomorrow night at the library."

"I thought you were debating your old friend Dr. Willows, who teaches at Deland University. He's the one who wrote a book about Central Florida," Penny Sue said.

Kevin stared in his glass uncomfortably. "I thought that too. It seems Willows changed his mind and invited Abby to take his place. Willows is going to moderate."

"Why is that a problem?" Ruthie asked.

Kevin took a seat at the counter, eyes still lowered.

"Because the lady's a bitchy witch," Guthrie blurted. "She had this, like, evil smirk when she told Kevin she was taking Willows' place. And she sneered that she looked forward to," Guthrie rolled his eyes, "taking Kevin to task." Guthrie gulped his scotch. "I think she's been stalking us." He turned to Penny Sue. "Remember the lady in the Books For Sale room? The one with blonde hair and a black outfit? That's her! She was in there for hours. Man, like, who would spend hours in a used book room? I'll bet she was watching us. She most likely knew you were Kevin's cousin. I think she's a black widow," Guthrie exclaimed with full drama. "You know, the kind of woman who lures men in, then slits their throats."

Penny Sue scowled at Guthrie. "Your imagination is running wild. But, I do remember her. She was wearing a good looking pants suit that caught my eye."

"Wait." I held up my hands. "She purchased a book from me, a really old book about the history of Florida. In fact, I thought it might be one from the rare books section that accidentally wound up in the sale room. I consulted a reference librarian before I sold it. Turns out it was donated to the library and not part of our collection. Abby only paid five dollars."

"Ha! She probably, like, ripped off the spine label and penciled in a price on the book. I'll bet it's a limited edition, million dollar book, and she got it for five bucks!"

"Guthrie, you're getting ahead of yourself," Kevin objected.

"What's new?" Penny Sue muttered as she stuffed a cracker in her mouth.

"Forget the book. Abby and I used to live together," Kevin said.

Our mouths dropped as one, except Penny Sue, who sputtered her cracker. "Sorry," she mumbled, snatching a sponge and wiping crumbs from the counter. "You lived together? When?"

"In graduate school at Yale. That's how Willows, Abby, and I know each other. We were all working on our Ph.D.'s at the same time. Abby and I fell in love, or so I thought, when we were researching Spanish Florida and Ponce de Leon. Shortly after we received our degrees, she up and left, taking our research with her."

"Man, I knew she was a black widow."

Ruthie poked Guthrie's arm. "Shh, let Kevin finish."

"Wait a minute." Penny Sue stared at Ruthie. "And don't poke me! He's my cousin and I'm allowed to ask a question." Then to Kevin, "She stole your research? Why didn't you sue or something? Your mother would faint if she knew you took that lying down."

Kevin shrugged. "Mom knew and wanted me to sue. But I was young and truly loved Abby. At first I was in shock and deep depression. By the time I snapped out of it, she'd published her Register Award-winning history of St. Augustine, which incorporated much of our work. If I had said anything then, it would have looked like sour grapes and possibly damaged my career."

"She stole it from you!" Ruthie said.

"Yes, but proving it would be hard. We did the research together. It was a joint effort. Separating out who did what would be close to impossible, so I decided to let it slide."

Guthrie drained his glass and plunked it down on the counter. "Good for you, man. Like Hugh Prather says, 'Peace of mind is more important than diarrhea.'"

Penny Sue gave Guthrie a sour look. "I've had a tiresome day. Can we please stay away from bowel movements? My head is full of library and Dewey decimals; I can't take New Age philosophy right now."

"Did Willows know the details of your split with Abby?" I asked. For Dr. Willows to spring something like this on Kevin at the last minute seemed awfully convenient, or rather inconvenient, to me. In fact, it was downright hateful. I thought he and Willows were friends, yet this was not the way a man would treat his buddy.

"Yes, Willows knew. The three of us socialized quite a bit." Kevin raked his fingers through his thick salt and pepper hair. "In fact, I've often wondered if Willows had something to do with Abby walking out on me. I suspected Willows had a crush on Abby, considering the way he seemed to show up wherever we went."

"Jealousy. Maybe he's harbored a grudge about your relationship with Abby all of these years and is trying to get even," Ruthie said.

Kevin went back to studying his wine with a hangdog look. "Or discredit me because I interviewed for the Chairmanship of Deland University's History Department. I'm sure Willows is my major competitor for the position, and there's no one who knows my findings on New Smyrna's history better than Abby. If Willows wanted to make me look like a fool, Abby's the best person to enlist."

"That's why she came over here acting so high and mighty," Guthrie said. "She's in cahoots with Willows and trying to psyche you out!"

Kevin stared at Guthrie for several beats. "You might be right."

Chapter 2

An extensive schedule of Founders' Day Celebrations preceded
the library debate over which city was discovered first, New
Smyrna or St. Augustine. The historical consensus said St. Augustine was first, founded by the Spanish in 1565. New Smyrna's
founding was attributed to a Brit—actually a Scotsman—Dr.
Andrew Turnbull, in 1768.

Leading the single largest attempt by the British to establish
a colony in the New World, Turnbull recruited some fifteen hundred indentured servants from the Mediterranean isle of Minorca
to make the voyage to Florida. Unfortunately, Turnbull and his
thug overseers were mean, rotten managers. That, plus Indian
attacks and a food shortage, eventually led the workers to revolt
and march seventy miles north to St. Augustine, where they
sought refuge.

Although the national flag that flew over St. Augustine
changed from Spanish to British, to Spanish, to the United States,
to the Confederacy, and finally back to the United States, the
true paradox of the whole mess was that the descendants of the
Minorcans, a large portion of Turnbull's New Smyrna colony,
made up the venerable families of St. Augustine today. There-
fore, as television and newspaper reporters often pointed out,
in a sense, New Smyrna was the backbone of present day
St. Augustine. Naturally, that notion fueled the competition

and newspapers in both cities were flooded with editorials criticizing the scholars and the debate. Dissension even erupted between the Minorcans and other factions within St. Augustine.

The debate was a good idea gone bad. A genteel, scholarly discourse had the potential of turning into a slugfest. The police and press established a presence in the library's parking lot hours before the event was scheduled to begin. Word of the satellite trucks and cameras spread like wildfire, meaning additional people from all camps suddenly decided to attend with the hopes of getting on TV.

I worked at the library that day, but planned to take off early in order to change clothes for the event. Like many modern libraries, the building was a sprawling, one story structure. The main entrance faced the parking lot and was comprised of automatic, sliding glass doors that opened onto a foyer and hallway leading to the auditorium and lavatories. The library proper was behind another set of glass doors that could be locked and were flanked by metal detectors. The layout was designed to allow meetings in the auditorium after regular library hours. Considering the crowd massing in the parking lot, it was a good thing the library could be locked down, at least providing the participants a quiet place to wait for the big show. The plan was to bring Kevin and the others into the main library through a side door hidden by a high plastic fence. The fence enclosed a picnic table used by the staff for breaks and lunches on pleasant days.

As the day wore on and the parking lot continued to fill, the Branch Librarian, Terry, told me to go home before lunch. When I showed up at the condo about noon, my news about the TV satellite trucks sent Penny Sue and Ruthie into a clothes frenzy. Actually, I was in a slight panic myself. The drab cotton slacks and tailored blouse were no longer appropriate. We decided not to say anything to Kevin or Guthrie about all of the hoopla, figuring Kevin might get nervous and Guthrie would surely tell Kevin.

We drove two cars to the library. Penny Sue and Kevin went in Ruthie's Jaguar while Guthrie rode with me. We parked in a gymnasium parking lot next door, at the direction of police, and Ruthie and I spirited Kevin to the side door of the library where I punched in the security code.

Guthrie and Penny Sue went in the front door, since they were scheduled to staff the library's entrance, passing out programs and directing guests to the auditorium that had been expanded to its full capacity. The anticipated crowd of scholars and government officials did turn out, especially groups from St. Augustine. The mere suggestion that New Smyrna was founded before St. Augustine caused blood pressures to soar and fingernails to curve into claws. Big bucks were at stake since an entire tourist industry was built on the premise that St. Augustine was the Ancient City.

Not to be outdone, the New Smyrna Chamber of Commerce, Ladies' Investment Club, and Association of Realtors organized a sizeable contingency of their own. This was economic war, and New Smyrna was not going to be outdone by a bunch of over-advertised promoters and a city with half its population, who barely counted as Floridians given their close proximity to the Georgia state line! Substantial bets had been placed on the outcome of the debate fueled by all the news coverage, giving the affair the feel of a horse race.

Everyone was dressed in their finest for the benefit of local TV. Penny Sue wore a three-year-old (unbelievable by her previous standards) jersey Chanel dress with a front slit up to her hoo-ha. The outfit would have been obscene except that she had the good sense to wear opaque tights. That was the extent of the Derby ambiance at the front door. Guthrie was dressed in his usual evening attire—an ancient madras shirt, wrinkled khaki slacks, and a skinny striped tie that may have served as a bungee cord from time to time. Penny Sue could barely contain her disdain for his outfit, giving him disgusted looks between her Southern sugary greetings.

In truth, Guthrie's outfit didn't really matter, since few guests even noticed it. To a person, they snatched a program, immediately flipped to Kevin's and Abigail's biographies, and studied their credentials like a racing form. Many additional bets were placed before attendees reached the auditorium.

Inside the library proper, Ruthie and I were also dressed in our best. Ruthie wore a classic Dolce & Gabbana square-necked shift with a pale pink shawl. My finest was a black pants suit I'd purchased at Talbots for half price. Ruthie tagged along to give Kevin moral support. We made small talk for several minutes, wondering if Willows and Abby were going to show up, when Guthrie banged on the glass doors that separated the main library from the packed foyer. Willows, Abby, and a tall, distinguished gray-haired man were squeezing through the horde behind Guthrie. The tall gentleman had his arm firmly around Abby's back and shoulder as he cleared a path; otherwise, the petite lady would have been crushed. I raced to the glass doors and punched the button to open them. Willows and Abby slid through.

"What a mob!" Abby said breathlessly as she smoothed her sleeveless silk sheath.

"It sure is." Willows was grinning from ear to ear.

"Didn't you get the message about entering through the side door?" I asked.

"Yes, but I ran into my old friend Peter O'Brien in the parking lot, so we accompanied him to the front door," Willows replied. "I wasn't expecting such a big crowd."

"Well, no harm done." I led them to a table next to the children's department that had been set up for their use before the debate. Each scholar lugged a laptop as well as assorted books and notes that they gladly dumped on the table. They took seats in upholstered chairs that had a good view of the front door. Willows stretched out lazily with a satisfied grin, watching the incoming crowd. Kevin had already powered up his computer and was reviewing his notes. Abby frantically dug in her purse and finally came up with a small leather-clad flask. She smiled.

"My throat is parched," she said hoarsely. "I could use a nip to settle my nerves. Is there a water fountain with cups around here?"

"There's one around the corner," I replied, hooking my thumb toward the children's area.

"I'll get you a cup," Kevin said with a chuckle. "I see you still need a little Jack Black courage before a performance."

Abby smiled wryly as she half-filled the small paper cup Kevin retrieved. She chugged the liquor. "Thank you. Would you like some?" She tipped the flask toward us. Everyone declined. "Come on, Kevin. You don't want a sip for old times sake?" Abby cooed.

He cleared his throat uncomfortably. "I've gone beyond those days." He reached in his pocket and pulled out a small container of breath strips. "Maybe you should take one of these, Abby. That stuff reeks to high heaven."

She ran her fingertips down his forearm before sliding two strips from the container. "God, Kevin, you've really stiffened up with age."

"No, I grew up," he countered, and stuffed the small plastic container in his pocket.

Ruthie was clearly not happy with Abby's flirtation. Normally filled with peace and love, Ruthie's lips drew tighter and tighter until they all but disappeared. Uh oh, a fight was in the making. The liquor sure hit Abby fast! Or maybe she'd had a drink earlier, I thought. Whatever the reason, Abby's antics had certainly rubbed Ruthie the wrong way. I needed to do something to diffuse the situation. "How rude of me," I blurted. "Can I get the rest of you something to drink before the debate starts? We have sodas and bottled water." Willows wanted a Coke while Kevin asked for bottled water and directions to the men's room.

I sent Kevin to the children's department bathroom so he could avoid the crowd in the hall. "I could use a soda myself. Ruthie, would you help me carry the drinks?" I asked, anxious to put some distance between the two women.

"Sure," Ruthie snapped, giving Abby a stern look.

We weren't gone very long but when we returned, Kevin was standing alone perusing the new books display.

"What happened to your colleagues?" I asked.

He nodded in the direction of the stacks to his left. "Seems they've found something interesting over there."

Willows and Abby were literally nose-to-nose in deep discussion. In fact, their noses would have touched if not for the books Abby clasped tightly to her chest. She was clearly telling Willows something he didn't want to hear. A moment later, she turned on her heel and started to walk away. Willows, one hand in his pocket until then, reached out, grabbed her upper arm and swung her around to face him. It was then that he noticed us watching them. He flashed a weak grin, said something to Abby, perhaps an apology, and strode towards us. I glanced at the table and realized Abby had left her computer behind, but was carrying all of her books. Strange. Was she afraid one of us would steal them? Abby started after Willows but she caught her toe on the carpet and dropped several books. Willows kept walking and didn't look back. Abby gathered her literary cargo, then rushed to catch up.

"Coke, just what I need," Willows said, pointedly avoiding my eyes and focusing on the horde milling in the foyer. "We have quite a crowd," he said with a wide grin. "It's not often that historians draw such an audience."

"It's not often that so much money rides on historical facts," I retorted.

Kevin's face twisted with confusion. "What do you mean, Leigh?"

"If you're right about New Smyrna pre-dating St. Augustine, a lot of tourist money is at stake."

"You're saying this quaint town could turn into a hectic tourist haven?" Kevin asked.

Willows chuckled. "Of course. What did you think this was about?"

"History!" Kevin said.

At that moment Terry stuck her head through the back door of the auditorium. "Show time! The place is packed, standing room only."

Kevin picked up his paraphernalia and clutched it tightly. He wore the expression of a man who suddenly realized he had no idea what he'd gotten into.

Predictably, the debate was heated. Abby claimed Ponce de Leon landed in St. Augustine in 1513, pointedly referring to her research with Kevin at Yale. Kevin did his best to maintain scholarly decorum over hoots and murmurs from the St. Augustine contingent. He questioned the generally accepted idea that New Smyrna's famous ruins called the Sugar Mill had been used for industrial purposes. Why did the structure have the design of a Spanish mission, and how to explain the religious artifacts found nearby? Kevin also pointed out that noted archeologists speculated the mission was constructed on Columbus' second voyage.

There was also the mystery of New Smyrna's Old Fort, covered by a mound of debris for most of its history. A restoration during the Depression unearthed the date 1513 carved on one of its massive coquina blocks. Who built it? Certainly not Ponce de Leon, even though the date coincided with his voyage. By all accounts, he didn't stay anywhere long enough to build such a substantial structure. Considering the style of its construction, Europeans had been in New Smyrna long before Ponce arrived. Who could it be? Columbus was a possibility, but the most likely explanation was Castilian slave traders who'd sailed northward from the Caribbean islands.

"That's a bunch of hooey!" A shout came from a bald man wearing a shirt embroidered with the logo of a St. Augustine real estate firm.

Kevin wiped his brow. "Actually, slave traders regularly raided the Bahamas as early as 1494. Considering the size of the islands, the native population could not have been very large. It's likely that able-bodied workers were quickly captured, forcing slave traders to sail north."

"Yeah? Prove it!" the realtor yelled back.

"Las Casas' *History* tells us that slave traders sailed northward from today's Dominican Republic in early 1511," Kevin responded. "New Smyrna could certainly have been their landfall, and that was probably not their only journey. It's possible traders first arrived much earlier and constructed the fort to store provisions and imprison the unwitting natives they captured. It doesn't take much imagination to see that the cubicles of what remains of the fort could have been holding cells. And, when one considers that newly quarried coquina must harden for one to three years before it can be used in construction, that puts landfall in 1511 or earlier."

"Screw you and Las Casas!" The bald realtor flashed a rude hand gesture and the TV cameras turned in his direction. "That document could have been forged!" Peter O'Brien, the distinguished man who'd ushered Abby through the crowd, grabbed Baldy's arm and ushered him to the side of the room. Peter was obviously delivering a stern reprimand, but Baldy kept his mouth shut.

The cameras swung back to the panel as Kevin delivered his most damaging evidence to rebut Abby's St. Augustine thesis— the fact that her various reconstructions of Ponce's voyage and landfall in St. Augustine did not account for Gulf Stream currents and recent discoveries about shifts in the magnetic North

Pole. When that information was factored into readings from Ponce's voyage logs, it put old Ponce's actual stops in the area between Ormond Beach and New Smyrna.

Abby viciously attacked the credentials of every study and academic Kevin quoted. At times she was so agitated, Abby slurred her words and mopped perspiration from her face. Willows did his best to provoke the controversy by lobbing sarcastic zingers, most of them aimed at Kevin, while mugging for the TV cameras. As the debate waged on, the audience's hoots, boos, and shouted questions ramped up.

Unable to contain himself any longer, the bald realtor took a swing at O'Brien who'd tried to restrain him earlier and decked a New Smyrna commissioner in the process. That's when the Branch Librarian, who'd stationed herself by the door to the main library, sensed danger and called the Sheriff's Department on her cell phone. Two burly male officers and a tall female I recognized as Deputy Heather Brooks appeared within minutes.

They didn't arrive a moment too soon. An older woman with tight, pink curls had just swung her purse and whacked a young lady sporting a large *New Smyrna Beach First!* button upside the head. *New Smyrna First!* retaliated with a roundhouse blow from her oversized handbag that knocked the old lady on her keester. The old lady's nose-pierced daughter lunged at her mother's assailant, grabbing *New Smyrna First!* by the hair and slinging her into an elderly group in the next row. An aristocratic woman was floored.

The cameras rotated for a closeup.

"Grab patience and might!" Mrs. Aristocrat shouted as her husband helped her up.

"Grab my ass! Might this!" Nose-Ring screeched, and snatched Aristocrat by her perfectly styled hair. The perfect style came off in Nose-Ring's hand. Flabbergasted, Nose-Ring flung the wig over her shoulder as if it were a dead rat. The hairpiece came flying back, skimmed the top of Nose-Ring's head and landed in Mr. Aristocrat's chair. The TV cameras focused in on a closeup as Mrs. Aristocrat dropped to her knees, hastily trying to reposition the wig. Then Mr. Aristocrat completely lost it and smacked Nose-Ring in the gut with his cane. Yet the crowning blow, literally, came when someone lobbed an open water bottle that hit Kevin squarely in the face. The plastic bottle splashed on a cameraman who shielded his recorder and made a hasty retreat.

That's when the deputies rushed in to separate the troublemakers. Terry, the Branch Librarian, was fortunately very nimble. She dodged a soda can, announced that the debate was over, and thanked everyone for their enthusiastic participation. She then ducked and ran out the back door.

Penny Sue, eyes blazing with her kung fu don't-mess-with-me expression, raced to the panel and ushered Kevin out of the auditorium. Hunched low in case there were other projectiles, Ruthie and I herded Abby and Willows out of the room, with Guthrie close on our heels.

"Kevin, are you all right?" Guthrie asked. "Man, those people are vicious! They should be, like, shot or put in jail!"

"You're going to have a big bruise," Penny Sue said, ignoring Guthrie and stroking Kevin's forehead tenderly.

"I'm so sorry," Terry said. "I never expected a historical debate to inspire such rage."

"Money," I replied. "There's big money at stake with tourism and real estate values."

"Yes, but this is a library!"

"Money trumps everything," I said, turning my attention to Willows and Abby. Willows didn't appear to be overly troubled by the brawl except for the fact that his comb-over hairdo was askew, but Abby was sweating like a whore in church.

"That bottle may have been intended for you," Ruthie told Abby. "You're lucky you didn't get popped in the face, the way

Willows was stirring up the crowd. After all, most of the audience was probably from New Smyrna."

Abby regarded Willows suspiciously and stepped aside.

"I didn't do anything wrong," Willows retorted with a palms
up. "I was merely trying to spur the debate."

"You certainly did that," Penny Sue said. "You incited a riot."
She stepped within inches of his face. Given her height in three-
inch heels, she looked down her nose at his thinning hair.
"Do you have investments in St. Augustine or something? Your
moderating sure didn't seem impartial to me." Willows backed
up. Penny Sue's kung fu mode was very intimidating.

"I'm horrified you'd suggest such a thing," Willows objected.
"I was absolutely impartial. I had nothing to do with that mêlée."

"Yeah, right," Penny Sue said, eyes narrowed.

Abby, looking flushed, asked directions to a bathroom.

"Here, I'll take you." Terry grasped Abby's elbow. They
headed to the children's department since attendees were still
being ushered out of the building under Deputy Heather's watch-
ful eye.

Terry returned shortly. "I believe Abby is more upset than
she let on. She was rubbing her chest and breathing heavily
when she went into the bathroom. I suspect she's having an anxiety
attack and needs some alone time to collect herself."

Collect herself or sneak a swig of Jack Black? I thought.

Terry turned to Penny Sue, Guthrie, and me. "I anticipated
the debate would go late, so I gave the cleaning crew the night
off. I sure didn't expect the audience to start throwing things!
There's a needlepoint meeting scheduled first thing tomorrow
morning. Could you meet me here at eight-thirty to pick up the
trash? I hate to impose, but don't want to call the regular staff
this late at night. I don't know about you, but I'm too tired to
deal with it now."

"Of course, we'd be happy to help," Penny Sue answered in
the gushy drawl she usually reserved for wealthy men.

"Thanks, I really appreciate it. I have to close up the back office now. When the audience clears, you're all free to leave. I'll turn off the lights and lock up."

"They can't clear out fast enough for me," Penny Sue said after Terry left. "I need a great big glass of Chardonnay."

Chapter 3

It was unusually cold for Florida and New Smyrna Beach—
mid-40s. Such temperatures were virtually unheard of in October,
a once-in-a-decade occurrence. Guthrie, Penny Sue, and I arrived
at the library simultaneously and parked our vehicles side by
side waiting for Terry to show up. Guthrie was in his Lemon
Aid VW bus that was outfitted to fix old (lemon) computers,
while Penny Sue and I were in my new VW Beetle. Both vehicles' heaters were running full blast since none of us had
wardrobes for such chilly weather.

Guthrie opened his window and motioned at Penny Sue. She
cracked her window enough to hear him.

"How long is this weather going to last?" Guthrie asked.

Penny Sue zipped her sweater to her throat and answered
through the small space at the top of the glass. "Ruthie says
it should pass in a day or two." Ruthie was our news junkie
and Weather Channel expert who put her heartless cardiologist
ex-husband through med school while working as a librarian. I
suppose that's where she developed a passion for information.
Given half a chance, Ruthie would watch cable news shows and
read newspapers all day long. "One must be informed," was one
of her favorite adages. Yet, deep down, I wondered if her obses-
sion with staying on top of everything didn't come from being
blindsided by her cheating husband.

"Bummer!" Guthrie rolled up his window.

Penny Sue hit the window's switch and shut hers, too. "Bummer is right. It never gets this cold in Florida. Our power went off last night. Did yours? I thought I'd freeze my butt off. I almost had a heart attack when I took a shower. The water was frigid!" She pulled down the visor and checked her lipstick. "I didn't bring clothes for this kind of weather. Did you?"

"I thought I was finished with winter, so I gave most of my warm clothes away when I moved down from Atlanta. I have two jackets—the one I have on and one I lent to Ruthie. Sorry."

"Never mind, I'll go shopping later. Your jackets wouldn't fit me, anyway." God's truth. If Penny Sue could get her arm in the sleeve, she surely couldn't button my jacket over her boobs. She'd always been buxom, but her perimenopausal weight gain added a few inches everywhere. Penny Sue flashed a smile at Guthrie, who was blowing on his hands. His old bus' heater was obviously not in tune with the times or temperature. "This being poor is awful!" Penny Sue groused. "I would normally call my housekeeper and have my cashmere coats shipped down. But I don't have a housekeeper anymore and, God willing, won't have a house either. I can't believe Daddy is putting me through this. He said I was muleheaded. Can you believe that? Muleheaded!"

I clamped my lips shut. Tar Baby was not going to say a word. I was not going to mention all of Penny Sue's husbands, messy divorces, excesses, and escapades that pushed Daddy to the brink. Penny Sue's investment and loss to Madoff was merely the icing on the cake. Judge Daddy told her not to do it, and she did it anyway. He was majorly annoyed. Fortunately, Terry pulled up beside us, giving me an excuse to ignore Penny Sue's question. I buttoned my jacket, hooked my pocketbook on my arm, and got out of the car. Penny Sue raced for the front door, beating Terry. Guthrie followed, hopping and flapping his arms like a spastic chicken. I arrived at the moment the doors slid apart and rushed into the foyer. Balancing a donut box in one hand, Terry was already keying in another alarm code and unlocking the glass doors to the library proper. Glorious heat bathed us as the doors opened.

Terry checked her watch. "We don't have much time," she said, putting the box on the counter and shrugging out of her coat. "Let's stage the auditorium for the needlepoint group. Then we'll make a pot of coffee and have a donut."

"Excellent plan," Guthrie replied, eyeing the box.

Whether spurred on by the donuts, a sense of duty, or need to warm up, we all rushed through the children's department to the auditorium. To say the room was a mess was an understatement. The initially neat rows of chairs were in complete disarray, with some overturned, attesting to the quick departure of patrons once the fights broke out and the law arrived. As if that wasn't enough, soda bottles, cans, crumpled programs and candy wrappers were strewn everywhere.

"Man, these people were, like, old-time Woodstock slobs!"

Terry and I stared at Guthrie. Little did he know what we routinely discovered in the book return bin! A few cans and wrappers were nothing in comparison to the baby poop, upchuck, and dead animals that sometimes accompanied book returns, particularly the ones that were long overdue and subject to hefty fines. Guthrie didn't know about that mess, because assigning a volunteer to book return duty invariably meant one less volunteer. Only paid employees with health insurance and retirement benefits at stake would put up with that horror.

"A donut's calling my name," Penny Sue said. "Let's get to work."

The motivational power of donuts is amazing. In less than 30 minutes we'd clamped shut the partition between the two halves of the auditorium, rearranged the chairs, and disposed of the garbage. The peace loving needlepoint club would never know there'd been a brawl the night before, unless they'd been there.

Terry went ahead to start the coffee. We quickstepped to the donuts, congratulating ourselves on our amazing coordination and industriousness. Guthrie reached the box first and opened the lid. His eyes went wide and his lips formed, "wow."

"Well, what's in there?" Penny Sue said. "Any Boston cream puffs?"

Guthrie's eyes went wider still, and he pointed a shaky finger across the open box top.

"Don't point at me. That's rude," Penny Sue admonished and grabbed at the box. He didn't let go. "Quit being selfish," she snapped. "Let me see."

"Bo-bo-bod," Guthrie stammered.

"Look, if there's only one Boston cream, I have dibs on it. I asked first," Penny Sue said.

He shook his tousled hair, still pointing. "Bod-dy," he finally managed.

Penny Sue was the first to follow his finger. "Oh, shit!" she screamed and ran down an aisle toward a pile of books. Guthrie ditched the donuts on the counter, and we followed Penny Sue into the stacks. Penny Sue was tossing books off of a woman's body, a couple of hardbacks almost nailing Guthrie and me.

"Heavens, it's Abby!" Penny Sue screeched. "Call 9-1-1."

Guthrie froze in place and screamed like a girl. I dashed to the checkout counter and snatched the cell phone from my purse. As I called 9-1-1, Penny Sue cleared the books from Abby, stretched her out on the floor, and began administering CPR.

"What in the world?" Terry started, then quickly assessing the situation, hotfooted back to her office. She returned with paddles and a portable heart defibrillator. Terry nudged Penny Sue aside and flipped the switch to the machine. "Clear," she shouted, slapping the flat paddles on Abby's chest. Abby's body arched upward as the current surged. Guthrie swung around and threw up.

Great, another Ruthie, I thought, remembering she had the same reaction to all of the bodies we'd encountered in the past. It wasn't that many, only four or five, but Ruthie threw up almost every time.

"Clear," Terry screeched again, adjusting a dial. Abby's body jumped even higher this time, but she didn't start breathing and her fingertips were blue. "Mouth-to-mouth," Terry screamed, bending forward.

"My technique is better," Penny Sue hollered, shoving Terry aside. Penny Sue began pressing Abby's chest. "1-2-3," she counted. "... 20-21-22," she continued. As Penny Sue pumped furiously, I assured Terry that Penny Sue knew what she was doing. She'd taken terrorist avoidance classes on account of Judge Daddy's constant threats from all of the nefarious characters he'd locked up. Meanwhile, the regular staff arrived and formed a circle around us, careful to avoid the pool of Guthrie's breakfast.

I forced myself to inspect the body. I'd done a stint as a candy striper in high school, back when I wanted to be a doctor, and had picked up a few things in the process. The bluish hue of Abby's fingertips was a sure sign that she was beyond help. Her right hand was clenched tightly as if she'd been holding something. Weird. I thought rigor mortis progressed from the head down.

"Out of the way!" Guthrie shrieked like a demon when the EMT squad arrived. Pushing people aside, he cleared a path for the paramedics and gurney.

Penny Sue was oblivious to it all. She kept pumping. "80-81-82."

"Penny Sue, it's time to stop. She's gone. Abby's hands are blue," I said

A medic knelt beside Penny Sue and tried to take command. She elbowed him in the stomach, tears coursing down her cheeks. "No! I'm not losing another one!"

Another one! Penny Sue was reliving her efforts to revive our neighbor during the 2004 hurricanes when Charlie, Frances, and Jeanne cut a path through Florida. All of her recent traumas had apparently fused into this one moment. The medic attempted to take over again, and Penny Sue belted him in the face. I grabbed her arm before she could deliver a karate chop. "Penny Sue, this is not your fault. This is not Clyde Holden."

She collapsed in my arms and bawled like a baby. "I tried," she wailed. "Tell Daddy I tried."

I inched her away so the medics could do their thing. Guthrie snuggled against us and cried, too. Geez, two of them! As the paramedics huddled around Abby, I kept moving backward, dragging Penny Sue and Guthrie into the haphazard mound of books. Finally, we were up against the stacks and could move no further, but it gave the EMTs enough room. It didn't take long. The first EMT on the scene stood and shook his head. "Call for a medical examiner," he instructed his partner, who manned the gurney.

As I clutched Penny Sue and Guthrie on each side, both sobbing at the mention of the medical examiner, Terry's face appeared within inches of mine.

"I thought Abby left with your group!"

I shook my head meekly. "No, we went before she came back from the bathroom. We debated checking on Abby, but we thought it might upset her even more if she was really having an anxiety attack. We felt sure she'd be out before you closed up. We left as soon as the crowd did."

Terry dropped to her knees. "It's my fault. I locked her in!"

"No, it's not your fault. Abby wasn't feeling well when you escorted her to the bathroom. You saw her rub her chest. She must have noticed when you turned off the lights and started to close up."

Terry rocked back on her heels. "The lights in the bathroom would have gone off. Only the night lights and exit signs would have been on."

"So, she had time to call out, right?"

Terry paused, thinking. "Yes, I would have heard her shout."

"And Abby wasn't incapacitated, because she made it from the bathroom to this place."

Terry perked up slightly. "That's right. It's a fair trek from the children's department to this stack. She couldn't have been deathly ill, at least not at that point."

Guthrie swiped at his eyes. "She had a cell phone, I saw her use it when she came in from the parking lot. Why didn't she call for help? There's not a scrambler in this building, is there?"

Terry shook her head. "No. Besides, she could have used the landline telephones. They were all working."

Penny Sue brushed tears from her cheeks. "Then why did she stay in the library and come here?"

Terry had just given Penny Sue, Guthrie, and me permission to take the rest of the day off when Robert "Woody" Woodhead, the local prosecutor, or persecutor as we called him, strode down the aisle flanked by a uniformed police officer and a suit—a New York detective transplant we'd encountered on an earlier visit. The paramedic shook his head at Woody, who turned to the crowd and announced loudly, "We need to clear the building. Please take your belongings and proceed to the front door." Woody signaled the uniformed officer, who stationed himself at the exit and inspected each person's belongings as they filed out. I assumed he was trying to ensure that no one made off with evidence. Meanwhile, Terry and the detective started a room-by-room search.

Guthrie, Penny Sue, and I struggled to our feet. I gave Woody a feeble smile. He just stared at us, shaking his head. It was hard to tell if his expression was one of disgust or disbelief. I hoped it was disbelief, because I thought we'd mended our fences and finally gotten Woody off our backs when we agreed not to press assault charges against his demented mother for pelting us with eggs. Woody the Worm had even brought us flowers as a peace offering. Yet the expression on his face told me the flowers had been an empty gesture.

Penny Sue, Woody, and I went back to college days, when Penny Sue dated him a few times during a visit some of our sorority sisters made to her father's beach condo. Everything was fine until my ex-husband Zack, then Penny Sue's boyfriend, showed up unexpectedly. Woody and Zack had words that escalated into a fistfight. Because of the *unpleasant situation*, Penny Sue dumped them both and eventually took up with her first husband, Andy Walters, who was the amiable, if dumb, captain of the football team. Because of a grudge over the *unpleasantness* and some other stuff, Woody had made our lives a living hell on two of our last three visits. The third visit, during the 2004 hurricanes, wasn't much better initially, but ended on a positive note. Heck, I hadn't seen Woody since then, and judging from the look on his face, I wasn't thrilled to see him now.

"I can't believe it," Woody led off. "A death, and you're involved."

Penny Sue's eyes shot darts. "We are not involved! We merely found Abby and tried to revive her."

"Abby? So you know the lady?"

"She was an acquaintance, a scholar from last night's debate here at the library. Dr. Abigail Johnston. We found her buried in these books when we arrived this morning." I swept my arm in a wide arc at the scattered volumes. "That's the extent of our knowledge and involvement."

"I'll need statements."

"No problem," I said, edging toward the door with Penny Sue and Guthrie in tow. "You know where we live."

No sooner had the words left my mouth than a scream came from the back workroom. We raced toward the shriek and found Terry standing on a chair next to the open door of the book return room. She was stuttering and blubbering and pointing at a trashcan. "Snake! A snake came out of the books. I think it's a rattler!"

We stopped dead in our tracks. Woody pulled a small pistol from his ankle holster and aimed at the wastebasket. A moment later, the detective arrived. Woody quickly explained the problem. The detective snatched a larger garbage can from a corner of the room, dumped its contents and held it upside down. "Cover me," he instructed Woody.

From the sweat beading on Woody's forehead, I thought Penny Sue probably would do a better job, but I wasn't getting involved. I held my breath as the detective tiptoed over to the wastebasket, gave it a swift kick, and slammed the other can over the snake. I give the guy credit—he had terrific reflexes. From what I could tell from my brief glimpse, the snake was about two feet long and did indeed have the color and markings of a rattler. We could hear the snake thrashing around inside the can. Woody was not going to give the vicious viper a chance to escape. He quickly yanked the plug of an industrial quality paper shredder from the wall and plunked it down on top of the can. "That should hold him," Woody said with a satisfied grin, as if he alone had saved the day. No one smiled back. Even the detective gave Woody a disgusted glance as he strode to the return room.

"Do you suppose the snake bit Abby?" Penny Sue ventured.

Terry hopped down from the chair. "No, the book room door was closed. The snake came out when I peeked inside. A dumb kid probably put it down the return chute as a prank. Well, this prank isn't funny. Someone could have been killed!"

"Looks like someone was," the detective said, pointing at an arm protruding from a mound of books that had spilled from the two overturned book bins under the slots. The only thing visible was a hand and navy striped shirt cuff.

"Get a medic over here," Woody called.

The detective knelt and felt for a pulse. He shook his head and began clearing books from the body. Within minutes, the person's head was exposed. It was a man with curly brown hair. The officer felt his neck for a pulse and shook his head again.

Standing on tiptoes, Penny Sue gazed across Woody's shoulder. "Oh my gawd, it's the weird man who hangs out in the magazine section, and I think he's dead!'"

Terry turned white as if she might faint. "Two?! Not two! How could this happen?"

Penny Sue and I were in a daze when we arrived at the condos. The sky was crystal clear and the sun had just peeked above the roof of our duplex. Normally, it promised to be an idyllic day. But things were hardly normal. The shock of finding two bodies had overloaded our circuits. We didn't speak the whole way home. I suppose we were both trying to make sense of the tragedy. Guthrie's VW Bus was already there when we arrived, and the door to my condo was ajar, which told me he was already filling Ruthie in on the details of the morning.

"Woody is a jerk," Penny Sue said. "Did you notice the way he looked at us? He assumed we were responsible or somehow mixed up in Abby's death. That whole forgiveness thing over his mother was a big crock. We should have pressed charges against the old biddy. Now it's too late."

I took the key from the ignition and opened my car door. "I'm afraid you're right. It doesn't seem like anything has changed with Woody. But the second body clearly didn't have anything to do with us. He can't possibly think we were mixed up in that death."

Penny Sue stared pensively. "Or the snake! I hate to be crass, but the other body probably saved us a lot of hassle."

"This is really bizarre," I said. "Under ordinary circumstances, I'd think the weird man killed Abby, but he was buried in books, too. What was he doing in the library after hours?"

"It was cold last night. He's probably homeless and hid in the book return room to stay warm. Then a snot-nosed kid pulled a prank with the snake, and the snake bit him. He tipped over the book bins when he struggled to avoid the snake and buried himself alive."

"That makes sense." I cringed. "A horrible way to go. Snakes give me the creeps."

"Me, too, but right now I'm worried about breaking the news about Abby to Kevin," Penny Sue said.

"Yeah," I mumbled, staring absently at her car and wishing I could forget the events of the morning. I canted my head at her big yellow Mercedes parked on the side of the driveway. "What's wrong with the Benz? You usually insist on driving since you hate my little VW."

"Something's wrong with the damned transmission, so I'm driving it as little as possible. It will cost a couple thousand to fix." Her jaw flexed. "Daddy has me on such a tight allowance until I sell my house, I'm really pinching pennies. I can't afford to get it fixed right now."

Tears welled up in her eyes. For a person who typically didn't give money a second thought and was used to buying designer clothes and spending like there was no tomorrow, being strapped for cash was traumatic. Throw in a couple of dead bodies, plus Woody's hassle, and you had the ingredients for a nervous breakdown. As wacky and outrageous as she could be, Penny Sue was a kind, generous person. I hated to see her go through so much embarrassment and pain over her investment loss.

"I'm sure Ruthie would lend you the money. After all, you'll get a lot from the sale of your house, it's being on a lake and everything."

"Not as much as you'd think. The real estate market is in the tank." Penny Sue sucked in air through her nose and let it out through her mouth. A yoga thing, I supposed. "I know Ruthie would lend me money, but I'm not going to ask. I'm bound and determined to prove to Daddy that I can stand on my own two feet. He thinks I'm a dizzy blonde, even if I'm not a real blonde. I'm going to prove him wrong." She squared her shoulders. "I'm going to show Daddy that I can make it on my own. I realize I haven't always behaved responsibly, but those days are over."

I had a hard time believing that, but decided to give her the benefit of the doubt. "You helped me after my divorce when I was down; I'm here for you. I'm sure Ruthie is, too."

Penny Sue nodded slightly. "I know you are, Leigh, and I really appreciate it. Right now I need your help to break the news to Kevin. Even though he and Abby split up ages ago, I sense he still has feelings for her."

I agreed. "First, let's consult Ruthie and Guthrie; then we'll all tell Kevin together."

Well, things didn't go exactly as planned. We headed inside my condo to formulate a strategy, only to find all three of them sitting on my sofa. It seems big mouth Guthrie had already spilled the beans. Ruthie got involved trying to calm both of them down. By the time we arrived, they were about cried out and fairly calm or exhausted.

Penny Sue knelt before Kevin and took his hands. "I tried to save her, Kevin. She was already gone."

A tear streaked down Kevin's face. "I know. Guthrie told me what you did."

Penny Sue squeezed his hands. "Can I do anything for you?"

Kevin swallowed hard. "Yes, call Mom. She and Abby's mother were friends. Mom will know how to get in touch with her. I think it's best that Mrs. Johnston hears the news from Mom rather than a strange policeman knocking on her door."

Penny Sue dropped his hands and backed away. "Sure, I'll do it right now." She all but ran out of the condo. I followed, sensing something was wrong. I caught Penny Sue as she angrily jerked open the screen door to her unit.

"What's wrong?"

"He wants me to call his mother!" she said through tight lips.

My hands went up in a *big deal* motion. "So?"

"So?!" Penny Sue screeched. "His mother is the Queen of Shit!"

"Penny Sue! How can you talk that way about Kevin's mother?"

"I didn't give her the name Queen of Shit, she gave it to herself! Aunt Alice was the Director of a Sewer Department in New Jersey. She *was* the Queen of New Jersey shit."

"Hold on," I said, grabbing her arm. "What's the big deal?"

Penny Sue stared at me as if I were an idiot. "Aunt Alice is the black sheep of the family, Momma's older sister. She ran away after high school and married a Yankee from New Jersey, no less. No one spoke to her for years until she had Kevin; then a truce was called."

"What's so bad about New Jersey?" I asked.

"New Jersey—gangs, Italian mafia, Russian mob! To succeed in that environment a person has to be tough. For a woman to succeed, they have to be doubly tough. Let's just say that Aunt Alice, in spite of her upbringing, doesn't cotton to Southern ways. She's going to yell at me no matter what I say."

"You don't know that."

"Yes, I do." Penny Sue opened the screen door that emitted its telltale rusty twang.

I tagged along and waited on the couch while she found her aunt's phone number and dialed. The conversation was stilted, Penny Sue giving Alice minimal details. Just when I thought Penny Sue had pulled it off, the doorbell rang and a voice sounded from the doorway. "Penny Sue? Is Kevin Harrington here? I need to speak with him." It was Woody's voice.

Penny Sue cupped her hand around the phone and motioned for me to deal with Woody. "No, Alice. Everything is okay."

Woody had started down the hall by the time I reached him. "Penny Sue's on the phone," I whispered, hoping he'd take the hint. The dumbbell didn't get it.

"I just need to speak with Dr. Kevin Harrington. I was told he's Penny Sue's cousin and is staying here," Woody said loudly.

No amount of hand cupping could block Woody's statement, and Aunt Alice apparently had ears like a cat. "Who's that in the background?" Alice demanded so loudly I could hear her in the hall.

Penny Sue held the phone away from her ear and grimaced. "It's nothing important. The police are just going through the usual hoops for an unexplained death. You know, they're tracing Abby's activities for the last day or so."

"What do they want with Kevin? For that matter, what the hell was Abby doing down there?"

Penny Sue giggled nervously. "Abby and Kevin had a debate at the library last night."

"What?" Alice thundered. Woody and I both heard that word. "Why was that worthless bitch involved? I thought Kevin was debating his swishy old schoolmate, Wallow, or something."

"There was a last minute change. Abby took Willows' place."

"Hmph," then a long pause as Aunt Alice digested the last piece of information. "I'll go over to see Abby's mother right away. I have nothing against *her*. Then I'm packing the Caddy and coming down. Expect me tomorrow evening," Alice said in a steely voice. "I assume you can put me up."

"Yes ma'am, no problem." Penny Sue was ashen.

Alice continued. "You tell whoever was yelling in the background that I'm coming and I have connections. You know what I mean? You tell that guy to lighten up on Kevin, or he'll be sorry."

Penny Sue hung up the phone, visibly shaken. "Crap! Alice is coming."

Ignoring Penny Sue's obvious distress, Woody rattled on like the insensitive jerk that he was. "Where is Dr. Harrington?" he demanded again.

Penny Sue swung around and wagged her finger in Woody's face. "You have no idea what you just did. Unless you have a search warrant, you are trespassing, and the person on the phone was my Aunt Alice, Kevin's mother, who's from New Jersey. Got that? New Jersey!"

Woody shuffled uncomfortably but finally managed, "New Jersey. Is that supposed to be a threat of some kind?"

Penny Sue clenched her jaw. "No, that's a fact."

Chapter 4

While Woody interviewed Kevin in Penny Sue's condo, the rest of us brainstormed in mine. Penny Sue was fit to be tied that Woody had waltzed into her condo uninvited and overheard Aunt Alice refer to Abby as a worthless bitch. The fact that Alice would arrive the next day and planned to stay at Penny Sue's place didn't do much for her humor, either.

"I need a drink. Any scotch left?" Penny Sue asked, brushing past Ruthie and heading for my kitchen. Guthrie raised his hand like a first-grader. "I could use a drink, too. I have some at my place if you're out."

I gave them both a disapproving look, but headed for the kitchen. Who was I to judge? Alice wasn't my aunt, and they'd both had quite a shock that morning. I reached into the cabinet and retrieved the bottle of liquor. As I handed it to Penny Sue who was already shoveling ice into highball glasses, I realized I'd had a bad morning, too. Scotch was a little strong for me, but I surely deserved a glass of wine. While Penny Sue and Guthrie sat at the counter sipping their drinks, I poured wine for Ruthie and me. We sat on stools beside them.

"Since this is my condo, I'll lead off," I said.

"Okay," Penny Sue agreed. "But there is one thing I must ask first. Leigh, may I please stay with you? I'd have to move into the guestroom with Aunt Alice and let Kevin use the master.

Even though the guestroom has twin beds, the thought of sharing it with Alice is more than I can stomach."

Unlike Penny Sue's condo which had a large master suite and one guestroom, my condo had three bedrooms. The master suite was smaller and space had been taken from the great room and owner's closet for a third bedroom. Both bedrooms were outfitted with a twin bed and shared a bath. Besides being beachfront, the layout and great price were major selling points for me. I had two grown children, Ann and Zack, Jr. The two extra bedrooms meant that I had a chance of getting them to visit at the same time and reuniting our family that had been torn apart by my rotten, money hiding, lap-dance fiend of an ex-husband. The fact that the previous owner was a friend of Penny Sue's and willing to hold the unit for me until my divorce settlement was finalized helped, too.

Ruthie had occupied one of my guestrooms since her father passed away. Both of her parents came from big money, and the house she shared with her widowed father after her divorce was a trendy mansion in Atlanta's Buckhead. As the only child, Ruthie inherited millions from both sides of the family. Excepting a penchant for simple, very expensive designer clothes and a Jaguar, Ruthie was as frugal as Penny Sue was extravagant. Of course, that dynamic was about to change, given Penny Sue's current financial circumstances. It was hard to believe, but Penny Sue might be forced to buy her clothes on sale at Talbots and Dillards with me.

"Of course you can stay here," I replied to Penny Sue. "Your father let me stay in his condo rent-free for months."

A tear welled up in Penny Sue's eye, and she took a gulp of her drink to hide it.

"You're welcome to stay with me, too," Guthrie added.

"What about Timothy?" Penny Sue asked.

Now Guthrie got teary eyed. Timothy was Guthrie's gorgeous, muscular boyfriend. They say opposites attract, but this was one pairing that was hard to figure. Timothy looked and acted like a man who'd stepped out of GQ. Guthrie typically looked like a person who'd stumbled in from a barn. "He's been transferred to Houston. How long depends on what happens to the space program."

Ruthie squeezed Guthrie's hand. "I'm so sorry."

I gave them the "halt" hand signal. "We've already had enough trauma and sadness for one day. Let's deal with our immediate problem; we'll grapple with the rest later. Agreed?"

Nods all around.

"As soon as Woody leaves, our immediate priority is to comfort Kevin," I continued.

Penny Sue perked up. "That's your department, Ruthie. You like Kevin and he likes you."

"I like Kevin," Guthrie mumbled into his drink.

"Okay, you're in charge of consoling Kevin," I said, emphasizing the statement with a hand chop. "We'll bring Kevin over here. Meanwhile, Penny Sue, Ruthie, and I will go to her place, change the sheets, put out fresh towels and pack up Penny Sue's necessities. I assume Aunt Alice will stay in the master bedroom so Kevin won't have to relocate."

"Yes," Penny Sue said emphatically. "I don't want Kevin going through my underwear drawer."

Ruthie flashed a mean look. "Why did you say that? He'd never do such a thing. Kevin's not a weirdo."

Penny Sue held her glass up for a refill. Guthrie followed suit. I took the glasses and headed around the counter. Penny Sue glanced sidelong at Ruthie. "It's been a helluva day, okay? I don't know why I said that—it just came out. It didn't mean anything. When I think of it, I'd rather Kevin went through my underwear than Aunt Alice."

"What's wrong with Kevin's mother, Penny Sue?" Ruthie asked

"She was born in the South, but didn't take her manners to the North. Her husband was a wuss, so she had to wear the pants.

She did well for herself and her family. But dealing with so many mafia types made her hard and tough. I know she had to do it to survive, but she's not a lot of fun to be around."

"Anybody home?" Kevin called from the front door.

"Sure, come on in," Ruthie and Guthrie shouted in unison.

Poor Kevin looked like death warmed over, as they say in the South. He took a stool next to Ruthie and folded his arms on the counter. He eyed Ruthie's wine. "I could use one of those."

"Of course." Penny Sue and I both hustled to the icebox, bumping into each other at its door. I finally stepped back and let Penny Sue take charge. Our drama queen had flipped into her School Marm persona. While I waited for her to serve Kevin, it occurred to me that the School Marm role might run on her mother's side of the family. Penny Sue had the trait, and it sounded like Aunt Alice did, too. Oh, joy. I might have to see a doctor about tranquilizers if my suspicion turned out to be accurate.

Penny Sue handed Kevin his wine and returned to her seat. As I put out a basket of chips and a plate of cheese and crackers, Kevin filled us in on his interview with Woody.

"Mom did me in," he said. "Woody was just gathering information until he heard Mom call Abby a worthless bitch when she was talking to Penny Sue." Kevin sighed. "Mom has never gotten over the fact that Abby walked out on me and stole my research. She wanted me to sue Abby. Actually, Mom wanted to have her roughed up, but I nixed that, and Mom gave in because she really liked Abby's mother."

I filed Kevin's last comment re: *roughed up* in my memory bank under, *don't mess with Alice!*

"What did Woody say?" Penny Sue asked Kevin.

"You know. 'Why did my mother say that?' which led to the fact that Abby and I used to live together. I think you know the rest."

"Surely they don't suspect you had anything to do with her death. You left the library with us," Penny Sue said.

"When Woody started, I thought it was a perfunctory interview. But when he honed in on Mom's bitch comment, it seemed I was suddenly a suspect." He gazed at us with dull eyes. "Abby walked out on me, and I was heartbroken, but I sure didn't want to kill her!"

"Of course not." Penny Sue patted his hand. "We don't even know if Abby's death was foul play. If it was, the dead man probably did it. Or," her eyes flashed, wheels in her head turning, "Abby killed the weird man and had a heart attack after she realized what she'd done." Penny Sue snagged a chip. "That's it! The weirdo hid out in the library and attacked Abby. She knew karate or something and killed him in the struggle. Then she had a heart attack when she realized what she'd done." Penny Sue took a bite of the chip and munched it slowly. "Yep, Abby killed the periodical guy, then died from guilt. The snake was an innocent bystander. By the way, your mother is coming down tomorrow."

"What?!" Kevin nearly fell off his stool.

Penny Sue took another chip and grinned weakly. "Your mother didn't like what she overheard from Woody. She's going to see Abby's mother this morning, then leave immediately. She should be here tomorrow evening."

"You're kidding," Kevin exclaimed.

"No. She's going to stay with you at my place, and I'll stay over here."

Kevin cradled his head in his hands. "This is going to be a disaster. She'll threaten everyone in law enforcement with her mafia contacts and before you know it, I'll be in jail. And, if that doesn't happen, I'll have to spend days playing gin rummy."

"I love gin rummy," Guthrie gushed. "I'll keep your mother company and off your back."

Kevin regarded Guthrie as if manna had fallen from heaven. "Do you really like to play cards?"

"Love it. Timothy and I used to play all of the time."

"My mother is difficult."

"No one could be worse than my Aunt Harriet, and she might be tolerable if she could play cards."

Kevin regarded Guthrie skeptically. "Are you sure?"

"Well, I can't entertain her 24 hours a day, but I'll help you out between my Lemon Aid business calls and volunteering at the library."

Kevin's eyes softened. "Thanks, Guthrie. I believe my mother would like you."

"Does she drink scotch?" Guthrie asked.

Kevin nodded. "You'll be two peas in a pod."

Penny Sue raised her hands and face to the ceiling. "See, Ruthie, it's just like you said—'the Universe provides.' Who would have guessed? Two people who love rummy and scotch."

Ruthie rolled her eyes. "If it will help, I'll run to the store and buy a case."

"I'll go with you if you're paying. I think we need to stock up on wine, too." Penny Sue flashed a mischievous grin. "But first, we need to move my stuff over here."

While Guthrie and Kevin morbidly sucked down alcohol, Penny Sue, Ruthie and I went next door to pack up Penny Sue's clothes and prepare for Aunt Alice's arrival. Ruthie and I changed the sheets and cleaned the master bathroom. Penny Sue packed up clothes and necessities. Close to an hour later, Ruthie and I had finished straightening the condo and headed for the front door. There were two large Hartman suitcases with hanging clothes draped over them and a huge woven basket of pill bottles.

"What in the world is that?" I asked, pointing at the pill basket.

"My amino-acids and vitamins," Penny Sue said airily.

She'd told us that she was on a health kick, making a complete change in her life. I guess the change didn't include alcohol. Still I didn't know about the supplements. "What are they for?"

"My personal trainer in Atlanta recommended that I read a book about neurotransmitters. She thinks mine are off."

Yes, Lord!

"The book says that certain amino-acids and vitamins will restore a person's brain."

Heavens, yes. You need them all!

Ruthie pointed at the basket. "Do you take all of those pills?"

"Not all of them, now. Actually, there were two books. The first book recommended one batch and the second recommended others. I think the second batch is better for me, so I only take about half of the bottles there."

I reached down and picked one up. "What's this for?"

"That's good for ADD, memory, sex drive, and stress."

I was stunned. That Penny Sue could recite that list of ailments was a testament to the supplement's benefit to memory. I also noticed that it was on the top of the pile, indicating that she recognized she had all of the problems, except a lack of sex drive. Of course, she wouldn't admit to sex problems if there were any. She hadn't dated anyone since she'd been in New Smyrna Beach, but neither had I! My memory wasn't so good, either. Geez, maybe I needed some of that stuff. "Where did you buy all of this? Is it expensive?" I asked.

"Not really. There's a place on the Internet that sells them for half price."

"Remind me to get the web address."

We all exchanged nervous glances when the car horn blared. Penny Sue swallowed hard and started for the front door, the rest of us followed. She paused for a deep breath and swung the door wide. One glance at the big blue Caddy—sand billowing from a quick stop—told me we were in for trouble. Aunt Alice must have really hauled it down I-95, it was only 6:30 p.m.. Apparently Kevin's mother shared some of Penny Sue's driving skills as well as personality traits.

Penny Sue forced her lips into a tight smile and offered a hand to the curly, gray-haired woman who already had a foot on the ground.

Aunt Alice waved Penny Sue aside. "I'm fine," she insisted. "I may be old, but I'm not crippled." Only about five-foot-four and slightly stooped, Alice projected the aura of a pro basketball player. Her polo shirt and neatly creased slacks looked as fresh as when she donned them for the long drive.

Kevin pulled his mother into a bear hug. "Mom, you didn't have to come down. I'm fine."

She patted his stomach. "I can see that. You've put on weight."

"Penny Sue and her friends are terrific hosts." Kevin quickly made introductions, his attention lingering on Ruthie.

Not to be slighted, Guthrie rushed to Alice and shook her hand. "Man, I couldn't wait for you to get here. Alice is one of my favorite names! I think it's a sign. Did you ever see the movie *Alice's Restaurant*? Man, that Alice was—" I gave his forearm a good squeeze. Guthrie cut his eyes at me, grinned sheepishly, and turned back to Alice. "Anyway, I hear you like scotch and playing gin rummy. They're, like, my favorites, and I've been looking for a buddy since my partner, Timothy, was transferred to Houston. He didn't drink, but he loved to play rummy."

Aunt Alice hauled back and gave Guthrie the once over. Apparently concluding he was a ditz and not dangerous, she started to laugh. "Are you always so hyper?"

Guthrie gave her a silly grin. "Sorry, I ramble when I'm nervous. If I talk too much, tell me, I won't be offended. It's just that I've really been looking forward to hanging out with you. I've been terribly lonely since Timothy left. Congress is a real pisser, you know, canceling the shuttle program and forcing Timothy to move to Houston. He's a brilliant fuels engineer. Now our astronauts have to hitch a ride with the Russians to get to the International Space Station that our country mostly built. Does that make sense to you? We build something that we can't get to.

And you know the Russians will charge top dollar for a ride. It's all a real stupid bummer—"

I squeezed Guthrie's shoulder.

"I'm rambling again, huh? Sorry, Alice. Can I call you Alice? My real name's Fred Fribble, but everyone calls me Guthrie. And don't worry—if anything comes up I can protect you. I have a Glock and I know how to use it. I protected the ladies here during the hurricanes."

Penny Sue gave him the squinty-eye. "His major contribution was eating all of the chocolate," she whispered to Ruthie and me.

Aunt Alice patted Guthrie's arm. "Son, you've got to calm down or you'll have a heart attack. Please call me Alice, and I'll call you Guthrie, okay?" She turned to Kevin. "Where's the loo? It was a long drive."

While Aunt Alice freshened up, Kevin and Guthrie carted her luggage to Penny Sue's master suite. Penny Sue had made a point of clearing out several drawers in her bureau for Alice, particularly the drawer with underwear.

As Alice unpacked, Penny Sue made a pot of Starbucks Special and set a plate of cookies on the coffee table in the living room. Kevin had pulled over the high backed rattan chair for his mother, and the rest of us sat on the sofa and loveseat, eyeing the cookies and wondering what had come over Penny Sue.

"Can I help you?" I asked, noticing the perspiration beading on Penny Sue's forehead.

"Yes. Would you please take this to the coffee table?" Penny Sue waved at a tray of cream, sugar, cups with saucers, and cloth napkins. Cups with saucers? Not our usual mugs? Cloth napkins? Boy, she was really putting on the dog for Alice. I squinted at the napkins that looked familiar. They were my napkins!

I sidled up to Penny Sue and whispered, "Don't be nervous, Alice seems nice. What's with the cloth napkins?"

"I found them in the utility room."

"Oh, yeah, I guess I forgot them when I moved next door. That was the only complete set of anything I got from my divorce, if you don't count the matching table cloth that Zack took."

As I said before, my sleazy ex works for Judge Daddy's law firm. The Judge always liked me and strongly *advised* Zack to be fair with the divorce settlement—split everything fifty-fifty—which the jerk did. He took half of everything. Half of the pictures off the wall; half of each set of china and crystal; all of the top sheets, no bottoms; one twin bed from Zack, Jr.'s room. He probably would have chain-sawed Ann's double bed in half if he had a chain saw and it wouldn't make him break a sweat. Considering Zack was responsible for the divorce in the first place by running around with a strip club dancer, to call him slimy was being kind. He'd also pilfered our life savings that he stashed in offshore bank accounts. If not for Judge Parker's intervention, I'd be living in a homeless shelter or tent instead of next door to Penny Sue at the beach.

"Alice really has you rattled, doesn't she?" I whispered.

Penny Sue clenched her jaw. "Momma's not here, so I'm the recipient of all of Alice's anger about the way the family treated her. Alice was raised Southern, so she knows how things should be done. With the big deal her parents made about her Yankee husband, I know she's going to point out any *faux pas* I make."

"I think you're wrong, she doesn't strike me that way at all."

"You don't know her," Penny Sue said squinty-eyed. "Momma told me."

"Penny Sue, that was years ago. The feud was between Alice and her parents, not you. She went on to become a high government official. I'm sure she doesn't give the olden days in Georgia a single thought."

Penny Sue handed me the tray. "Yeah, she had to worry about the Mafia."

"Come on, Kevin's a great guy who loves you. Y'all get along fabulously."

"Sure, he takes after his father."

I had just arranged the cups, saucers and napkins on the table when Alice came in from the bedroom.

"Mom, take this chair," Kevin said, ushering her to the rattan chair that resembled a throne.

"Coffee, anyone?" Penny Sue appeared with the Mr. Coffee pot. "It's Starbucks Special!" That was added to blunt the genteel slight of a Mr. Coffee instead of a silver serving pot.

Alice glanced at the cookies, and then at Guthrie who was wide-eyed, as surprised as we all were by the formality. "I'd really prefer a scotch, if you have it," Alice said.

Guthrie raised his hand. "I'd like one too, please ma'am."

Penny Sue's face fell to her boobs. So much for her efforts at Southern hospitality. "Of course, there's scotch and wine."

Noticing Penny Sue's crestfallen expression, Kevin, Ruthie and I asked for coffee. Each of us also took a napkin and cookie.

Alice picked up a napkin. "I haven't seen lace napkins in twenty-five years. I thought they went the way of the abacus."

Penny Sue's jaw flexed. I jumped in to take the heat. "That was my idea. We wanted to pull out the best for our initial meeting since we're planning to have pizza delivered for dinner. We didn't want you to think we were beach bums. The napkins belonged to my grandmother."

Alice winked. "They're very pretty, but you don't have to put on airs for me. This is the beach."

Guthrie grinned like a Cheshire cat. "Man, I'm really glad you said that, because I don't have any cloth napkins. I use paper towels." He waved his arm. "Only Bounty, though, not the cheap stuff."

Penny Sue handed Alice and Guthrie their drinks. Alice took an appreciative sip. "No airs. I'm here to help Kevin."

I noticed that a stomach cramp seemed to hit Kevin at the comment. Fortunately, the phone rang. Penny Sue answered. "Aunt Alice, it's for you."

"It must be Myrna, Abby's mother, about the funeral arrangements." Alice took the phone, mouthed some pleasantries then listened for a long time. She hung up and turned to Kevin. "There's not going to be a funeral or memorial service anytime soon. Myrna and the authorities down here want an autopsy. But Myrna has a copy of Abby's will. She left all of her books and research notes to you, Kevin. Myrna has to clean out Abby's apartment and wants me to pack up the things at the timeshare Abby rented here at the beach. Myrna's going to ship all of Abby's books and notes down here to you. Myrna said she told the New Smyrna police to give you any of Abby's research they found."

Kevin hopped up, spilling his coffee. "To me? We broke up fifteen years ago! Why me?"

Alice blew out a long sigh. "I suppose Abby felt guilty about stealing your research."

Kevin sat down, dabbing at his trousers with the lace-trimmed napkin. "I can't believe this. I don't want the research. I've spent years trying to put the whole affair behind me."

Alice gave her son a stern look. "Well, Kevin, it's come back around. You'll just have to deal with it."

Chapter 5

Penny Sue and I were scheduled to work at the library the next day. This time, she wore slacks and a silk blouse with flat shoes. She also insisted on driving her Mercedes.

"I thought you didn't want to drive the Mercedes because of the transmission," I said.

"Yeah, that and I wanted to leave it for Kevin to use. Now that his mother's here, he can use her Caddy. Besides, I'd like your opinion on the transmission. You know how some repair shops are. They'll replace the whole engine when all you need is a fan belt, especially now with the economy so slow. I'll bet Mercedes sales are in the tank." She stopped at the intersection of our sand driveway and Highway A1A. "Listen for a clunk when I accelerate." She made a right turn and floored it. The engine whined, obviously straining, then came a jerk and grinding sound as the transmission shifted to a higher gear.

I glanced sidelong. "No question about it, your transmission needs work."

"Darn, I hoped it was my imagination. I can't afford to have it fixed right now."

"Just keep the car parked. Ruthie and I don't mind driving. Your Dad called last night. Did he have any news on your house?" I asked.

"He didn't admit to anything, but I think something's cooking. He's mailing a power of attorney down here for me to sign.

He said it was merely a precaution in the event a deal materialized. That's all I could get out of him. He's trying to torture me, Leigh."

"He is not."

"Yes he is. He wants to teach me a lesson, as if having to sell my house isn't lesson enough. He also wants to oversee my investments from now on. I'm not a child, and I won't agree to that." She thumped her chest. "I'm not the only person who lost money to Madoff. Most of our friends invested with him. Ruthie and Daddy are the only people I know who didn't jump on the bandwagon."

"I didn't."

"Well ... okay, you were smarter than I was."

"Or luckier. Zack handled our finances."

"Maybe it's a good thing he was distracted by the stripper. If he hadn't been so busy getting lap dances, he might have gotten caught up in the Madoff scheme. Ruthie says there are no accidents, and even the worst disasters can have a silver lining. Maybe that's yours. Did you ever think of that?"

I gave her a disgusted look as she parked at the library. "I promise, that thought never crossed my mind," I said as we headed toward the front door, passing a Volusia County deputy at the entrance.

"I guess they're still investigating," Penny Sue said.

"Yeah, that's probably a crime scene tech." I pointed to the aisle where Abby's body was discovered. A large area was roped off with yellow crime tape. A young woman in khaki slacks and a green polo shirt was examining the books on the floor and sorting them into boxes. Every now and then she stopped to take a picture. "I guess they're searching for evidence, like a weapon or Abby's blood."

Penny Sue shivered and glanced away. "It gives me the chills. I hope they let me work in the reference stacks or do something that's a long way from this part of the library."

"I'm sure Terry—" I caught sight of a man with a bad comb-over hairdo in the row next to the crime scene. He pulled out a book, fanned the pages, then peeked through the void to the other side. I elbowed Penny Sue. "Look, that's Dr. Willows!" As we watched, he replaced the book, glanced from side to side, and repeated the process, this time removing two or three volumes. "He's spying on the technician. You know, I believe the roped off area is the place where he and Abby had the disagreement before the debate."

"I wonder what he's up to?" Penny Sue stomped off after him. Willows was peering through an empty space to the other side and didn't see her coming. When Penny Sue put her hand on his shoulder, he jumped, bumping his head on the shelf. "Dr. Willows, what brings you here? Doing a little nosing around?"

"Uh, uh..." he stammered, rubbing his ear. He stared at us with an embarrassed grin, obviously trying to come up with a plausible excuse. Apparently, nothing came to mind. He cleared his throat. "You've got me there. I confess that I was curious about Abby's death, so I swung by to see what was going on. Such a tragedy. She seemed in perfect health, yet to die so young. It's hard to believe. I heard there was another body, too."

"Yes," Penny Sue replied curtly, looking him in the eye.

Willows shoved the books back on the shelf. "You're Kevin's cousin, Penny Sue, right?"

She nodded.

"I was actually on my way to your place to see how Kevin's holding up. I stopped here on a whim. How is Kevin doing?"

"Very well, under the circumstances. My Aunt Alice, his mother, drove down last night."

"Kevin's mother." Willows fidgeted some more. "This probably isn't the best time for a visit. It was thoughtless of me not to call first." His eyes shifted from side to side like a caged animal. "I should go, I need to prepare for a class this afternoon. Nice seeing you." He inched away. "Give my best to Kevin. Tell him to call me anytime if he'd like to talk." Willows all but ran out of the library.

"What do you think he's up to?" Penny Sue asked.

"Maybe nothing. He could simply be curious, like he said." I took her arm. "Come on, we're late. We need to sign in."

"Just another minute." Penny Sue rounded the bookcase and hung over the crime tape. "Good morning," she called to the technician, whose nametag read Jane. "I'm Penny Sue Parker, one of the people who found Dr. Johnston's body."

Jane gave her a "so?" shrug.

"My cousin Kevin was Abby's former fiancé. They went to college together and she willed her books and research papers to him. What's going to happen to all of those books?"

The technician stood. "I don't know anything about the deceased's will. The books that belong to the library will eventually be reshelved. Anything else will be held until the investigation is complete. After that, they'll go to the next of kin."

"Some of Dr. Johnston's historical research is very valuable. Did you notice the man peeking at you through the bookcase? He's a historian who'd probably like to get his hands on her notes."

Jane waved at the stacks on each side. "Yeah, I saw him and a lot of other gawkers since I've worked the case. I think the entire St. Augustine Chamber of Commerce and Realtors Association were here yesterday. Don't worry, both crime scenes are secured at all times. I can't go to the bathroom until a deputy or another tech arrives. The big dogs in Deland want a thorough investigation. With two unexplained deaths, this is potentially a big liability lawsuit."

"Of course, I hadn't thought of that. Carry on." Penny Sue gave her a silly salute and left. Jane did an eye roll and went back to sorting the books.

I worked checkout, and Terry was kind enough to assign Penny Sue to the children's department so she wouldn't constantly be confronted with bad memories. That was good for Penny Sue and me. My workstation in checkout had a good view of most of the library, and I couldn't help but notice a lot of gawkers from the New Smyrna and St. Augustine debate crowds who came in during the day. To a person, they peeked through the shelves, just as Willows had done. The debate itself hit a sore spot with business interests in both cities. The fact that St. Augustine's First City advocate—Abby—was found dead seemed to fuel the flames of dissent, since there were many more officials from St. Augustine who showed up asking questions.

I felt like I'd been chewed up and spit out by the end of the day, what with my regular duties and answering questions about Abby's death. It seems most of the St. Auggie people knew I was connected to Kevin and Penny Sue, so many of the conversations were downright adversarial. A few times it felt like the old days when I was arguing with Zack. Needless to say, it took all the control I could muster not to smack a couple of them. Based on the accusations they made about Kevin, they deserved to be decked. I watched the clock, counting the seconds until five o'clock. At the moment Terry announced that the library was closing, I rushed to the back room, snagged our pocketbooks, and headed to the children's department. Penny Sue was already coming out with a dazed expression.

"Now I know why I never wanted children," Penny Sue said. "They're messy little things." Her silk shirt and slacks were covered in an unidentifiable substance.

"What happened?" I handed over her purse.

"It was finger paint day, and I worked with a couple of kids who couldn't keep their hands to themselves."

"I'm surprised that was a problem. You have plenty of experience fending off suitors with wandering hands."

"Yeah, but you can't belt a kid," Penny Sue groused as she opened her car door. "I did run into a guy from the debate, though.

Remember the gray-haired man who came to the debate with Abby and Willows? The one who reeled in the loud-mouthed baldy. The tall, well dressed guy at the back of the room? I met him in the hall." She reached in her pocket. "He gave me his card. Peter O'Brien. He's Baldy's boss and president of a real estate firm. Nice guy. He was reading the flyer for Wii bowling posted on the bulletin board. Peter said he might come; he'd been thinking of buying a Wii game machine. He also apologized for his employee's behavior and said he hoped there were no hard feelings."

"Hmm. I wonder why he singled you out."

Penny Sue gunned the Mercedes' engine and took a right out of the parking lot. "Coincidence. He probably came down to snoop around about Abby's death, then noticed the bowling announcement." She grinned and wiggled her brows devilishly. "Or maybe he liked my looks. He wasn't wearing a wedding band."

My jaw sagged. Honestly, Penny Sue was the most man crazy woman I'd ever met. You'd think three husbands and divorces would be enough. But no, she thought almost every man she met was her soul mate. That's a lot of souls, she must have had a jillion past lives. "I thought you were waiting for Rich, your true soul mate." Rich was a man Penny Sue fell in love with and followed to Bike Week. It turned out he was working undercover for the Feds on a drug ring and got caught. The biker gang almost beat Rich to a pulp, so the authorities shuttled him into police protection. "Wasn't he supposed to be getting out of protection soon?"

"Something must have gone wrong. I haven't heard a word since that one phone call when he said he thought he'd be back soon because the bad guys were finally behind bars."

"No anonymous flowers for his little Honey Bunny?" I teased. Before, Rich stayed in touch with Penny Sue by having a fellow agent send roses to her. Honey Bunny was her nickname. Ruthie and I discovered it in a telephone message and kidded her about being a *Looney Tunes* character. She didn't think that was funny.

Penny Sue curled her lip at me. "No flowers. Of course, he may not know I'm down here. If he tried to find me in Georgia, he'd discover my house was on the market. I hope he doesn't think I've remarried or something."

"He's a smart, resourceful guy. I'm sure he'll check down here. One of the drug cases was probably postponed."

Penny Sue took a left from Route A1A onto our sand drive-way that flanked a wooden beach walkway. "I hope you're right. Still, I'd have a drink with Peter to pass the time." Penny Sue parked beside Alice's Cadillac, just as Alice and Ruthie were getting out of it. "I wonder where they've been. I thought Alice was playing cards with Guthrie today."

"Ruthie could use a hand. We picked up Chinese," Alice shouted.

I caught sight of large boxes in the backseat. Geez, how much did they buy? I started to open the back door of the Caddy. "Not that—" Ruthie started, "—over here, I'm afraid I'll spill it." She was sitting on the edge of the seat holding a corrugated box filled with about a dozen food containers.

"Let me have it." I took the food and headed for the front door that Penny Sue held open. "Smells good," I said over my shoulder, suddenly realizing that I was starving. "What did you buy?"

"Some of everything. Guthrie's coming to dinner." Alice followed me into the condo. "Kevin, I need some help out here," Alice hollered. He stepped from his room holding a book. "You need to bring in the boxes from my backseat."

"What is all of that stuff?" Penny Sue asked.

"We cleaned out Abby's timeshare. For a person who was in town for two weeks, Abby packed heavy or did a ton of shop-ping. Shorts, swimsuits, and sandals—she was clearly here to enjoy herself. She only brought three business dresses and suits, so work was low on her list of priorities. She must have done a fair amount of book shopping, too. We found a bunch of old history books in boxes with labels from the Muse and Family Book Shops in Deland.

"I guess the books belong to Kevin now. Take them to your room," Alice instructed as Kevin passed us, carrying two obviously heavy boxes. "No sense in shipping them to Myrna. There's enough of the other stuff."

"How's Abby's mother taking this?" I asked.

"All business. I think she's in shock and so busy with details it hasn't hit her yet."

Ruthie nodded. She'd recently been through the same ordeal when her father died in his sleep. Facing a huge shock that didn't register at first, Ruthie was so occupied with funeral arrangements and seeing to the needs of her father's long time valet, Mr. Wong, and the housekeeper, that she ran on automatic. Mr. Wong, as old as her father, was willed a sizeable sum to cover the costs of assisted living in a very upscale Atlanta facility. The housekeeper also received a sizeable inheritance, and she was given the use of one wing of the mansion for as long as she lived, since her close friends were neighboring housekeepers. Once all of that was taken care of, Ruthie closed up the rest of the house and came to stay with me.

When the reality of the situation finally hit her, it hit hard. Ruthie was massively depressed and only left the condo to visit Cassadaga, a nearby town of spiritual mediums, where she hoped to make contact with her father's spirit. I always drove, fearing she might receive a troubling message. The message services were fairly interesting, and I got some advice from a spirit I was sure was Grammy Martin, since most of the messages were in the form of Bible quotations. Grammy was a staunch Southern Baptist with a photographic memory who quoted the Bible for virtually every occasion.

Ruthie received a few cryptic messages that might have come from her father, but nothing definite or comforting. One of the mediums explained that it sometimes took time for the deceased to adjust to their new environment (I guess that's what many call Heaven and New Ager Ruthie called an Attractor Field), so it might be months before communication was established with her father. Months. I shuddered. I loved Ruthie, but she had begun to get me down, and I didn't totally believe all of that New Age stuff, except maybe the part about vibes being contagious. At one point, I felt so depressed I bought some of the American Indian sage and cedar to burn in the condo to clear the energy. That was a first for me. I generally avoided burning the stuff, since it smelled like marijuana and had gotten us in trouble on more than one occasion. Thankfully, I didn't have to resort to burning the smudge wand. With Kevin's arrival, Ruthie gradually emerged from her funk.

Kevin brushed past with another box of books, followed by Guthrie, who lugged two very large suitcases. "Man, where should these go?" Guthrie asked breathlessly.

Alice started to speak, but I interrupted. "In the utility room." With spirit messages, bad vibes, and Indian herbs fresh on my mind, I thought it best that Abby's stuff be stored as far away as possible. In fact, its mere presence might attract her spirit. I supposed it was a kindly spirit, since she'd willed her books to Kevin. Even so, given our track record, I didn't want to take chances. I called Ruthie and Penny Sue aside to express my concern.

"Good point," Ruthie said seriously. "It sure wouldn't hurt to sage the place."

"What about the books in Kevin's room?" Penny Sue asked.

"They're probably okay," Ruthie replied, "because Abby just bought them. They don't have her vibes yet. But she'd surely have an energy attachment to her clothes and other personal belongings."

"Leigh, do you still have that cedar and sage smudge stick?" Penny Sue asked.

"Yes, I picked up a new one in Cassadaga a few weeks ago. Should we do this in front of Aunt Alice?"

Penny Sue went wild-eyed. "No! She'd have a cow, and I doubt Kevin would be much better. How can we get rid of them?"

At that moment, Guthrie scooted by en route to the car for another load. I snagged his arm. "Guthrie, we need your help."

"Anything, Commander." He gave me an arm-across-chest salute.

Commander. I thought he'd finally dropped that foolishness. Guthrie thought I saved him from drowning during one of the hurricanes, so he'd pledged to be my slave forever. That was a jaw dropper! I didn't save his life. All I did was unzip his sleeping bag and pull him off of the air mattress that was floating around our flooded condo. "Let's drop the Commander thing," I winked, "you know, for Alice. Are all of Abby's suitcases in the utility room?"

"Yeah, that lady must have been a real clotheshorse. Her suitcases are huge and weigh a ton. I mean—"

"Guthrie, we need you to get rid of Alice and Kevin for a while so we can smudge Abby's stuff in the utility room. There may be bad vibes."

"Good thinking, considering she's dead and all. Yeah, there may be some really bad vibes on that stuff considering—"

"Can you think of an excuse to get them out of the house?" I whispered.

His face scrunched up with excruciating thought. "Well, I have some brownies cooling on my counter."

"Excellent. That's a terrific idea, but we'll need some time. Can you think of a reason to keep them away for a least a half hour?"

"Well, I have this really good bottle of scotch that Timothy gave me. Twenty-five years old. It was a going away—"

"Perfect!" I twirled Guthrie around and nudged him in Alice's direction. The old boy did a masterful, if garbled, job of convincing Alice and Kevin to come to his condo for the brownies. Both were bemused by his jabber but agreed to help him out.

"We'll be back in a flash," Guthrie said with a big wink as they trooped out, the screen door slamming behind them.

"Hurry," Penny Sue screeched to me. "Go get the smudge stick. We don't have much time and I don't want Alice telling Daddy about this."

I dashed next door for the smudge stick and a lighter. We assembled in the utility room, and Penny Sue stuffed a towel under the door to contain the fumes. I lit the wand. Just like old times, it smelled like marijuana. As Penny Sue and I fanned the smoke all over the luggage, Ruthie said a prayer and several incantations urging Abby to go to the Light and promising that her spirit would live forever. It didn't take long to fill the small enclosure with smoke, and Penny Sue started to cough.

"That's enough," Penny Sue wheezed. I drenched the wand with water from the utility sink. "We'd better get out of here fast or our clothes will reek." I hid the wet wand behind the laundry detergent as Penny Sue kicked the towel away. "Okay, we have to be fast." Penny Sue jerked the door open and we dashed out. We stood in the hall, sniffing. "Do you smell anything?"

Ruthie answered, "I do, but it may be our clothes."

"Turn on all of the exhaust fans and open the windows," Penny Sue commanded. We did as she instructed, not wishing to tangle with her School Marm persona. Meanwhile, she grabbed a can of air freshener from the bathroom and doused us all with it.

"That'll probably ruin your silk blouse," Ruthie said quietly.

Penny Sue raised her arms with a wild expression. "Who cares? The darn thing is already trashed by the finger paint."

A moment later, Alice trooped in, led by Guthrie who carried a pan of brownies. Kevin brought up the rear, cradling a full bottle of scotch. Guthrie shrugged as if to say, *I did the best I could.* Penny Sue backed to the kitchen counter and ditched the air freshener.

"Man, this looks like a good batch. I wanted them to have a drink, but Alice thought it would be rude. I told her you wouldn't care, but she said the Chinese food was getting cold."

Alice marched down the hall, sniffing as she went. When she reached us, her eyes narrowed. "What's that smell?" she demanded.

"You're downwind from the brownies," Penny Sue ventured.

Alice rolled her eyes. "Give me a break! Do you think I was born yesterday? I was Director of the Sewer Department, and I could sniff marijuana out in the midst of all the shit. Got rid of us so you girls could take a little toke, eh?"

Penny Sue's hands flew up like cornered rustlers did in the old Westerns. "No, we were not smoking marijuana." Ruthie and I nodded.

Aunt Alice took a few deep breaths. "Don't try to shit a shitter, much less the Queen of Shit!"

Ruthie came to Penny Sue's aid. "Honestly, it's not marijuana." She studied her nails for a beat. "It was my idea, so don't blame Penny Sue. I was afraid that Abby's things might be contaminated ... that's the wrong word ..." Ruthie stroked her forehead and gave me a pleading glance, "oh, crap, ... have bad vibes. So we used the old American Indian technique of burning sage and cedar to clear the energy."

Guthrie slid the brownies on the counter. "Alice, it's really a common thing. Like, people do it all the time. In the olden days people did it at all the pot parties—" Guthrie stopped, realizing what he'd said, "to ... clear ... the energy." He skulked to the great room without another word.

Kevin shifted nervously behind his mother, who was giving us a very stern look. A look that reminded me so much of Grammy Martin that I tensed, expecting an onslaught of Bible quotations. Lying never worked with Grammy, so it was best to come clean. "Alice, we're telling the truth. We only smudged Abby's suitcases." I strode past her to the utility room and swung the door wide. The cross flow from the open windows sucked the sage/ cedar stench into the hall. Alice followed and watched skeptically as I reached behind the box of detergent and retrieved the wet smudge wand. "See, this is what you smell."

Alice sniffed it gingerly and was about to speak when a familiar voice came from the front doorway.

"I gather from the smell that you're up to your old habits, Penny Sue. I'm here to see Kevin Harrington."

Chapter 6

Old habits die hard, or at least they do with Woody. So much for our truce. He knew the smell was from sage and cedar. We'd told him that a number of times and showed him the smudge wand in the course of several investigations. We were not dope smokers or murderers. Why couldn't he get that through his thick skull? Just because Penny Sue dumped him in college, he was determined to make our lives as miserable as possible. Never mind that we hadn't pressed charges against his demented mother for threats and property damage, or that we'd accepted his apology and thanks. He'd shown his true colors—he was a weasel.

Kevin passed the bottle of scotch to Penny Sue and met Woody at the door. "What can I do for you?"

Alice whipped out of the utility room holding the smudge wand and stood beside her son. "I'm Alice Harrington, Kevin's mother. What was that rude comment about the smell? It's part of an American Indian ritual. Who are you and why are you such a bigot?"

Woody stepped back, clearly not used to being so blatantly challenged. "Uh, I'm not a bigot. I'm part American Indian myself."

"If that's true, I'd think you'd show more respect for your ancestors' customs. Who the hell are you to come in here making snide remarks and demanding to see my son?"

Woody looked as if he'd been punched in the gut. "I'm the local prosecutor assigned to the investigation of Dr. Abigail Johnston's death."

"As a government employee, I'd think you'd show more respect for your employers, the taxpayers."

Go, Alice, go, I thought.

Woody did a palms up. "I apologize for being flip. I know Penny Sue; we go back a long way."

Alice folded her arms and regarded him coldly. "I'm a retired government official myself, from New Jersey. Up there, a comment like that could land you in a garbage dump. I suggest that you work on your manners."

Woody squared his shoulders. "Is that supposed to be a threat?"

Alice smiled sweetly. "No, son, merely a suggestion. Charging in like a wild animal rarely gets results."

Silent until then, Kevin chimed in. "What do you want? We were about to sit down to dinner. I'm surprised you didn't have the courtesy to call ahead."

Since Kevin outweighed Woody by at least seventy-five pounds, and Woody didn't have his usual contingent of uniforms, Woody caved. "I'm sorry. If this isn't a good time, I can come back tomorrow."

Alice answered. "That's a good idea. We typically sleep late."

We nuked the Chinese food and had a fine dinner. Guthrie's brownies, his signature dish, were even good. "No nuts," he announced, because I'd once fibbed that I was allergic to nuts, fearing his brownies were laced with real marijuana. Well, he made such a big deal about the movie *Alice's Restaurant* that I mistakenly thought involved spiked brownies, I was afraid to eat his. Turns out I was wrong about the movie and his brownies. They were good old Duncan Hines Double Chocolate. Of course, Guthrie later gave spiked brownies to our competitors to help us win a charity race, but he swore that was the last of his stash, and we forgave him because it was for a good cause.

"Why do you think Woody wants to talk to me again?" Kevin asked, as Penny Sue served coffee.

"He's torturing me," Penny Sue said, pouring a cup for Alice. "We dated a few times in college, and I dumped him. He's held a grudge ever since."

"Seems he'd be questioning you, then," Alice said.

"He probably will at some point. I'm sure he's using Kevin's relationship with Abby and the debate to get back at me. Woody doesn't have anything on Kevin; he's playing games."

Aunt Alice sipped her coffee thoughtfully. "If that's the case, he's playing with fire. Anyone who messes with my son is messing with me."

Kevin winced. "Mom, I'm sure it's nothing. Woody's merely dotting the I's and crossing the T's for his bosses. The fact that Abby and I were engaged and that she willed her research to me probably raised some eyebrows."

"I'll bet I know one," Penny Sue said, as she dumped the last dollop of Baileys Irish Cream into her coffee. "Willows. He was at the library snooping around today. Given half a chance, I think he'd steal Abby's books and stuff."

"Willows?" Kevin repeated. "He probably would like to get his hands on her notes, when I think about it."

"Did you stay in touch with Abby?" Alice asked her son.

"No! I did my best to put her out of my mind. I was stunned when I heard she was taking Willows' spot in the debate. If I'd known, I'd never have agreed to participate. The whole thing took me by surprise."

Alice studied her coffee for a second. "Kevin, when did you find out that Abby was taking Willows' place?"

"The day before the debate."

"Abby had already been in New Smyrna Beach close to two weeks, according to the super at her rental agency," Alice said.

Kevin's jaw went slack. "You think it was a set-up? Why would Willows do that? We weren't great friends, but there wasn't any animosity between us."

Penny Sue gave Kevin her School Marm serious look. "Because you interviewed for the chairmanship of Deland University's History Department!"

"Yes, but ..."

"Isn't that why you came early?" Penny Sue said. "For the interviews and to get the lay of the land."

"What are you getting at?" Kevin asked.

"Willows is up for that spot, isn't he?" I asked.

"I'm sure he's a candidate. But how does Abby figure into this?"

Ruthie jumped in. "Was Abby qualified for the position?"

"Certainly. She won the Register Award."

"On the basis of your research," Alice added quickly.

"Mom, what are you suggesting?"

"Willows and Abby were in cahoots," Alice said.

"No way," Kevin almost shouted. "They were friends, nothing more."

"Kevin," Aunt Alice said sternly, "you're naive, always have been. You're honorable and think everyone else is. Everyone isn't."

"If they were up for the same position, what did they have to gain by conspiring against me?"

Alice arched a brow. "I can think of several possibilities."

"Such as?" Kevin asked.

"Figure it out." Alice held up her cup. "Any more of that Baileys?"

Penny Sue fidgeted, embarrassed. "Only some cheap stuff— Saint Somebody's Irish Cream. Sorry, I'm on a tight budget."

"That's fine, honey, it's going into coffee. I won't be able to tell the difference."

Woody called Penny Sue's cell phone at nine the next morning and woke her up. "Why are you calling me?" she asked drowsily.

"To make an appointment to interview Kevin Harrington."

"He's next door," she mumbled. "I'm staying with Leigh."

"Oh."

I was sipping coffee at my kitchen counter next to Penny Sue's room and could hear the conversation. She'd put the phone on speaker mode as she stumbled to the bathroom.

"Why are you tormenting him?" Penny Sue called. "Kevin loved Abby—he wouldn't hurt her. You're just being mean by scraping scabs off old wounds."

"Penny Sue, I'm not trying to be difficult. County officials in Deland are all over me. A lady and a man died in a public building. There are potential lawsuits at stake. In spite of what you think, this isn't personal. I have to examine everything. Kevin was once engaged to Dr. Johnston, and as I understand it, their parting was acrimonious. Something about her stealing his research?"

"Who told you that?"

"A reputable source; that's all I can say."

"If you want to speak with Kevin, call my condo number." Penny Sue started to recite it but he stopped her.

"I have it. Sorry to have bothered you."

"Woody, Kevin's mother has a lot of New Jersey contacts. Tread softly. Don't go locking Kevin up on a whim. After the Italian/Russian gang war during the hurricanes, I'm sure you know what I mean. If Alice happened to mention this to someone, who mentioned it to someone else, who knows what could happen. Get my point?"

"I appreciate your concern, but I'm a big boy. I know how to handle these situations."

"I hope you do." Penny Sue flushed the toilet.

We were loading the dishwasher when the postman arrived with an Express Letter for Penny Sue. It was the power of attorney form from her father. She gave me a guilty look as she asked to borrow Ruthie's Jaguar. "I have to get these in the mail right away," Penny Sue said.

"You're welcome to use my car, Penny Sue," I said with a wry grin.

"I've already imposed on you too many times. I won't be long," she said to Ruthie. "I'll just take them to the Coronado Post Office on Flagler Avenue." Ruthie nodded.

I slapped the air playfully. "Come on, Penny Sue, admit it. My car is a tight fit for you."

She raised her chin regally. "It is not too small; I fit in it just fine." She turned and wiggled her fanny. "The seats in Ruthie's car are softer."

Ruthie and I took our coffee to the table on the deck. The temperature was back to normal, and a pleasant breeze blew from the south. The water was calm, at least for the Atlantic, since there were no whitecaps on the horizon.

"This would be a good beach day. Do you have any plans?" I asked Ruthie.

"Kevin and I may start sorting and cataloguing Abby's books. He suspects he may already have a number of them and intends to donate duplicates to the library."

"You really like him, don't you?"

Ruthie's pale cheeks flamed. "Yes, I do. He's smart and a kind, gentle soul. I've been waiting for someone like him for a long time. I was beginning to believe such men didn't exist. I felt like I knew him the moment we met."

Wow. Her statement was a shocker. I knew they were attracted to each other, but I had no inkling of the depth of Ruthie's feelings. "Do you think you'd ever remarry?"

She stared at a sailboat on the horizon. "Maybe, if I got a proposal from the right man."

"Is Kevin right?"

"I believe he is, but marriage is a two way street." She glanced across the top of her coffee cup. "Actually, at our age, people live together. There's not much sense in getting married, since I certainly don't plan to have children."

I smiled. It was music to my ears to hear Ruthie say she'd even consider living with a man, because I had a feeling a proposal was in the offing. Kevin was a methodical man who, like Ruthie, had been burned in love before. He was merely taking his time. The recent mess didn't help matters any. "I don't doubt that a proposal will come, in time. But Kevin teaches at Columbia University. Would you be willing to move to New York City?"

Ruthie took a sip of her coffee. "I have plenty of money, so we could afford a place in the suburbs. Besides, I believe Kevin will get the chairmanship at Deland University, in which case we'll live down here."

"I'd love that! My fingers are crossed for you both. I hope Abby's death and Willows don't mess up the deal. Do you really think they were in cahoots? What does your intuition say?"

"I think there was something between them, but it's more complicated than we know." Ruthie paused in thought. "I can't put my finger on it. In some way, they were both enemies and allies. But I feel certain that Willows is feeding information to Woody to make Kevin look guilty. How else would Woody know that Kevin and Abby were once engaged?"

"Yeah, I had the same thought about Willows. Maybe he and Abby were allies to embarrass Kevin in the debate, but enemies over the chairmanship," I ventured.

"Could be, but we don't know for sure that Abby was a candidate for the position."

"Didn't you say she brought three business outfits?" I asked.

"Yes. Abby only needed one for the debate. Maybe the others were for job interviews. She also brought a lot of resort wear," Ruthie said.

I noticed sea gulls headed our way and instinctively ducked and covered my coffee. The reaction went back to our college days, when a flock of birds dropped a stinky load on Penny Sue's head that slopped into her drink.

Ruthie noticed my reaction and started to laugh. "Thank goodness we dodged that bullet," she said, gazing at the birds flying into the distance. "You know, since the Founders' Day Committee was paying for Abby's plane ticket, maybe she simply decided to make a vacation of the trip."

"True," I conceded.

We sat in silence for a long while, enjoying the warmth of the sun and beauty of the pristine beach. Suddenly, the realization hit me that Penny Sue would return any minute. There was something I'd been dying to ask Ruthie and preferred to ask without Penny Sue's presence. "Ruthie, tell me if I'm being too nosey, but I'm curious. Since Kevin arrived, I've noticed that you've started venturing out on your own. Where do you go? Are you just riding around to clear your head and gather your thoughts?"

Ruthie's face lit up. "I'm looking for a place to open a bookstore. You know, there isn't one on the island, and I think I've found the perfect place. There's a vacant lot on Flagler Avenue, midway down, close to the coffee shop and that new deli. I'm going to call it *Hungry for Knowledge,* and there'll be an area with tables so people can bring their coffee and sandwiches from the local delis to eat while they peruse books. I visited a store like that in Colorado and loved it."

"Ruthie, that's brilliant and perfect for a former librarian! How long have you had this idea?"

"Since Kevin came home from his interview. At that moment I just knew he'd get the position, and I'd move to New Smyrna Beach."

"You never said a word about it!"

"There's a New Age adage that talking dissipates energy while silence gathers it in. I wanted the energy to build up for this idea, because it feels so right. Please don't tell Penny Sue; you know she can't keep a secret. With her big mouth, my store's energy will spread to the four corners of the globe."

No sooner had the words left Ruthie's mouth than the front door banged open. "Hey, y'all. I picked up a six pack and some hoagies for lunch from Publix supermarket. Leigh, your friend Jennette says 'hi.'"

We ate lunch on the deck, enjoying the sun and generally speculating on the causes of Abby's and the other man's deaths. We resorted to calling him *the other man* because of Ruthie's strident objection that he was not a bum, even though *bum* was the consensus of the library staff. Whatever. Our discussion was pure speculation since we had no facts, so it went nowhere until an evaluation of the debate and the agitated realtor who slugged a New Smyrna Commissioner came up. It was then that Penny Sue remembered her meeting with Peter O'Brien and his intention to return to the library for Wii bowling.

"To be so angry, that realtor must have had a lot at stake. I think we need to check him out," I said.

Ruthie nodded. "Could be. He was unusually agitated."

Penny Sue's eyes sparkled. "I can do that. Peter, the guy's boss, is going to play Wii bowling today." She glanced at the clock. "I need to change, but I can make it if I hurry. I'll see what I can wheedle out of Peter. Don't worry if I miss dinner. I'll try to get him to go for drinks." She changed into a low cut blouse and capris.

"You can take my car," Ruthie shouted as Penny Sue charged out at a fast trot.

Ruthie and I exchanged a knowing glance. Only a wealthy, good looking man could draw such a fast response from Penny Sue.

Chapter 7

"*Is everyone decent?* I've got a good looking man with me!" Penny Sue hollered as she opened the front door.

Ruthie and I were watching *CSI* reruns in the living room. It was nine o'clock, and the tone of Penny Sue's voice told us she'd had a glass or three of wine. She and Peter O'Brien, the St. Augustine realtor who was Willows' friend, appeared a moment later. Peter was lugging a cardboard box that was obviously heavy, since his face was pinched with effort. Penny Sue made quick introductions, which were about a minute too long for Peter.

"Where should I put this?" Peter asked, perspiration starting to bead on his face and drip into the box.

I almost said, "In Penny Sue's bedroom," then realized her room was probably a wreck with underwear draped over the lampshade or hanging from a door handle. I motioned to a corner of the dining area. "That corner's fine for now. What is it?"

Penny Sue was already in the kitchen area of my great room fumbling with Mr. Coffee. She motioned to a barstool. "Peter, have a seat. Let me make some coffee. You have a long drive ahead."

He sat at the far end of the bar, angled so he could see us all. "That would be nice," he said to Penny Sue. Then to us, "The box is full of books."

"Would y'all like some?" Penny Sue asked. "Caffeinated. Peter needs to stay awake." Ruthie and I declined. We didn't need to stay awake; under normal circumstances, this was close to our bedtime. Penny Sue finished scooping coffee grounds and dumped in water. A moment later, the rich smell of French vanilla coffee filled the room. "We ran into Woody as we were leaving the library. They've finished the on-site investigation. These are the research materials Abby dropped when she ... well, you know. He gave them to me to take to Kevin, said it would save him a trip. Tacky, if you ask me. Woody is just plain lazy."

I wanted to follow up with questions about the investigation, but thought better of it, seeing how Peter was from St. Augustine. It's not that I thought Peter had anything to do with Abby's death; still, he was on the opposing side of the First City debate and probably not a big fan of Kevin and his theory. No sense dragging up controversial subjects. "Have you been bowling all this time?"

Penny Sue blew on her coffee before taking a sip. "No, we bowled a couple of hours, then went to the Riverview for dinner. You know, Wii bowling is really fun, almost like the real thing." She gave Peter a saucy wink. "Mr. O'Brien won the roll-off. He can put spin on the ball and everything."

Spinning the ball wasn't his only talent. Peter had obviously spun Penny Sue's head. Her true soul mate, Rich, was at least temporarily forgotten.

"Y'all should come next week," Penny Sue went on. "I think you'd like it. Your clothes don't get dirty and you don't have to wear those ugly, smelly shoes they have in real bowling alleys. There's another tournament next week and Peter's coming.

"He's working on an exciting business deal down here," she continued. "With the demise of the shuttle program, there's a possibility that the government, needing money, may be willing to sell off part of the Canaveral National Seashore Park. That's prime real estate and a terrific investment. He's put together a high level team of historians, environmentalists, archeologists, and lawyers to help convince the government." She pointed to his empty mug and Peter nodded. Penny Sue refilled it and passed the cream.

Peter swung around to face Ruthie and me. "This is all very preliminary, but a major unspoken reason for the park's existence was to provide a controlled buffer for the Kennedy Space Center. Without the shuttle program, there's really no need for the buffer. Private launches will likely be made from Cape Canaveral which is government-owned." He stared at Ruthie. Penny Sue had obviously mentioned Ruthie's huge inheritance. "It's a great chance to get in on the ground floor of a very upscale development on prime real estate. There isn't much undeveloped waterfront property left in Florida."

"Isn't your real estate firm in St. Augustine?" I asked. "Why are you interested in property down here?"

Peter grinned across the top of his coffee. "Because there isn't much left to develop up there. Besides, the weather here is better."

Ruthie was no fool, for all her seeming innocence. "Isn't that prime turtle nesting territory?"

Peter's smile diminished but didn't disappear. "Yes, that's why I've assembled a team of eminent scholars, and I plan to preserve and protect all of the environmental and archeological features like the Indians' Turtle Mound."

"That's nice to hear," Ruthie said, but didn't sound sincere.

Peter set his coffee mug down. "Well, I should be going. I have over an hour's drive ahead of me. Nice meeting you ladies," he said. "You really should try the bowling. It's amazingly realistic." Peter winked at Penny Sue. "I'll be back. I have to defend my championship. It seems the local champ wasn't there tonight. I heard a lot of mumbling that I wouldn't stand a chance against him." Peter grinned widely. Nice teeth. "I can't ignore that challenge."

"No, you certainly can't," Penny Sue gushed in her buttery drawl. She cradled his elbow and ushered him to the front door.

I turned to Ruthie. "How long do you give that one?"

Ruthie sniggered. "Until a richer or handsomer man shows up. Of course, she's not a one-man woman, so she could easily keep a couple on the string."

"I heard that!" Penny Sue shouted from the hallway.

"Boy, that was quick. No long kisses or passionate groping?" I said.

"Tacky, tacky, tacky." Penny Sue stomped to the kitchen, grabbed the bottle of Irish Cream and dumped it in her coffee.

"Come on, Penny Sue, I'm merely stating a fact. You're the one who juggled an Atlanta Falcon and a Brave at the same time."

She sat down, curled her lip, and gave me the old snake eye. A moment later a corner of her mouth turned up. "It wasn't just two; you forgot Lyndon. Three." She grinned smugly. "I juggled three good looking, rich men. If ya got it, flaunt it."

I smacked my forehead with the palm of my hand. "Of course, how stupid of me to forget Lyndon, the sleazeball who tried to manipulate you to retrieve the evidence that he was a thief."

She reared back. "He wasn't a thief, Lyndon bought those turtle eggs, even if it was illegal. And he really liked me—"

"Wait," Ruthie said forcefully. "Forget that stuff—it's old history. What did you find out about the rude realtor who works for Peter? That was the reason you went bowling in the first place."

"Oh, yeah." Penny Sue took a sip of coffee and put on her serious face. "Well, I had to be coy, since I didn't want to tip my hand. The guy's name is Willy, and he's a hot head. Peter has no proof, but he suspects Willy might sniff white powder on occasion. Peter would have fired him long ago, except Willy's father is a St. Augustine bigwig who owns a fair amount of land in the historic district. Willy's family goes back generations."

"So? Do you think Willy had a reason to kill Abby or the other guy?"

"We didn't get that far," Penny Sue replied. "Like I said, I had to be cagey. But if his family owns a lot of land, they stand to lose a fortune if Kevin's New Smyrna Beach theory turns out to be true."

"Yeah, but that doesn't give him a motive to kill Abby. Besides, aren't we jumping to conclusions?" Ruthie asked. "We don't know that Abby was murdered. Maybe she had a heart defect or something, and died of natural causes."

"It's pretty unusual for two people to die in a library on the same night," Penny Sue shot back.

"True," I said. "I wonder if the autopsies have been finished and if there was any connection between Abby and the bum."

"Don't call him a bum," Ruthie objected. "It's disrespectful. His spirit could be here right this minute."

I looked up at the ceiling and spoke to the unseen spirit. "I didn't mean to be disrespectful. I was parroting what most people at the library call you. I apologize. I was thoughtless."

"Any way we can find out about the autopsies?" Ruthie continued.

"Woody sure isn't going to tell us." Penny Sue turned to me. "What about your friend, Deputy Ted?"

"I haven't seen or heard from him in months. He may have gone back with his wife for all I know. Heather Brooks is a better candidate."

"Good idea. How can we reach her?"

"We certainly shouldn't call the Sheriff's Office; we need to keep this low key," Ruthie said. "A couple of times when I was out riding around, I noticed her car in the public lot on Hiles. She was probably looking for speeders or doing her reports."

"Yeah, police stake that out all the time. We should make a point of looping by there whenever we go out. We'll stumble across her," Penny Sue agreed. "I'm sure she'd be more likely to talk without an audience."

"Guthrie and I will try to get the scoop on the ... dead man. Is there anything else?" I asked.

Ruthie gazed at the box in the corner. "Someone should go through that box, in case there are incriminating notes or other clues. Is her computer in there?"

"Yes." Penny Sue yawned. "Ruthie, you and Kevin are prime candidates for that job. You're already cataloging the boxes Alice got from Abby's room."

"The fact that Mrs. Johnston asked for an autopsy tells me that Abby didn't have a congenital condition or a serious illness her mother knew about. Unless they were completely estranged, a mother would know." The instant the words left my mouth I thought of Ann and Zack, Jr. If they were seriously ill, would they tell me? Would they hide it so I wouldn't worry? The little boogers better not! I was going to call them first thing in the morning.

Penny Sue had the day off, so I called my daughter Ann from the privacy of my car parked in the library lot. After a stint working at the U.S. Embassy in London, she was now living in Washington, D.C., studying for a master's degree in International Relations. I caught her before she left for class.

"Are you sick?" I asked. No sense beating around the bush.

"No! Why do you ask?"

"Have you talked to your brother? Is he all right?"

"I spoke with him on his birthday. He seemed fine then."

"If you were injured or had a horrible disease, would you tell me?"

"Of course. Mom, what's up? Penny Sue's down there, isn't she? You always act crazy when she's around." Ann sucked in a breath. "Lord, y'all haven't stumbled over a body again, have you? Every time Penny Sue goes to Florida, someone ends up dead."

"This wasn't our fault."

"It never is. Penny Sue is a magnet for murder and mayhem."

"You sound like your father."

"Well, it's true. Why do you think I'm sick?" Ann asked.

"Oh, I'm just upset. A lecturer at the library turned up dead. She was a young woman, only in her forties." *About my age!* "Her mother didn't know of any health problems. It made me wonder if you and Zack, Jr. would tell me if anything was wrong, or if you'd try to shield me from bad news."

Ann sighed. "Mom, I'd tell you if I had problems. You'd be the first person I'd call. I'd want your support."

Tears welled in my eyes. "Do you promise?"

"Yes, cross my heart. I'll tell you first if I'm ever sick. Do you want to know about cramps and colds?"

"You don't have to go that far. Just swear you'll tell me if there's anything serious."

"I will. So what's the deal with the dead lady? You're not accused of a crime, are you?" Ann asked anxiously.

"No, but her death is suspicious, and the police are taking an unusual interest in Penny Sue's Cousin Kevin."

"The professor?"

"One and the same."

"Mom, if you're not a suspect, please don't get involved. I'm having a hard enough time with my thesis without having to worry about you."

"Okay, darling. Forget I called. I'm being silly." I checked my face in the rearview mirror. No tracks of my tears. "I need to go or I'll be late for work. I love you, sweetheart. Be careful."

"You're the one who needs to be careful!"

I worked checkout, which was fairly slow. The crowds had thinned considerably since the crime tape had been removed.

There was only an occasional question from patrons about Abby, and the library's gossip level was back to normal. Whenever I got a chance, I quizzed my coworkers about the identity of the so-called bum. No one knew the dead man's name, and he didn't appear to have checked out any books. The only comments were that he seemed too clean to be homeless, and he did more people watching than reading. Not much to go on. It appeared Heather Brooks was our best hope for finding out about the man's death.

By afternoon, the day was really dragging. I kept checking my watch, but the hands did not seem to move until about four o'clock. That's when a disheveled man dressed in khaki slacks and a wrinkled dress shirt, with sleeves rolled up to his elbows, rushed in the library and made a beeline for the magazine section. He had sandy blond hair in dire need of a trim, and a round, boyish face. He did a three-sixty degree inspection of the library, then raced toward me.

"Has a slender fellow with curly hair been in the magazine section today?" he asked with a distinct British accent. "A bloke about my height. He comes here often, I understand."

Could he be talking about the dead bum? "Uh, there is a gentleman that fits that description."

"Has he been here in the last two days?" the Brit asked anxiously.

I wasn't certain we were thinking of the same person, but in any event I sure as shootin' didn't want to break the news that his friend might be dead. "Let me get the branch manager. She may know something. I'll only be a minute." I scurried to the back room, found Terry, and quickly explained the situation.

"Goodness," she said, eyes round. "I have no idea how to handle this. I guess I should refer him to the police."

Terry followed me to the front and introduced herself to the man, who said his name was Leonard Kydd. "There was an accident involving an unidentified male. He may be the man you're looking for. The best thing you can do is contact the Volusia

County Sheriff. Come to my office, and I'll call them for you. Are you a relative?"

Panic crossed Leonard Kydd's face. "No. I have a cell, I'll phone myself. I appreciate the information. Have a nice day," Leonard mumbled over his shoulder as he pounded out of the library.

"I don't know if he's going to call the Sheriff, but I am." Terry turned on her heel and hurried to her office.

Guthrie and Alice were stretched out in lawn chairs, sunning themselves in the parking lot when I arrived home. A cool wind was blowing from the north and the beach was shadowed by the condo this late in the day. A small patch next to the front door was one of the few spots in full sun. Guthrie tipped his glass at me as way of greeting.

"Alice and I are resting up from a full day of investigation. Man, I think we're on to something."

I shut my car door. "Good. I had an interesting development, too. I'll fill you in later. Now I need to get out of these clothes and put my feet up. Where's everyone else?"

"Kevin, Ruthie, and Penny Sue are in your living room going through Abby's computer and books."

My living room? Great. How come I always end up with the short end of the stick? I slung my purse to my shoulder. "I'm beat. Any plans for dinner?"

Alice answered. "We're sending out for seafood—my treat. That's why I told Kevin to take the books to your condo. Penny Sue's dining room table is bigger than yours. I thought we'd eat at six-thirty."

"That's fine. We can fill each other in over dinner." I started for my front door.

Guthrie held up his cell phone. "Just call me with your order after you change. I already have everyone else's."

I snuck into my bedroom, drew a bath, stripped and sank into the tub. The warm water and solitude were heavenly. My solitary, peaceful life had suddenly been turned upside down and I felt like I was back in the sorority house. Only I wasn't 20 and didn't have the energy I did back then. I wasn't used to so much company and commotion.

Don't get me wrong—Ruthie was an ideal houseguest. She liked to meditate, watch TV, and clean. The cleaning part was fine with me, since it wasn't my strong suit unless I was upset about something. That's when I cleaned the floors and closets, sometimes even straightening the drawers in the kitchen. The amount of effort was in direct proportion to my distress.

As guests go, Kevin was on par with Ruthie, since his favorite pastime was reading. Penny Sue was a disaster waiting to happen. Fortunately, she typically wasn't in residence, except now that she'd lost her fortune and was trying to sell her house in Georgia. Even Guthrie wasn't too bad, until Timothy moved to Houston. Before that, Guthrie only dropped in for an occasional drink after working on old computers all day. But Alice had completely disrupted our social equilibrium, such as it was. She was a take-charge, brusque woman used to calling the shots. I felt my life was out of control and I was merely a staff person—a lot like my marriage to Zack. Although the water in the tub was growing cold, I was getting hot at the mere thought of my worthless ex-husband.

Stop! I told myself. Alice was not Zack, and we were doing all of this to help Kevin. Woody obviously thought Kevin killed Abby, yet there was no way that gentle man could murder any-one. We also knew Woody was a jerk. We would not allow Woody to railroad Kevin for Abby's death. From what Penny Sue said, it was in our best interest to clear Kevin before Alice felt com-pelled to call in her New Jersey gang connections. After our run-in with the Italian and Russian mafias, I did not want to draw their attention again! What if Alice's contacts made the connection between us and the mob carnage during the 2004 hurricanes? Lordy, we could be sitting ducks that even Alice and Judge Daddy couldn't protect.

Our seafood dinner was delicious, particularly because I didn't have to cook it. I took my last bite of blackened grouper and gazed across the table at Alice as I chewed. For such a little bitty person, she had one helluva big personality. Of course, if her husband was as timid as Penny Sue claimed, and her family disowned her, circumstances forced Alice to develop a tough skin. I cut my eyes at Penny Sue, who sat at the head of the table. At about five-eight, her personality matched her height, yet the two women were eerily similar. I hadn't known Penny Sue's mother well, bless her soul, but suspected Momma Parker possessed the same grit. I suppose the Judge's presence was so overpowering, her strength didn't shine through very often. A lot of Southern women were like that—it went back to the Civil War—a soft, sugary veneer over a stainless steel backbone.

Penny Sue stood. "Who'd like decaf?" Everyone did, except Guthrie, who wanted a scotch.

One benefit of Alice's visit was that Penny Sue's alcohol consumption had diminished considerably. That was good, because I couldn't afford to keep her in booze and the way she chugged it before Alice's arrival, I considered starting an Al-Anon or AA chapter. Penny Sue always liked her wine, but she'd started drinking more than usual after she lost her Madoff investment. Ruthie speculated that Penny Sue was self-medicating the anxiety over her financial situation. She was far from poor by normal standards, yet poverty stricken in comparison to her old lifestyle, which was in the league of reality shows about housewives in Atlanta and Orange County.

Once the coffee was passed around, we were ready to process the day's events. Guthrie's thoughts came fastest.

"Well," he said dramatically, "I had a service call at a house on North Beach. Man, that house was huge! It had this fancy stacked-stone wall with a wrought iron gate and we had to, like, identify ourselves before they'd let us in. I thought it was strange that someone that rich would have old computers. Didn't you?" he asked Alice.

She rolled her eyes. "Yes, it was strange."

"An-nyway," Guthrie continued with a shoulder gyration, "they had been robbed which forced them to pull out their old computers. The police were there and had picked up some guys on the beach in a big van filled with stolen equipment. The cops were questioning them in the driveway, when an Englishman stormed up asking if the suspects knew a man called Splash." Guthrie took a sip of his drink. "Now, what kind of a name is Splash? The crooks said they didn't know him. Then the Brit said Splash often hung out at the library." Guthrie took a big swig this time. "The cops shooed us away, and I had to fix the computers, but that's strange, don't you think?"

Alice glared at Guthrie. "Get a grip! Of course it's strange. Splash is obviously the dead guy found at the library."

"I agree." I thunked down my mug. "A Brit named Leonard Kydd came to the library this afternoon asking about a guy who visited the magazine section. Terry told him a man fitting the description had been found dead. Leonard left immediately, clearly upset."

"It must be the same person," Penny Sue said. "How many Brits are in New Smyrna Beach?"

Kevin canted his head. "A lot, I'm afraid. A huge English contingency attended the Founders' Day celebration, since New Smyrna was an English colony established by Dr. Andrew Turnbull."

"So, these Turnbull people might want to discredit you, too," Ruthie mused. "If your theory's correct that New Smyrna was first settled by Europeans as early as the 1400s, then that takes Turnbull down a notch."

Kevin's eyes widened. "I hadn't thought of that."

"Did you find anything on Abby's computer?" I asked.

"A large folder is password protected—we couldn't get in," Kevin said. "I tried everything I could think of—her social security number, her beloved poodle's name, her birth date—nothing worked."

"Don't worry, I know a person who can find the password." I turned to Ruthie. "Fran's son, Carl, can do it. Remember how he decrypted the FBI's computer during Bike Week?"

She grinned. "Of course, I completely forgot about that."

"I'll give Carl a call. If we get into Abby's computer, we might at least find out if she was a candidate for the Deland University chairmanship."

"And why she brought three business suits," Penny Sue added.

"I can't take another *Criminal Minds*," Ruthie said forcefully, as we turned on the TV in my condo. "I had horrible dreams last night. How about *Numbers*? I like that show."

"You were terrible at math," Penny Sue said.

"Yes, but the show's upbeat and the math is real. We can learn something," Ruthie countered.

I grinned. It was good to be back in my condo with just the three of us and the usual banter. "I vote for *Numbers*," I said. "*Criminal Minds* is starting to scare me, too. How about a Baileys on the rocks?"

Penny Sue scowled. "We're out of Baileys. We only have that cheap stuff."

"So what? All Irish cream liquor over ice tastes the same."

"You're probably right. Okay, I can go with *Numbers*. The curly haired mathematician is cute. I think I could learn math if I had him for a teacher." Penny Sue batted her eyes impishly.

"Fat chance! I doubt that Adonis could teach you math. That was your worst subject, too," I said.

"That was only because the professors were old. I would have paid attention to a young hottie and might have learned something."

"Learned what? Or, would you have taught him a thing or two?" I winked at Ruthie.

Penny Sue's lips stretched to a devilish grin. "There are probably a few pointers I could share."

"I'm sure of that," I exclaimed, remembering her story about the party where a man leaned forward to kiss her hand but licked her Wonder Bra-ed boob instead. Poor Rich—wherever he was—surely didn't have a clue about the true Penny Sue. I made the drinks, turned off the lights, and we settled around the TV to watch the cute professor. Perhaps we really would learn something useful.

About halfway through the show, just as the professor came up with a terrorist-catching algorithm, there was a scraping sound on the glass doors facing the ocean.

"Did you hear that?" Ruthie whispered. She had the TV clicker and turned down the volume. We strained to listen.

"It's a palm frond scratching against the door," Penny Sue said.

Ruthie didn't buy the explanation. She slunk out of the glow of the TV and peeked through the vertical blinds. "No, someone's out there!"

Penny Sue and I scattered from the TV's glimmer and sneaked a look for ourselves. There was a shadow at the junction between the two sliding glass doors.

"Is Lu Nee 2 on?" Penny Sue whispered.

"No, she's in your condo," I whispered back.

"Well, is the alarm on?"

"I don't have an alarm," I admitted.

"No alarm? Do you at least have the liquid taser?" Penny Sue hissed as she crept to her bedroom, no doubt going for her .38.

"I never brought it over when I moved from your condo."

"Crap!" Penny Sue crawled back with her gun. "Ruthie, scoot over to the light switch for the deck and turn it on when I give you the word."

"Me?"

"Yes, you!"

As Ruthie made her way to the light switch, I crept to the phone in the kitchen, crouched behind the counter, and dialed Penny Sue's condo's number. Kevin answered. I quickly explained the situation and told him where to find the liquid taser.

With Ruthie in position, Penny Sue shouted, "On!" The deck was filled with light, and Penny Sue jerked open the vertical blinds. Two men were hunched at our door, one holding a long, metal slim jim. Blinded, they stumbled backward, tripped over the deck's low railing and fell onto the sand dune. A moment later, Kevin and Alice appeared on the deck next door. Kevin carried the taser, while Alice packed a large pistol. Kevin fired several shots at the would-be intruders, who by then were hightailing it toward the beach and out of range. Thankfully, Alice didn't feel a need to shoot, since they were on the run.

I flipped a switch in the kitchen and the great room lit up like a Christmas tree. Kevin squatted outside the glass doors, while Penny Sue inspected them from the inside. A moment later she stood up, holding a broomstick that I'd wedged in the track of the sliding doors so they couldn't be opened.

"This is your security system?" she demanded hotly.

I folded my arms defensively. "I couldn't afford anything else with all of the repairs from the hurricanes. Besides, everyone uses them. You did."

Hand on hip, Penny Sue gave me a squinty-eyed look that would have fried the devil. "And it didn't work, remember? Kevin," she screeched. "please give me the taser and bring Lu Nee 2 over here right now."

Kevin glared at Penny Sue. "What the heck is Lu Nee 2?"

Chapter 8

Lu Nee 2 is a robot. It was named after Lu Nee 1 that was a Furby. A drug-smuggling criminal didn't cotton to Lu Nee 1. The ruthless thug slammed little Lu Nee into a closet and busted its brains out. Talk about mean! How could someone smash a cute toy? Such cruelty surely deserved a life sentence in the poky. The perpetrator actually was incarcerated for drugs and money laundering but died of a heart attack before the trial. Ruthie said it was karma—his hard heart did him in.

Penny Sue bought Lu Nee 2 because her condo didn't have an alarm system, and we had been stalked by numerous despicable hoodlums on our first visit. The robot was intended to act as a security guard, since it sensed motion and called out, "Halt, who goes there?" If nothing else, the R2D2 look-alike alerted inhabitants to an intruder. The robot was also supposed to be a maid, fetching drinks, snacks, and what not. Unfortunately, Penny Sue never mastered the remote control for that task, leading to a lot of broken stemware and spilled drinks.

Yep, our first trip was a real mess. I tripped over a body and pretty soon it seemed everyone was out to get us. Things became so bad that Ruthie's father, rest his soul, arranged to have a liquid taser sent to us from a company he'd invested in. The prototype weapon looked a lot like a kid's super soaker water gun, except this booger was no toy. It shot electrified saline solution that could stun and disable multiple subjects. The technology was under development for the Army. They were going to outfit a new version of Abrams tanks with the system, so instead of mowing down the enemy with cannons and machine guns, this device would squirt them into a stupor. A win-win. The soldiers were immobilized and no one was killed, unless, of course, someone happened to have a pacemaker that shorted out. The liquid taser was a marvelous invention that had saved our lives on several occasions.

Penny Sue opened the back door and let Kevin and Alice in from the deck. Ruthie had already dialed 9-1-1 and was talking to the dispatcher. Alice stomped in circles, muttering that she never had a clear shot.

Kevin handed the taser to Penny Sue. "What is Lu Nee 2?"

"It's the robot in the big closet."

Kevin was perplexed. "Why do you want that toy?"

"It's not a toy; it's a motion-detecting security system," Penny Sue snapped. "You probably need to charge it first. There's a cord wrapped around its arm."

A knock on the front door was Kevin's cue to leave. He bolted out the back and across our condos' shared deck, as Ruthie answered the door. It was Deputy Heather Brooks and a young patrolman.

"Is everyone all right?" Heather asked, as she strode past us to the glass doors.

"Yes, we were watching television in the dark when we heard a scraping noise on the glass," I said. "I suppose the burglars thought the TV glow was a nightlight and the place was empty."

"They were trying to lift the pole in the door's track with a slim jim," Penny Sue added, leading Heather to the deck. "We called Kevin next door at my place, and I got my .38. When we turned on the floodlights, two men scattered. Kevin got off a few shots with the taser, but they were out of range." Penny Sue pointed across the dunes. "They went that way."

With flashlights and guns in hand, Heather and her partner followed the footprints down to the beach. We watched from the deck, straining to keep them in view. They came back up the walkway from the beach a few minutes later.

"Long gone," Heather said. "There were tire tracks on the beach; they must have driven down here."

"But driving is prohibited on this part of the beach because of the sea turtles," Ruthie blurted.

Penny Sue gave her a sour look. "Burglars couldn't care less about turtles, Ruthie."

"Of course," Ruthie agreed, her face crimson. "I wasn't thinking."

"There've been a rash of burglaries," Heather continued, stooping to examine the juncture of the glass doors. "Has anyone touched this?"

"No," Alice said quickly before Penny Sue could answer. "Do you think you can lift a print?"

"Maybe. See, there's a handprint here where they pushed the door to insert the slim jim. I'll get a crime tech out here right away. We think these robberies are tied to a meth operation in the area."

"I thought you'd already arrested those guys," Alice said. "Guthrie and I saw them on North Beach today."

"Yeah." Heather stood and stretched. "City police arrested two men, but we don't think that's all of them. Last I heard, they were still being questioned. Your guys may be part of the same gang. A good fingerprint would help a lot. Tommy," she said to her partner, "call for a crime tech."

"Will do." He headed to the patrol car.

Heather regarded me seriously, holding the pole. "Leigh, you know this isn't much of a security system."

"I told her the same thing," Penny Sue snapped. "She needs a real security system like I have."

"Wait a minute. You used a pole in your door track for years, until your condo was robbed and we were almost killed," I retorted.

"Well, Leigh, you should have learned a lesson from that," Penny Sue replied in her School Marm tone.

"I'm not made of money like you used to be."

That stopped her. Penny Sue pouted and her eyes narrowed to slits.

I gave her a palms up. "Sorry, that was a low blow."

"Yes, it was." She turned her back on me.

"Ladies," Heather interrupted. "You're both upset. Let it go. This isn't the time for good friends to argue."

Penny Sue glanced at me, her jaw muscles twitching. "I guess we are on edge."

"Yes, it was a mean thing to say. I'm truly sorry."

She turned to face me. "It was hateful," Penny Sue said haughtily, "but I forgive you. I know you would have installed an alarm if you could afford it. Lord, life is expensive, isn't it?"

"It is on the beach." I gave Penny Sue a hug.

"For godssake, give me a break!" Alice stuffed her pistol in the pocket of her robe. "I can't stand blubbering women." She marched out the door, back to Penny Sue's condo.

"Who is that?" Heather asked.

"The Queen of Shit. My aunt from New Jersey, Kevin's mother."

"Does *the Queen* have a permit for that gun?" Heather continued.

"I have no idea." Penny Sue paused, thinking, then continued with a sparkle in her eye. "It's probably hot, a throwaway from a mob shootout. Why don't you check it out? Maybe you can arrest her."

Heather snickered. "No way I'm getting in the middle of your family squabbles." She handed me the pole. "I think I'll wait in the car for the city crime tech."

"City? Why are you here? We live in the city."

"There's a new cooperative agreement between the city and county. Whoever's closest responds. I was close. Besides, the entire beach is county property."

* * *

Woody arrived with the technician. "Leigh, I heard you'd had a break-in. Is everyone all right? Was anything stolen?"

"How did you hear?" Penny Sue asked suspiciously. "Am I still on your watch list?"

"I got a call because I live in your neighborhood, remember? No matter what you think, I'm not out to get you."

"Sure seems that way," she drawled.

"Hey, if everyone's okay, I'm out of here," Woody said curtly.

"Penny Sue!" Ruthie frowned at her.

Penny Sue glanced from Ruthie to Woody and let out a long breath. "Woody, I'm sorry. I was rude. I'm on edge."

He turned halfway to the front door. "Forget it, apology accepted. I'm glad to see no one was injured."

We were finishing sodas, when the crime tech and Heather came in from the deck. "We have several good prints," Heather said. "It's late. That's it for now, but I'll need statements from everyone tomorrow. My shift is about to end." Heather grinned. It was close to eleven p.m.

"How about nine?" I asked. "I would just as soon get it over with."

"That works," Heather said. The crime tech left, but Heather lingered. "Leigh, with the recent break-ins, a security system or real locks for the back doors are a good idea. All of the robbers have come from the beach. I think you can have holes drilled and pins installed to lock those doors pretty cheaply. I'd do it, if I were you."

Ruthie spoke before my sleep-deprived brain had a thought fully formed. "Don't worry, we'll order a high tech security system tomorrow. I'm buying."

"And my robot will provide security for tonight. It has a motion detector," Penny Sue bragged. The words were barely out of her mouth when a mechanical voice cried, "*Whoops. Where did that come from?*" Lu Nee 2 zig-zagged toward us, bumping into the walls along the way. I cringed—the walls had recently been painted. A shame Kevin wasn't much better with the remote control than Penny Sue.

"Is that your robot?" Heather asked, stifling a snicker.

"Yes," Penny Sue replied defensively.

"Then I suggest you put 9-1-1 on speed dial."

The night was uneventful, not a single peep from Lu Nee 2, and our interviews the next morning went smoothly. The fingerprints on the doorway looked promising, and Heather hoped they would identify the culprits. She'd also learned that an old Volvo was seen speeding down the beach toward the Flagler Avenue beach access ramp shortly after the attempted break-in. She speculated it was the getaway car our intruders used. Heather promised to keep us informed of any developments.

"Do you have another minute?" I asked Heather. "We wondered if there was any news on the man found dead at the library. Does anyone know who he is or how he died?"

"I can't talk about an ongoing investigation except to say that an autopsy is being performed."

"Well, a Leonard Kydd came in the library looking for a friend that matches the dead man's description. We referred him to the Sheriff's Department and he said he'd call them. Do you know if he did?"

Heather was suddenly all business. "I don't know anything about it. What did he look like?" I described Kydd, stressing his British accent and frantic behavior. "Please call me if you see him again. I'd like to speak with this guy." Heather handed me a card with her cell phone number, just as the radio on her belt spit static. She waved a thanks and headed out, already listening to her radio.

"Heather knows more than she admits," Penny Sue said.

I nodded. "No doubt about it."

As soon as Heather left, Ruthie started calling alarm companies. Two companies were available that afternoon, and a third could make it the next day. Penny Sue and I were sipping coffee and munching cinnamon raisin toast. Ruthie joined us at the kitchen counter.

"What do you have planned today?" I asked Ruthie.

"Besides getting bids on the alarm system, Kevin and I will probably work on cataloguing Abby's books." She motioned to the stack of boxes against the wall that had grown in size since I last noticed. "UPS delivered several boxes from Abby's mother yesterday. I took the delivery, since Alice was out with Guthrie and Kevin. Penny Sue had run to the store."

"Did you smudge them?" Penny Sue asked with a panicked expression.

"Yes, I did it as soon as they arrived. Those books came from Abby's apartment, so they are loaded with her vibes."

"Good." Penny Sue took a bite of toast and held up a finger while she chewed. "You know, Ruthie, Abby might not like the idea that you have her stuff, considering you and Kevin are becoming pretty tight. She might try to haunt you or something."

"I had that thought," Ruthie replied, "so I used extra sage."

Great. I not only was embroiled in another death, and had Penny Sue living with me, but now there was the possibility that my condo might be haunted. I rolled my eyes to the ceiling. *Why me, Lord?* It was Penny Sue. Stuff like this only happened when she was around.

Thankfully the telephone rang, diverting my attention from the spirits and hauntings. Penny Sue lunged for the phone, no doubt hoping it was Peter O'Brien. In a split second, her demeanor changed to surprised horror.

"Who, why?" she screeched. "Hold on," Penny Sue said to the caller. Then to us, "It's Alice. The New Smyrna Beach police just took Kevin into custody!" Back to the phone, she said, "I'm going to put you on the speaker if that's okay. Leigh and Ruthie are here."

I guess Alice said 'yes,' because her quivering, shrill voice filled the room. "They said there was a warrant out for Kevin in New Jersey. Failure to Appear, FTA, for a traffic accident! New Jersey wants him extradited. But, Volusia County wants to hold him as a material witness pending the results of Abby's autopsy. They think he's a flight risk if he leaves Florida. It's a big, made-up crock if you ask me. New Jersey authorities discovered his whereabouts when Volusia County ran a search on Kevin."

"For goshsakes, Heather from the Volusia County Sheriff's Department just left. The two groups must have passed each other," Ruthie exclaimed.

"See, it must be a set-up!" Alice yelled. "I'm calling my contacts at home."

"Aunt Alice, please don't do that. It will complicate things—" Penny Sue started.

"—and may put our lives in danger," I jumped in, recalling the terror of the Russian and Italian mob shootout in our complex a few years ago.

"How could it affect you?" Alice demanded.

"Please come over so we can explain," I pleaded.

Guthrie arrived at our front door before Alice. Since he usually drank his coffee, or whatever, on his balcony that overlooked our parking lot, he saw the two sets of law enforcement arrive and witnessed Kevin being led out. Guthrie was on our doorstep the moment the cops left. Alice appeared before we could close the door. She has holding a scotch and her cell phone.

"I just left a message for my contact at an Italian family. I won't say who," Alice blurted, mad as a hornet.

"Aunt Alice, we asked you to wait," Penny Sue said.

Five-foot-four Alice instantly seemed to telescope to ten-foot-six. "My only son was led away in handcuffs! Did you really think I'd do nothing?"

"There are things you don't know," I said gently, guiding her into the great room. "Coffee, anyone?" I asked, half expecting Guthrie to request a scotch.

"Black," Guthrie replied, as he sat at the counter. "Believe it or not, I have a job in Daytona Beach at the Medical Examiner's. Can you believe it? I may be able to sneak a peek at Abby's autopsy report. There was a power outage last night that screwed up their system, and some of their computers are really old."

"Can I go with you?" Alice asked, taking a big gulp of scotch.

For once, Guthrie gave the scotch a disapproving look. "Alice, this is a state facility. Man, we can't go in smelling like booze, or I'll lose the job. My contact is a buddy from the olden days, if you get my drift, but he's clean and sober now. A single whiff of alcohol and I'm off the list."

Alice handed her drink to Penny Sue and motioned to the sink. "I'll have a cup of black coffee," Alice said. "So what's this stuff about endangering your lives?" she asked me.

I gave her an abbreviated version of the New Jersey gang war during the 2004 hurricanes.

"I didn't know that," Alice said. "This could be a problem, not only for you, but for Kevin."

Penny Sue's eyes went wide. "You didn't call any Russians, did you?"

Tiny Alice flashed a tiny smile. "I did make one call to an old acquaintance."

I threw my head back. "Oh, crap."

Penny Sue's eyes bored holes in me. "Don't talk to my Aunt like that!"

"I'm sorry, Alice, but we don't need to be in the middle of another mob war," I said.

"Tell me again, why was Kevin arrested?" Ruthie asked Alice.

"He's actually being held by Volusia County as a material witness to prevent his extradition to New Jersey. I know the cops think I'll be able to get him out of jail in Jersey; they said as much."

"Why does New Jersey want Kevin?" Ruthie pressed.

Alice's shoulders slumped, the look of an old woman who was worn and tired but refused to give in to age. "A turnpike pileup where a woman was killed." She sighed. "It was all because of a domestic dispute. The husband had been drinking, the couple argued, and the wife fled in her car. The husband went after her, and Kevin happened to be behind the husband on the turnpike. Well, there was a minor fender bender ahead. The wife hit her brakes, but the husband's reflexes weren't very good, so he hit her hard. The poor lady was squished. Kevin was able to stop and only sustained minor damage, but he was subpoenaed to appear in court for the prosecution. The husband was charged with DUI and vehicular manslaughter. The trial was postponed, and Kevin swears he never received a notice that it had been rescheduled." Alice gritted her teeth. "The process server says otherwise, so now Kevin's FTA in Jersey."

"Gracious, what a mess," Ruthie said, cutting her eyes at Penny Sue. "And all because of alcohol."

Penny Sue's eyes narrowed. "You don't know that. There was probably a lot more to the couple's argument than alcohol. Besides, Volusia County is holding Kevin as a material witness for Abby's death." Penny Sue had flipped into her Jessica Fletcher persona.

"If that's true, they must have ruled out natural causes," Ruthie mused.

Penny Sue started to pace. "We need information on the autopsies, and we need to find out who the dead man was." She planted her feet and stared at me. "What was the name of the guy looking for the bum?"

"Don't call him a bum!" Ruthie snapped.

Penny Sue rolled her eyes. "Excuse me. The dead man, is that all right?"

"Leonard Kydd," I said quickly, hoping to prevent our own domestic disturbance. "What Kevin really needs is a lawyer. Penny Sue, do you suppose your dad can recommend someone?"

"Sure, I'll give him a call."

"Ladies," Guthrie interrupted, "I have to go. I'll try to do some snooping at the Medical Examiner's office." He turned to Alice. "If you can get the scotch odor off your breath, you can tag along as my assistant. But you can't be aggressive. Don't ask any questions. And, man, please don't threaten anyone."

Alice looked contrite. "Agreed. You call the shots."

"While you're doing that, we'll track down Kydd. Can you call off your New Jersey dogs?" Penny Sue asked Alice.

She snatched her cell phone and headed for the door. "I'll try, but those guys move fast. Guthrie, when are you leaving?"

"In an hour."

"I'll gargle mouthwash and be at your bus by then."

Chapter 9

As soon as Guthrie and Alice left, Ruthie folded her arms and slumped on the counter.

"You're not going to get sick, are you?" Penny Sue shrieked, inching away.

I bolted from my stool and stroked Ruthie's back at arm's length. Ruthie had a weak stomach that was known to act up in tense situations, and I was not in the mood for puke so early in the morning.

"I'm fine. I just can't believe Kevin's in jail and Alice called in the mafia." Ruthie reached for my telephone. "If any of the alarm companies can install a system today, I'm buying it. We don't have time to lose, and Lu Nee 2's *Halt, who goes there?* doesn't cut it for me."

"God's truth," Penny Sue replied, en route to the taser positioned on the coffee table. She ejected the battery pack and plugged it into the wall. "Is there any more of the saline solution?"

"I believe there's another bottle in your condo," I said.

"I'll call the company and get them to express ship some more." Ruthie held up her finger to silence us when the alarm company answered. She talked for a few minutes, then hung up disgustedly. "They don't keep an inventory. Everything has to be special ordered after the inspection." The second company wasn't any better. "Darn it, they don't stock anything, either. I guess we're on our own for a few days."

"We should spend the night in Penny Sue's condo. It's alarmed, and we really shouldn't leave Alice there alone. Two of us can sleep in Kevin's room and the other—"

Penny Sue's jaw muscles contracted. "Well, I'm not sleeping with Alice, even if it's a king-sized bed!"

"I'll sleep on your sofa. You can sleep with Ruthie," I said quickly. Penny Sue snored like a sailor. Of course, she didn't believe us and refused to be tested for sleep apnea, saying a stupid mask would ruin her sex life. We tried to tell her that dying would be worse for her sex life, but she wouldn't listen. Muleheaded. Judge Daddy had her pegged right.

Ruthie's eyes went wide, no doubt picking up my thought about the snoring. "I'm shorter, I'll sleep on the sofa," she said.

"For heavens sake, you're buying me an alarm system. Sleeping on the sofa is the least I can do."

"Yes, but I've stayed with you for weeks," Ruthie said in a honey dripping tone. She really didn't want to sleep in the same room with Penny Sue. "The alarm system is the *least* I can do. I want to sleep on the couch."

"Hush." Penny Sue clapped her hands to silence us. "I'll sleep on the damned sofa." She snagged a piece of toast, took a bite, and started to chew. "Besides," she finally said, a smile tugging at the corner of her mouth, "the sofa pulls out into a queen-sized bed."

Ruthie and I exchanged a relieved glance. "Well, if you insist." I reached for the breadbasket, but stopped with my hand suspended in mid-air. "If that's a sofa bed in your living room, why didn't you pull it out for Guthrie when he stayed with us during the hurricanes?"

Penny Sue canted her head and took a sip of coffee. "I didn't want to encourage him to stay."

"That was mean, Penny Sue. Guthrie had an injured knee," I said.

"With drippy, frozen meat tied to it. Do you think I wanted that mess on my chesterfield?"

"Guthrie used the frozen food on his knee so he could conserve ice." Ruthie came to his defense.

"Yeah, but it *was* nasty." I could understand Penny Sue's position.

"The worst was the chicken." Penny Sue grimaced. "Remember how he showed up at our door with a frozen Perdue roaster strapped to his knee with an Ace bandage?"

I chuckled. "And it kept sliding down his leg!"

"Laa, and Ruthie kept pulling his chicken back up to his knee." Penny Sue started to laugh.

"Oh, Lord, that was funny." I was giggling now.

"What's so funny about that?" Ruthie asked, clearly confused. "The man needed help."

Penny Sue wiped tears from her face. "Honey, a man whose chicken reaches his ankle does not need help."

Ruthie didn't get it. "What? What?"

"Never mind, sugar, it's not important." Penny Sue tensed her lips to keep a straight face. "I'll sleep on the couch."

I swallowed a laugh and changed the subject. "I don't really think the authorities would go to the trouble and expense of extraditing a person for a traffic accident. I'm with Penny Sue; I believe this has something to do with Abby's death. So, the sooner we figure out what happened to Abby and ... the man ... the sooner things will get back to normal. Penny Sue, call your dad about an attorney, then you and I should see what we can find out about Leonard Kydd and his friend."

"Yep, let's get at it." Penny Sue hooked her pocketbook on her shoulder. "I'll call Daddy from the car. Don't forget the extra saline, Ruthie. We may need it."

Our first stop was the library; it was payday and I needed the money. I'd gone overboard on a birthday present for Zack, Jr., and my credit card bill was due any day. His college sweetheart moved to Vail with him, but dumped him for a rich Olympic skier. I thought I knew how Zack, Jr. felt, and I wanted to cheer him up. So, I went all out with silk underwear and North Face ski bibs with a matching jacket. Considering Zack's 27 years old, I guess I really couldn't identify with his feelings after all. Another girl had moved in before his birthday cake was digested—maybe before the candles were blown out. Ah, youth. Such resiliency!

Penny Sue opted to sit in the car and call her father. I swept through the front door of the library to the back room, signed for my check, and was hoofing past the circulation desk when a familiar face caught my eye in the magazine section. It was Leonard Kydd! I stuffed the check in my purse and headed down a row of books so I could catch him by surprise. At the end of the aisle, I paused to appraise the situation. Although Kydd held a magazine at eye level, he was really gazing across the top at the patrons. Hmm, just like his partner used to do. There was no longer any doubt in my mind that Kydd was connected to the dead man. As Kydd watched the front of the library, I slid in from the side and sat next to him.

"The man found dead was your friend, wasn't he?" I whispered. Kydd jumped close to a foot out of his seat.

"What? Who are you?" He closed the magazine and started to leave.

I clutched his arm. "Listen, I have a friend in jail that's somehow connected to your friend. It appears you've taken your buddy's station here at the library. I want to know what you're looking for. You realize there's another death involved, don't you? I think we should swap information and work together. If we don't, things could get ugly. Not only are the police on the case, but so are some mafia types."

Kydd stared at me incredulously. "Mafia types?" He studied me for a moment. "Hey, I know you. You're the lady I spoke with at the checkout desk."

"One and the same. I'm not trying to cause trouble; I only want to clear my friend. I believe we'll both get what we want by working together. Why don't we go somewhere and talk?" Heavens, I couldn't believe I was using that line. I sounded like Penny Sue, who suddenly appeared in front of us with her hands on her hips.

"I thought the hogs got you," she said to me, all the while giving Kydd the up and down. He apparently passed inspection, because her shoulders dropped and her faced morphed into the Scarlett O'Hara expression.

"Penny Sue Parker, meet Leonard Kydd," I said.

He rose and extended his hand. "My pleasure," Leonard said in his thick British accent.

She fluttered her lashes demurely. "Likewise."

Likewise? God, now Penny Sue had flipped into her version of English gentry. Honestly, her personality changed so fast, I almost had whiplash. Yet, I needed to intervene before all her flipping blew our chances with Kydd. "Why don't we go have a cup of coffee or a bite to eat? I'm famished," I fibbed.

"I'm starvin' too," Penny Sue added, her attention fixed on Leonard.

Starvin' for what? I thought wryly. *Food or a man?*

Kydd's eyes shifted from Penny Sue to me. I suppose he decided we weren't too dangerous, because he agreed.

"That new restaurant, the Upper Deck, has a cozy lounge on the first floor that's the perfect place for good food and getting acquainted," Penny Sue gushed. "Happy hour starts at noon."

Penny Sue's emphasis on *acquainted* and *happy hour* made my skin crawl. The lack of male attention had definitely taken a toll on her, and she'd always been fascinated by Brits, Europeans, and foreigners in general. There was no doubt that her focus was on affairs of the heart and not on the affairs of her Cousin Kevin.

"It is a nice place," I assured Leonard, who was obviously leery of Penny Sue. "Do you have a car?"

"A rental."

"I drive a small Volkswagen, so you may want to follow me."

Penny Sue did some more eyelash fluttering. "I'll ride with Leonard and show him the way."

Why didn't that surprise me? Soul mate Rich was completely forgotten. Penny Sue was back on the prowl.

Penny Sue was snuggled close to Leonard on a sofa when I arrived. I made a quick stop to deposit my check at the bank next door, so they beat me to the restaurant by several minutes. His body language said Penny Sue was too close for comfort, because his back was against the overstuffed arm with his knees angled toward her. I reckon he planned to kick her if she lunged for him. I sat in a chair facing them on the other side of a coffee table.

"I ordered Pinot Grigio for us. It's two for one." Penny Sue grinned.

"Thanks." I leaned across the table and addressed Leonard. "I don't believe I introduced myself. I'm Leigh Stratton. I live nearby and work at the library."

"Nice to put a name with your face," he said crispy, glancing at me briefly before cutting his eyes back to Penny Sue. She was definitely making him nervous. Lucky for him, the waitress arrived with our drinks. He made a grab for his, but couldn't reach it from the corner of the sofa. "It seems to be a little tight. Do you mind?" he asked Penny Sue.

"Oh, so sorry," she said demurely, batting her lashes as she took a sip of wine and scooted to the side.

Honestly, Penny Sue was so obvious. I was happy she wasn't wearing false eyelashes. At her first wedding she did so much lash fluttering, a false eyelash fell off. We were chatting by the champagne punch when I noticed that one eye looked a lot bigger than the other. I mentioned it and she went berserk. "It's sable," she shrieked, "and cost a fortune!"

Next thing you know, a hoard of men were on their hands and knees searching for the darned lash as if it were a contact lens or her diamond ring. It was a sight. Black, tuxedoed butts crawling around Penny Sue like a swarm of ants. Judge Daddy finally called off the hunt and drew Penny Sue to the dance floor. It was then that I took a sip of champagne and found the creepy thing at the bottom of my glass. It looked like a big, dead centipede. I haven't cared for champagne since.

"Leonard," I led off, "did Penny Sue explain the situation on the way over?"

"I gather her cousin is in jail for missing a court date, but you ladies believe it's a ruse. The real reason he's being held is because he's suspected of killing a former lover, such lover having been found dead in the library on the same night a man was found dead there as well."

"Yes, a man who regularly staked out the magazine section like you did today. Who was he, what was he doing, and why are you here? It's too coincidental for both deaths to occur at the library on the same night."

Leonard let out a long sigh. "Well, I suppose the police have retrieved fingerprints and will know his identity soon enough, if they don't already have it. The man was William Duffy, a freelance reporter working on a story for my employer, *Vainglory*. Bill's initial idea was to do a story about surfers; however, he stumbled on something sinister, something he refused to discuss until he was certain of the facts. Even I don't know what he was working on."

"That's why you were in the library?" Penny Sue asked, holding up her glass for a refill.

"Yes, I wanted to see if I could discover what he found out. Whatever he was researching, I know he first encountered it at the library."

The server arrived with two more glasses of wine. I told her to give them both to Penny Sue. I had to drive, and if Penny Sue got smashed, she might at least stop batting her damned eyelashes. "Did you notice anything?"

Leonard shook his head. "You were the most unexpected event."

Penny Sue grinned so wide her gums showed. She clearly thought he was referring to her. I figured Leonard meant my sneaking up on him.

"Surfing? What's the big deal about surfing in New Smyrna Beach, besides the fact that the best waves are in Shark Shoals, which explains why New Smyrna is sometimes called the Shark Bite Capital of the World? Of course, that's all based on the number of bites. The national news never explains that most injuries are mere scratches from a surfer putting his foot in the mouth of a shark going after small bait fish," I said, pointedly ignoring Penny Sue and her smug grin.

"It was the Shark Bite Capital angle that initially drew Bill down here. He quickly realized just what you said, yet in the process discovered that some of the best surfers on the East Coast hailed from New Smyrna Beach. Something to do with small, but tricky, waves forcing surfers to develop extraordinary skill. In the course of his surfer research, he stumbled on something else—a really big story, he said."

As Leonard and I talked, Penny Sue was ogling him in her sex-starved, kewpie doll mode. The wine on an empty stomach had clearly hit her.

"Do you believe his secret was important enough to get him killed?" I asked.

Leonard took the first taste of his drink, one eye fixed on Penny Sue. "Probably. I'd worked with Bill before and he wasn't usually so guarded. That told me it *was* a big story, which is why I kept funding his stay. Yet, I can't imagine how his death could be related to the lady scholar."

"Maybe Abby stumbled onto his secret, so he offed her," Penny Sue said.

"Not likely. Bill was a gentle man," Leonard replied, clearly relieved Penny Sue had stopped staring at him.

"Yes, and it doesn't explain how Bill died," I said to Penny Sue. "Leonard, did you talk to the police?"

"No, I thought I'd do my own investigation first. I know the authorities will eventually identify Bill and track me down. Bill worked in Iraq, so his fingerprints are on file. It's simply a matter of time."

I'm sure it was, but I'd also promised Deputy Sheriff Heather Brooks, our only police ally, that I'd let her know if I found him. "Considering Abby's death and the fact that Kevin Harrington is being held for extradition, I think the picture is larger than you imagined. Please talk to the authorities. We know a deputy who is sympathetic and discreet. Would you speak with her? I'll set up a meeting."

Penny Sue had finished her second glass of wine and moved on to the third. Her eyelids were beginning to droop. "Yes, Leonard," she put her hand on his arm. He cringed. "Heather is *very* discreet."

I motioned to the wine. "Forgive Penny Sue; she hasn't had much to eat today. If you believe the police will find you anyway, why not meet with a sympathetic officer? I'm telling you, there are some tough cops in this town who'd love to make your life miserable. We've been down this road before. Then there's the possible mafia problem."

"How does the mafia figure into this?"

I paused to choose my words carefully. "Penny Sue's aunt, Kevin's mother, was a New Jersey government official. She's retired now, but has a lot of her old contacts. You know what I mean? When Kevin was arrested, Aunt Alice called in some favors from friends up north. She didn't know that Penny Sue, Ruthie (whom you haven't met), and I have bad blood with those groups. If Kevin isn't cleared and released from jail immediately, the situation down here could become complicated."

Leonard downed his drink in one gulp. "When you put it that way, I'm more than happy to meet with your police friend. I don't want any trouble with the mafia. I live in New York."

"Good. I'll try to set up a meeting in a neutral location, like a parking lot or my condo. How can I reach you?"

He stood and handed me a business card with his cell number. "Please keep that confidential." He glanced at Penny Sue.

I pocketed the card and smiled. "I'll guard it with my life, and I'll call when I have a meeting arranged."

"Very well. It's been a pleasure. Since I don't have much time before the authorities are involved, I'm going back to the library."

Penny Sue struggled to her feet. "It's been a pleasure, likewise. I hope I seen you again soon."

"I look forward to it." Leonard couldn't get out of the restaurant fast enough.

Back in my car, I took a left and headed home. Penny Sue needed some food and a nap.

"Are you all right?" I asked.

She leaned back against the headrest. "Yes and no." She paused a beat, "Do you have any ice cream?"

The workings of her mind were beyond logic. "I may have some Rocky Road."

"That's fitting. Rocky Road. I like the nuts."

"What's wrong, Penny Sue? You're acting strange. Leonard isn't that good looking."

"No offers on the house."

"You'll get one; it's just a matter of time. Your big lot on a lake is prime real estate. I think the market's starting to come back."

"Yeah, but when? I need money now. You know what this means? No new clothes and I can't button my jeans. I feel like a feather bed tied in the middle. I never thought my life would come to this," Penny Sue said mournfully. "I know it's that damn nursing home across the lake that scares people off."

"It's a very up-scale progressive living facility. Half of the tenants are retired executives and high ranking military officers. The grounds are lovely. I'm sure it won't affect the sale of your house."

"Bad vibes. People there die all the time. Maybe we should smudge it." She closed her eyes and fell asleep before we reached the condo.

I led a groggy, half smashed Penny Sue to her room and closed the door. Ruthie gave me a knowing look and turned her attention back to a man in the living room, no doubt one of the alarm technicians who was working up an estimate. A shame Penny Sue was asleep, because she would have tripped over herself getting to this man. Six-foot-one, brown hair, a dark tan, and bulging biceps—this guy was an unusually fine specimen of manhood. While the technician explained the equipment and costs to Ruthie, I started making cream cheese and olive finger sandwiches. They were Penny Sue's favorite, so I figured I'd let her doze for a while, then coax her into eating something.

"I plan to make a decision soon. How fast can you get the equipment and begin installation?" Ruthie asked the technician.

"I can usually get the equipment in one day, as long as it's ordered by three o'clock. We're pretty busy now because of all the break-ins on the beach, but we have an opening for to-morrow. A part was out of stock, so we had to reschedule that installation. If your parts are available, you could take the slot."

"If you can install our system tomorrow, we have a deal," Ruthie said.

"Fine, I'll call the office and get back to you within an hour." He checked his watch. "I haven't had lunch, so I'll grab a bite nearby. I'll need a signature before the order is actually placed."

"No problem, George. I'll be here."

"Good looking guy," I said, holding up the plate of sand-wiches after the technician left.

She nodded. "He's married with kids."

"Too bad, Penny Sue would go ape over George." I fixed us both a plate and sat next to Ruthie at the counter.

"What's with Penny Sue?" Ruthie asked between bites.

"It was happy hour at the Upper Deck. Three glasses of wine on an empty stomach. She'd talked to her father, who said she hadn't received any offers on her house. I reckon she was drowning her sorrows."

"Geez, that's awful. Why didn't you just come back here? Why go to the Upper Deck?" Ruthie asked.

I filled her in on Leonard Kydd and William Duffy. Thank goodness the dead man finally had a name, so we wouldn't upset Ruthie by calling him a bum. "Leonard agreed to meet with Heather." I rummaged through my purse for Heather's card. "I probably should act fast. I don't want to give Leonard time to change his mind."

I phoned Heather and explained the situation. She was en route to a domestic call, but could swing by in an hour or so. "I'll try to reach Leonard and will leave you a text message," I told Heather. "Be careful. I read somewhere that domestic calls are among the most dangerous."

"Yeah, you have a chance of reasoning with a hardened criminal. It's nearly impossible to deal with angry family mem-bers—emotions run too hot. I'll check my messages when I'm finished. I'm anxious to speak with Kydd. We can meet at the parking lot on Hiles."

"Good deal."

I sent a text message to Leonard, figuring he wouldn't answer his cell if he were in the library. I typed *pls call* and hit send. I'm sure there's a shorter method that kids use, but this was new territory for me. I was a texting novice. Penny Sue had

shown me how to do it only a few days before. It was complicated. You had to double and triple press the keys since I had an
old phone, according to Penny Sue, who owned a fancy
BlackBerry. I felt like Wilma Flintstone in a Joan Jetson world.
I supposed I should hire a ten-year-old to teach me all about cell
phones, iPhones, berries, apples, pears, or whatever. No sooner
had I pressed the send button for Leonard's message than Heather
called. She was headed our way and would meet us in the
parking lot at Hiles and A1A.

"Heather's on her way. I hope Leonard hasn't changed his
mind," I said.

Ruthie studied me for a moment. "He'll call," my intuitive
friend said with certainty. Once again, she was right. My phone
rang a few minutes later. Leonard would come directly.

"Do you want to ride with me?" I asked Ruthie.

"I have to wait for George's call. Besides, Penny Sue would
be fit to be tied if we both left without her."

"Good point." I snagged my purse and headed out, I wanted
to beat Heather and Leonard to the parking lot so I could make
proper introductions. I also didn't want to take the chance that
Leonard arrived first and didn't wait. Guthrie pulled into the
parking lot just as I put my car in reverse.

He screeched to a stop, billowing sand, and yelled out of his
window, "Man, we got some scoop!"

"Hold it," I called back. "I won't be long."

Alice got out of Guthrie's VW bus and gave me a pinched
look as I drove away. I'm sure she wasn't used to being put off.

I beat Heather and Leonard to the parking lot, but only by a
few minutes. Leonard arrived first in his blue rented Malibu.
Heather came a few minutes later in her Volusia County Sheriff's
Impala. At close to six feet, Heather was an attractive brunette
with a belt full of weapons and gadgets that said, *Don't mess with
me.* I had seen her back down manly men, two at the debate,

with a mere I-mean-business stare. I sensed Leonard flinch when
she got out of the car.

"Hi, Heather," I called in a purposely light tone intended to
relax Leonard. "Did you set the husband and wife straight?"

She laughed. "Husband and wife? It was worse than that—a
mother and teenaged daughter. Seems the mother refused to let
her daughter go to the Slithering Lizards concert, and a fight
broke out. Somewhere in the fray, the mother doused the daughter
with whipped cream, and the daughter retaliated with Lysol spray
and Cheese Whiz. The kid was holding her mother hostage in
the bathroom when I arrived."

I pointed to a blob of cheese on Heather's shirt. "I see you
got in the line of fire."

She chuckled. "Only a dribble as I slapped on cuffs. Then
the kid started crying and the mother yelled at me. Geez, Mom
was the one who called in the complaint! Naturally, she refused
to press charges. I gave them both a stern lecture and left. I hate
these domestics. They call the police, yet rarely press charges."
She flicked the dab of cheese off her shirt. "I assume this is
Mr. Kydd."

The three of us leaned against his car as he relayed the same
information to Heather that he'd told me earlier.

"So you don't know what William Duffy was looking for in
the library?" Heather asked.

"No idea, only that it was a major story and he wasn't ready
to talk about it yet."

Heather turned to me. "You work at the library, don't you
Leigh?"

I nodded.

"Have you seen anything unusual?"

"Nothing other than Duffy. The entire staff noticed him.
He was hard to miss since he staked out the magazine section
almost every morning."

"Surfers, then something else. Whatever he stumbled on probably got him killed," Heather mused.

"It was murder?" Leonard asked shrilly.

Heather waved off the comment. "I was thinking out loud. I don't know anything about the cause of death. Could have been a stroke, for all I know. The detectives don't keep me informed. I will pass on his name, in case they haven't identified the body.

"If it was Bill, who should his family contact to claim the body?" Leonard asked.

"The Florida Medical Examiner, District 7. Since he died in a county building, I'm sure an autopsy is being performed."

"Will the results be made public?" Leonard asked.

"I don't know. It depends on the status of the investigation. There are two bodies involved here." Heather gave Leonard her card. "Call me if you notice anything unusual at the library. Leigh, keep your eyes open but try not to raise suspicions. We don't want to scare off the people Duffy was tracking."

I nodded tentatively, wondering if I should keep it from Guthrie and Penny Sue. They worked at the library, but could they keep a secret?

Chapter 10

Ruthie and Penny Sue were carrying their clothes and other necessities next door, when I arrived home from the meeting with Heather and Kydd.

"George can install the alarm system in your place tomorrow," Ruthie called over her shoulder. "It will only take one day. Go get the stuff you'll need for the evening. Guthrie's gone to Publix for fried chicken."

Loaded down with enough paraphernalia for a month, including all her vitamins, Penny Sue huffed, "Please hurry. Guthrie and Alice are about to bust to tell us what they found out at the Medical Examiner's. And they have to go back tonight."

"Did the Judge find a lawyer for Kevin?" I asked as the screen door closed, hitting Penny Sue on the butt.

"Yeah, the attorney is checking on Kevin at this moment. Now scoot, we're on a tight schedule," Penny Sue said.

I scooped up a nightgown, robe, work clothes, a few toiletries, and hurried to the guestroom at Penny Sue's place. Ruthie was already changing the sheets on Kevin's bed.

"Do you know what Guthrie found out?" I asked Ruthie.

"No. They wouldn't talk until you got back. I think Alice is mad that you didn't wait to hear the story."

"You know I couldn't wait."

Ruthie tucked the sheets under the mattress. "I explained it to them, but Alice still seemed peeved. Penny Sue told them all about Leonard Kydd, but they still wouldn't talk. Guthrie has to go back to the Examiner's office tonight to finish the job, and Alice said they didn't have time to tell the story twice."

"The old my-way-or-the-highway, huh?" I said.

Ruthie smiled. "I'd say that sums it up." She fluffed a pillow and tossed it to the head of the bed. "Alice is a very strong-willed woman."

I moved my toiletries to the bathroom and placed the open suitcase on the floor against the wall. "Keep that in mind if you and Kevin ever get really serious."

"I've done some thinking since we last spoke. I think one marriage is enough for me. Living together would be okay, but no legal stuff, especially now that I have the inheritance. I don't want to jeopardize Jo Ruth's future legacy."

Boy, that was a switch! I couldn't help but wonder if the thought of Alice for a mother-in-law had something to do with Ruthie's change of heart.

Jo Ruth was Ruthie Jo's one and only daughter, who had almost finished her residency in psychiatry at Duke Medical School. With Ruthie's wispy good looks, her cardiologist father's brain, and a looming huge inheritance, Jo Ruth was a catch for anyone. We all joked that it was good we had a shrink in the fold to guide us through old age. In fact, Penny Sue could probably use a little counseling now. Yet, was Jo Ruth's inheritance truly the reason Ruthie had suddenly soured on remarriage? Maybe, maybe not. At our age, living together was as good as being married and a lot less messy if things didn't work out.

My marriage musings were interrupted by the unmistakable screech of the rusty screen door spring and a few familiar grunts. Guthrie had clearly arrived. "Ready for the drama?" I asked Ruthie.

She let out a long sigh. "As ready as I'll ever be."

Alice and Penny Sue were already arranging the food buffet style on the kitchen counter. Guthrie had purchased a large bucket of chicken, potato salad, cole slaw, bakery rolls and a coconut cream pie. He was first in line, holding a plate impatiently.

"Man, we don't have much time," he said to Alice. "We have to get back to the Medical Examiner while the cleaning crew is still there, but before the night shift arrives, if we want to get a look at those files."

"I know," she said tersely, plunking a piece of chicken and scoop of potato salad on her plate. I sliced the pie, in the interest of time, while everyone else filled their plates. It was a good thing I'd eaten a few of the cream cheese and olive finger sandwiches I'd made for Penny Sue earlier in the day. A single chicken leg, a dab of cole slaw, and one roll were all that was left. By the time I took my seat, Guthrie had wolfed down his food and started telling their story.

"The bodies were in another room, but we heard the doctors talking. The man's name is William Duffy, just like Penny Sue said. The tox report hasn't come back, but a doc thinks Duffy died of compression asphyxiation."

"What's that?" Penny Sue asked. A stern look from Alice stopped Penny Sue's fork in mid-air. "Never mind, I'll look it up later. Please continue."

"There was one fang mark on Duffy's finger, but they doubt he got enough venom to kill him. They suspect he panicked when he saw the snake and pulled the bins of books over on himself." Guthrie shook his head ruefully. "Smothered. A tough way to go."

"The young doctor said the snake bite could have caused a convulsion," Alice added.

Guthrie nodded. "Yeah, it could have been a convulsion."

Guthrie was obviously going too slow for Aunt Alice's taste, because she took over. "A heart attack was the immediate cause of Abby's death, but they don't know why. Her heart looked healthy, so they can't make a determination until they get her tox report." Alice checked her watch. "Guthrie, let's go. With any luck I'll be able to find the files on Abby and Duffy and sneak a peek. There may be things the doctors didn't talk about."

He headed for the counter with his plate. "Sure, as soon as I have a piece of this—"

Alice stood and hitched her purse in the crook of her arm. "No, now!"

Guthrie put his plate down. "Yes, ma'am. I'll have my pie later."

Penny Sue, Ruthie and I served up pieces of pie and adjourned to the living room. "This stuff is good," Penny Sue muttered between bites. I was glad to see she was drinking coffee and had recovered from her earlier funk and libations. "Heavens, I hope Alice doesn't get caught snooping through the files. All we'd need is for her to get arrested."

"God's truth," I said.

Ruthie was silent, staring into her coffee.

Penny Sue nudged Ruthie. "Are you listening?"

"Oh, yeah. I was thinking about Kevin. I wonder what he had for dinner." She held up her plate. "I'll bet he didn't get coconut cream pie."

"Now, don't go getting all sentimental on us. This is a small town and they probably buy their food from Publix Supermarket, too. Remember how Aunt Bee on the *Andy Griffith Show* used to feed the prisoners in Mayberry. They always got the meal she was serving at home. Dessert and everything. New Smyrna Beach's local lock-up is so small, they probably have a contract with a nearby restaurant. Kevin will be out soon. The lawyer Daddy found should be meeting with him right now." Penny Sue suddenly turned to me excitedly. "Oh, you don't know! Daddy called while you were gone. He said the lawyer was on his way to visit Kevin ... and ... I've gotten an offer on my house! Daddy wouldn't say much except that the offer was very promising. I'll tell you, if that deal goes through, I'm going to manage my money a lot better this time. No more of all-of-the-eggs-in-one-basket, no matter how promising the investment looks. I'm spreading my investments around from now on. And I'm going to be frugal. Only one or two designer outfits per season. The rest of the time I'll dress like you, Leigh."

"Gee, thanks. Is that supposed to be a compliment or an insult?"

"I just meant that you're better at managing money and more careful with your clothes budget. After all, you are an accountant. I didn't—"

I waved her off. "A good place to start is at the New Smyrna Ladies' Investment Club that meets at the library. You might learn a lot."

"You're right. Those women are all skinny and dressed to kill. Maybe they get discounts at the upscale department stores," Penny Sue said.

I shook my head. "No, I meant you might learn how to invest. I believe they pool their money and have created their own little mutual fund. All of them don't wear designer clothes like you and Ruthie, but they are well dressed."

"And skinny. Maybe they went in together and hired a personal trainer."

I would never understand the workings of Penny Sue's mind. For a person wolfing down pie, skinny was a strange thing to harp on. "I think they meet tomorrow at the library. Ten a.m. as I recall."

"Ruthie, do you want to come with me?" Penny Sue asked.

"No, I have to stick around to oversee the alarm installation. I'm going to use Poppa's financial advisor for the time being, and I have my eye on another investment."

I knew Ruthie was referring to her bookstore, but the comment went right over Penny Sue's head.

"The alarm system!" Penny Sue swung around to me. "Did you arm Lu Nee 2? You know it has that remote control TV monitor. If anything happens, we could see it from over here."

"Did you figure out how to work it?" Ruthie asked.

"No, but I found the instructions. I thought you and Leigh could decipher them. I believe we should keep a remote eye on the place tonight in case the burglars come back. I wonder what they're after. Your place doesn't look fancy enough to have a lot of electronics and expensive stuff."

I reared back. "First you make fun of my wardrobe and now my condo. Penny Sue, that is too much even for you!"

"Wait." Ruthie signaled stop. "She makes a good point. We should go next door and get our jewelry and other valuables. Leigh, then you and I will figure out how to operate Lu Nee 2's video," Ruthie smiled sweetly, "while Penny Sue does the dishes."

I smirked. "That's a good plan."

The instructions for the robot made no sense at all. English was clearly not the first language of the booklet's author. After more than an hour of arguing and frustration, we broke down and called Carl, our friend Fran Annina's MIT genius son. He happened to be home and agreed to come over.

Already a millionaire in his late twenties, Carl lived with his widowed mother and was still single, since his passion was science and not the opposite sex. I'd tried to fix him up with my daughter Ann, but they didn't click. I reckon it had something to do with the fact that Carl and his best friends were *Star Trek* fans whose favorite indulgences were Trekkie role playing games (in full costume). Ann wasn't ready to be a Klingon. Even though Carl spent most of his time inventing GPS and stealth technology for high tech firms, the Trekkie thing was a deal buster. Sigh. Ann didn't marry a millionaire, but her few dates with Carl made her take a second look at the old diplomat she dated, and almost married, while an intern at the U.S. Embassy in London. In comparison to Carl, the old guy was sluggish and stuffy, Ann said, and she wasn't ready to waste her youth. Hallelujah! I'd be forever grateful to Carl for bringing Ann to her senses.

It took Carl about fifteen minutes to set up the remote view feature for Lu Nee 2. We all huddled around him, listening intently to his instructions on the remote camera's operation, with the hope that one of us would understand and remember it, when Guthrie burst through the door.

"Man, we got a problem!" Seeing Carl, he stopped short and did the hand across chest salute. "Hey, dude. Good to see you. Kill any Romulans lately?" Carl returned the Klingon greeting.

"Cut the foolishness!" Penny Sue shouted. "What's the problem, and where's Alice?"

Guthrie did some head and hand gyrations that basically asked if he could talk in front of Carl.

"Spit it out," I said. "Carl's a friend we trust. Did something happen to Alice?"

A pained expression flashed across Guthrie's face. "Yeah. She's locked in the Medical Examiner's building."

Penny Sue's face turned so red I thought she might explode. "How could you let anything happen to my aunt?"

"Kevin's mother," Ruthie threw in.

"Man, it wasn't my fault. While I worked on the computers, Alice went snooping around. Well, when the night shift came in, they hustled me out of the building since I was in a sensitive area. I tried to find Alice, claiming I'd left a voltage meter somewhere, but this big, mean looking doctor, like, pushed me out of the door and told me to come back tomorrow. He said he'd put the meter on the receptionist's desk if it turned up. What should we do? What if Alice hid in the refrigerated room with the bodies?"

Ruthie's hand went to her heart. "Gracious, what should we do?"

"Calm down," Carl instructed. "There's nothing to worry about. This is no different than my war games. We'll get her out. I have a slew of strategies up my sleeve. Guthrie, do you know if they have two or three shifts?"

"I think two. See, I didn't check my answering machine until after nine this morning. The Medical Examiner apparently called in the middle of the night and wanted to know if I could come in at four a.m."

"Okay, the current crew will probably leave at four. We can get Alice out then," Carl said.

"But, they have these fancy electronic locks," Guthrie objected.

Carl smirked. "No problem. I can get through them in a minute."

"What if there's an alarm system?" I asked.

"Five minutes," Carl replied.

"Yes, but what if she's hiding in the cooler? Alice is old. She could catch pneumonia if she's stuck there until tomorrow morning," Ruthie said.

Carl stroked his forehead. "You're right. We should probably try a diversionary tactic first. Something to get the night crew out of the building while another group sneaks in and finds Alice. How large was the staff, Guthrie?"

"I only saw four. All doctors and lab techs, I guess."

"Any commotion will likely draw them all out. Do you want me to call my buddies?" Carl asked. My stomach knotted at the thought of a Klingon assault.

Silent until this point, Penny Sue flexed her jaw. "No. I've got an idea. Ruthie's so skinny and pale she can fake an illness. How about Leigh bangs on their door, screaming for a doctor. Ruthie will be lying on the ground in a fetal position. As everyone runs to help her, I'll shoot them with the liquid taser." Her eyes flashed.

"No shooting, Penny Sue," Ruthie said tensely. "And, I do not look sick! I have a milky complexion."

"Wait, I've got a better idea," I said. "Penny Sue, you're dramatic and have a more commanding presence than I do." That made her smile. "You bang on the door and lay on the dramatics about Ruthie. If you lay it on thick, they'll all come running.

Guthrie and I will slip in to look for Alice. Carl will drive the getaway car."

"You're right—I do have a commanding presence and could do a better job of attracting their attention. You know, I took a drama class once. The teacher said I had a wide range and a unique style," Penny Sue bragged. "Even so, I'll hide the taser beside the building in case the staff comes back too soon. Then I'll shoot them."

"No shooting!" Ruthie insisted. "Just pretend you're having a heart attack or something."

Or you're pregnant and having contractions, I thought wryly. I did a mental cheek slap at having such ugly, catty thoughts about one of my best friends. But hey, Penny Sue'd insulted me a couple of times recently. What goes around comes around. At least I had the good sense to keep my mouth shut.

"Man, that's a good idea," Guthrie said. "What if they don't come out?"

"Then we'll wait until their shift ends, and I'll get us into the building," Carl said.

"What car do we take? There will be six of us, and my Lemon Aid bus isn't very fast."

"I need a few instruments from my workshop. I'll come back with my Bronco."

"Good deal. Let's do it." We did a sloppy high five.

Chapter 11

Carl had a big, black SUV, the kind you see on the TV detective shows. A good thing, because the back cargo area was packed with equipment—a satellite dish, car batteries, several black metal boxes with a lot of dials and lights, a tool kit, and assorted handheld instruments. When Carl said he could get us into the building, I believed him. I just hadn't expected an all-out alien attack. I suppose he wanted to be prepared for anything.

The five of us were piled in the van, headed north on I-95. Carl took a left on International Speedway Drive, named in honor of the Daytona 500 car race, and a right into the government complex that housed the Medical Examiner's office. We'd worked out a cover story before we left New Smyrna Beach.

Penny Sue and Ruthie's car broke down, and they were waiting for help, when some sinister looking men pulled up behind them offering aid. The men tried to force Penny Sue and Ruthie into their van, but the two broke away and ran to the government complex. When they reached the lawn in front of the Examiner's office, Ruthie collapsed. She supposedly had asthma. To make the story look real, they both smeared dirt on their clothes before we left our condo parking lot. Penny Sue even put a couple of twigs in her hair.

Guthrie and I were dressed in black so we could hide in the darkness before sneaking in the building to find Alice. Guthrie

owned a black tee shirt with FBI stamped on the back that I
wore. Since the staff might recognize Guthrie, if we happened to
be caught, I could pretend I was arresting him. Penny Sue groused
that it wouldn't be an issue if we'd just let her bring the liquid
taser, but Ruthie insisted there would be no shooting. Carl told
us not to worry. If we were caught we should put our hands over
our ears and hightail it back to the SUV. He could disable the
medical staff with sound waves. That was the point of the dish.
Having a genius friend sure comes in handy.

For the most part we were silent for the entire trip, each of us
mentally rehearsing our part in the charade about to unfold. Carl
parked at the intersection of a cross street close to the Medical
Examiner's lot. We piled out of the van and headed to our marks,
as they say in the theater, while Carl opened the rear window
and positioned the satellite dish.

Guthrie and I pressed ourselves against a chain link fence
on the side of the building, close to the door, as Ruthie curled up
in a fetal position on the ground about fifty yards away. With
everyone in place, Carl gave us the high sign, and Penny Sue
went into action.

"HELP! HELP! We need a doctor," she hollered, banging on
the door. "HELP! My friend is dying!" She banged so hard I was
surprised the glass didn't shatter. "MURDER! HELP!"

Well, the girl did have a unique style, as her drama teacher
said, because her performance drew the entire staff. The burly
doctor who'd kicked Guthrie out of the building earlier in the
day opened the door, the rest of the staff huddled behind him.
Before he could get a word out, Penny Sue grabbed him by the
arm and pulled him out of the building screaming, "My friend is
dying! Our car broke down and some men tried to kidnap us.
She has asthma. She collapsed. You've got to help!" Ruthie was
heaving loudly and twitching. Someone said, "I'll call 9-1-1,"
and Penny Sue screamed, "No, the men are following, you have
to come out and protect us."

A slight bald guy in a lab coat pushed past the big doctor and raced toward Ruthie. "Come on," he yelled. "This isn't Central Park. I'm not going to stand around like a wuss and watch someone die!" That's all it took for the entire group to rush to Ruthie's aid. As the bald doctor examined Ruthie, Penny Sue was blubbering hysterically and hanging from the neck of the big guy. The others formed a barricade facing outward, as if on the lookout for the kidnappers. The moment the staff left the building, Guthrie snagged the door before it shut and we both slipped through.

He pointed to double doors directly ahead. "You check the cooler. I'll check the offices down this hall." He hooked his thumb to the right. "Hurry."

Hurry was an unnecessary command. I flew through the doors whispering, "Alice, it's Leigh. Are you in here? Alice. Alice." She wasn't in sight. The place was dimly lit, cold, and creepily sterile. I stopped in the center of the room and gazed at a bank of lockers. Lockers—the kind they store bodies in. Dead bodies—one of them was probably Abby. Mangled and dissected bodies. A wave of nausea swept over me, and I swallowed my gorge trying to summon the nerve to open a locker. Surely Alice hadn't crawled in one of those. Still, she was pretty gutsy and might do it in a pinch.

I clenched my teeth and tiptoed toward the bottom locker on the left, when a metal door suddenly hit my leg. Yeow! I must have jumped halfway across the room as a scene from *Night of the Living Dead* flashed through my mind. Frozen in place, I watched a skinny leg extend from a compartment below a countertop. Then another leg, and hands. Old hands. Glory, it was Alice! I rushed to help her to her feet.

"Well, it sure took you long enough," she gripped, straightening her shirt indignantly.

"Sh-h," I whispered and guided her to the reception area. Guthrie was headed our way shaking his head. The sight of Alice put a spring in his step and in an instant he was hustling us out of the door and across the parking lot toward the SUV. It wasn't a minute too soon. Ruthie was sitting up, and the tall doctor had pulled free of Penny Sue's grasp. "I'll call the police," he said, clearly eager to get away from Penny Sue and her screeching. At that moment, Carl jogged toward the group calling, "Mom, I've been so worried!" Everyone stopped what they were doing, except two women who moved to block Carl's path.

"No, it's okay," Ruthie said weakly. "That's my son. We called him when the car broke down and left a message on his voice mail."

Carl picked Ruthie up and gave her a bear hug. "I was so worried. I found your car and have been riding around searching for you. You should have stayed with the car." He set Ruthie down and turned to Penny Sue. "Are you all right?"

She grinned thinly. "Yes, I'm just shook-up. It's a long story. These nice people helped us."

"I should still call the police," the burly doctor said sternly.

"Call the police?" Carl asked incredulously.

"Some men in a van tried to kidnap us," Ruthie told him.

"There was no van close to your car," Carl replied.

"We got away and ran." Ruthie turned to Burly. "Don't call the police. I just want to go home. We didn't see their license plate or anything—it was dark and we were so scared."

The slight doctor who vowed he wasn't a wuss patted Ruthie on the shoulder. "Take care of yourself. You should probably buy some pepper spray."

"Thank you all for helping my mother." Carl herded Ruthie and Penny Sue toward the SUV. "And I promise they'll buy pepper spray. In fact, I'll buy it for them myself."

They piled into the SUV, and we took off slowly. "Wow Ruthie, that was, like, an academy award-winning performance," Guthrie said.

"Carl wasn't bad, either," Penny Sue added with true admiration. "He almost had me believing he was Ruthie's son."

"When you play war games, you learn to think on the fly. I heard the comment about calling the police and figured I'd better intervene."

"How in the world could you hear that comment?" Ruthie asked.

"The dish," Carl replied. "It can pick up and send sounds. Hey, Guthrie, can you reach the dish and pull it back so I can put up the back window?"

"Sure, man, no problemo."

Alice was sandwiched between Guthrie and me in the backseat, her arms crossed across her belly. I assumed it was because she was cold. Wrong. "Well, doesn't anyone want to hear about my day?" she asked tersely, pulling a manila folder out the bottom of her shirt.

Guthrie's eyes were saucers. "Wow, is that what I think it is?"

Alice grinned smugly. "Part of Abby's file that I found on a counter. I haven't had a chance to look at it, but I heard a lot while I was hiding under the counter."

"Well, don't keep us in suspense," Penny Sue said.

Alice leaned back and rolled her shoulders. She was clearly playing her part for all it was worth. "Like Guthrie and I heard earlier, Duffy died from compression asphyxiation. The tox report arrived and proved there wasn't enough snake venom in his body to kill him. The poor fellow was suffocated by the weight of the books." She hugged the folder to her chest and took a deep breath. "They also got Abby's report. The heart attack was caused by an overdose of nicotine."

"Nicotine?" I echoed.

Guthrie scooted forward excitedly. "I noticed Abby was wearing a patch on her arm when she came to tell Kevin she was going to debate him. It must have been a nicotine patch! I'll bet she went to the bathroom to sneak a cigarette. Maybe she was having a panic attack and thought a cigarette would calm her nerves. She could have smoked two or three, which was probably enough to cause an overdose."

Alice smirked at Guthrie. "Exactly what I think. Nicotine poisoning proves that Kevin had nothing to do with her death. And, since I know New Jersey won't insist on extradition, Kevin should be released tomorrow morning."

I looked askance at Alice. "You know they won't insist on extradition?"

"How can you be sure?" Ruthie chimed in.

"I have sources," Alice said.

Penny Sue turned around to face us. "Which was it, the Italians or Russians?" she asked Alice.

Alice arched a brow. "Both."

Carl dropped us off at Penny Sue's condo. Everyone was exhausted, so there was no offer of coffee or a liqueur. Even Guthrie immediately headed up the hill to his condo, mouthing a weak "good night" over his shoulder. We went straight inside Penny Sue's unit, set the alarm, and checked Lu Nee 2's status next door. We'd left the lights on in my condo, and Lu Nee's control panel showed no intruders during our absence. Alice tossed her folder on the dining room table, declaring she was too tired to deal with it. The withering look she flashed in our direction said we'd better not touch it, either. No problem. We were too worn out to think about anything other than making up Penny Sue's pull-out sofa bed, which we did in record time. A half hour later we were settled in our beds, make-up and all, and drifting off to Never Never Land.

I felt like my head had barely hit the pillow when an *Alert Intruder* sounded from Lu Nee's control panel. I was the first to locate the box with the tiny television screen on the kitchen counter. Next door, Lu Nee was buzzing and screeching, *Halt!* as its head rotated to scan the room. The scan picked up two young men standing beside the stack of boxes in my dining area. Still groggy, I couldn't remember how to stop the scan and zoom in on the perpetrators. Penny Sue and Ruthie were leaning over my shoulder, yet they couldn't remember how to stop the scan either. It was good old Penny Sue who found the intercom button and yelled into the box, "The police are on their way!" Meanwhile, Ruthie gathered her wits and hit the panic button on Penny Sue's alarm. A deafening blare filled our condo and sent the burglars on the run. Lu Nee 2 caught their backsides as two slender males, probably in their teens or early twenties, scurried out the sliding glass door. The pole for the track, my security system, was lying in the middle of the floor. This time they'd succeeded in jimmying the door.

Penny Sue raced to the linen closet for the taser as Alice pounded down the hall with her long barreled pistol. Ruthie flipped on the deck spotlights just as a loud knock sounded at the front door. "Sheriff!" a male voice shouted. It was Tommy, Heather Brooks' young partner. "Is everyone all right?" he asked excitedly. We said we were and that it was the unit next door that had been burglarized. We motioned to the sliding glass doors that led to the deck, where Heather stood surveying the scene. It was one of those foggy beach nights when the humidity hugged everything like a wet blanket.

"A car was waiting again," Heather said. She glanced at Penny Sue holding the taser, and Alice with the pistol, and grinned. "They got away. No shooting tonight, ladies."

Alice stuffed the pistol in the pocket of her velour robe and headed back in the house. "Damn, then I'm going back to bed."

Heather motioned to my condo, where Lu Nee 2 was still screeching *Intruder Alert! Intruder Alert!* Salty dew was streaming down the glass doors. Heather shrugged. "The likelihood of lifting fingerprints from this mess is slim to none. Come on, Leigh, let's do a walk-through to see if anything was stolen."

I punched the button on Lu Nee's head to silence it. "I don't believe they had time to get much. Lu Nee 2 went off immediately, and Ruthie pushed Penny Sue's panic button a moment later. I saw two young men head for the boxes stacked against the wall, but the robot's head kept swiveling, so I couldn't see if they took anything. By the time Lu Nee's camera went full circle, they were headed out the door. I believe their hands were empty, but I couldn't swear to it."

"What's in the boxes?" Heather asked.

"Books and a laptop computer."

"Are they valuable?"

"Some of the books could be; they're pretty old," Ruthie answered. "They belonged to Dr. Abigail Johnston. She willed them to Kevin, who was her former research partner."

Heather stroked her bottom lip, thinking. "You're talking about the lady who died at the library? She willed her books to the man who's now sitting in jail as a person of interest?"

Ruthie's eyes flashed. "Yes, but Kevin had nothing to do with Abby's death. He'll probably be released in the morning—"

I was standing behind Heather, facing Ruthie. I shook my head to shut her up. The last thing we needed was for Ruthie to say something that connected us to the Medical Examiner and the file Alice stole. Fortunately, Ruthie got the point.

"He'll probably be released tomorrow," Ruthie continued, "because his lawyer met with Woody this afternoon."

Heather studied Ruthie. She was a terrible liar, and her normally pale skin was red as a beet. Heather apparently chose to ignore the obvious. "Do you have an inventory of the books, so you can tell if anything is missing?"

"Kevin and I started one," Ruthie said, "but didn't get very far. The books we logged are all on the top, so it should be easy to determine if any of them are missing."

I jumped in. "And the thieves didn't have time to dig through the boxes before the alarm went off. We should be able to determine if anything was taken pretty quickly."

Heather checked her watch. "Tomorrow's soon enough. I've pulled another double shift and I'm beat. Will you be available tomorrow afternoon?"

"I'm sure we can make arrangements," I said. I was scheduled to work, but felt sure Terry would give me the afternoon off.

"Good. Leigh, did you think about an alarm system of your own?" Heather asked, giving Lu Nee 2 a distasteful look.

"Yes," Penny Sue fired back. "One's being installed tomorrow."

Heather nodded approval. "It's pretty strange that someone would try to break into your condo two nights in a row."

"God's truth. Especially since there isn't anything valuable here," Penny Sue said flippantly.

Nothing valuable? The nerve! If I'd been holding the taser, I would have shot her in the butt. Tommy saw my reaction and stepped away. Heather picked up the cue to leave.

Chapter 12

We were sitting at Penny Sue's kitchen counter, sipping coffee, having just polished off some cantaloupe and a basket of
bagels with cream cheese. Alice wasn't up yet. I was dressed for
work, while Penny Sue and Ruthie were still in their robes.
Even though I was absolutely exhausted from the previous night's
escapade, there was a place in me that longed for the normalcy
of the library. Checking in books, sorting books for shelving—it
was like a meditation. And I only expected to work half a day so
I could get in a nap after the interview with Heather.

At eight a.m. on the dot, Penny Sue's BlackBerry played the
Georgia football fight song. "Who in the world ..." she started,
then hopped down from the stool and took a seat in the living
room. "It's Daddy."

Ruthie and I exchanged a puzzled look. The Judge knew
Penny Sue was rarely awake so early. In fact, she'd still be asleep
on the sofa bed if the odor of the French vanilla coffee I made
hadn't roused her. After all, I had to go to work. My first thought
when her phone rang was that I hoped the Judge was okay. I'm
sure Ruthie wondered if he had news about Kevin. We watched
intently, as Penny Sue stared at her feet and listened without
interrupting, a rare occurrence in itself. Then a smile stretched
her lips and her eyes lit up like the Fourth of July.

"How much was that again?" she asked. A pause. "You're
sure the deal will go through?" Another pause. Then her tone

changed from subdued to sassy. "You've known about this for weeks and didn't tell me?" A long pause. "Yes sir, I understand. Thanks Daddy, I love you." She hit the off button and blasted halfway to the ceiling. When she came to earth she danced a jig and sang, "I'm in the money. I'm in the money. Money honey. New car, new clothes, and I won't need a full time job. My prayers have been answered!" She planted her feet, looking happier than she'd been since she arrived. "Hell, I think I'll join that New Smyrna Beach Ladies' Investment Club at the library. It meets today, doesn't it, Leigh?"

"Yes, at ten o'clock. What just happened?" I demanded. "Details, woman, details."

"You know that old folks home across the lake—"

"It's a progressive community, not an old folks home," I corrected.

Penny Sue blew me off. "Whatever it is, they want to expand with some very upscale duplexes and buy up all the property around the lake. Daddy's known this was in the works for a long time and turned down their first offer. Well, my house was the last piece of the pie, so they upped the ante. Daddy got six million! Can you believe it? Six million!"

"Don't go crazy, Penny Sue," Ruthie advised. "Without a good investment plan, you could run through six million pretty fast."

Penny Sue forced herself to be serious. "You're right, of course. I'm turning over a new leaf. I'll buy a new car and some clothes, but I'm going to be cheap and sensible like Leigh. I'm going to be responsible. I'll start today by joining the investment club, then I'm going to drive my Mercedes to the dealership and trade it in on a new one. No more embarrassing clunk, clunk for me. Praise the Lord, my ship has come in!"

Alice scuffed down the hall, looking like a woman who'd been to hell and back. For all her New Jersey bravado, the previous day had taken a heavy toll on her. "What's all the commotion? Can't a person get a decent night's sleep around here?"

"Penny Sue sold her house," Ruthie exclaimed.

Alice struggled up on a stool and motioned for coffee. I poured a cup and passed it across the counter. She took a long pull of the black coffee. "I'm happy for you, Penny Sue. Judging from the singing and carrying on, I gather you got a good price for it."

"Yes ma'am. Thanks to Daddy, I made out very well."

Alice nodded. "I always liked your Dad, he has a good head on his shoulders. Did he have any news about Kevin?"

"No ma'am, he had a meeting and only had time for my news. However, I'm sure he'll check on Kevin as soon as he gets a break. One of the junior partners may be doing it now."

"Not necessary. I have that lawyer's cell number and will call him in a little while." Alice took another swallow of coffee. "Leigh, would you fetch the file I found at the Examiner's office? I tossed and turned most of the night wondering what it says. I never got a chance to look at it. Being stuffed in that tiny cubicle, it's a wonder I didn't suffocate. I suppose I should know what it says before I call Kevin's attorney."

I retrieved the file and we all gathered around her, peering over her shoulders. The file contained two sheets of paper titled "Dr. Abigail Johnston." The first sheet was a stylized drawing of the front of a woman's body. The other sheet was the outline of the back. Superficial markings on the body were penciled in with annotations down the side of the page. Except for a scar on her right arm and a faint circle above one boob marked "adhesive outline," the first page was uninteresting. The second page was intriguing. There was a butterfly tattooed on her buttocks and several faint circles labeled "adhesive outline." On her right shoulder blade was a filled in circle marked "nicotine patch (21 mg.)." However the real standout was a square adhesive marking on the back of her upper left arm that had a number of dots drawn inside. The dots were circled in red with a question mark and the annotation read "high and irregular concentrations of nicotine on the skin."

Alice studied the dotted square. "What do you suppose that means?"

"Maybe Abby put on a patch the day before and it buckled in the heat," Penny Sue said. "You know, steam from a shower, getting caught in the rain, or perspiration could make tiny pockets in the glue so the patch didn't stick evenly. Maybe the salt in sweat can dissolve nicotine and cause it to dribble around."

Alice drummed her fingers on the counter. "Possible. I really don't know anything about those transdermal patches they use nowadays."

"Neither do I, but the good news is that nicotine can't possibly be related to Kevin." I glanced at my watch. "I've got to run if I'm going to get to work on time. Penny Sue, the New Smyrna Ladies' Investment Club meets at ten o'clock. You'd better get hopping."

"Yeah, I want to look good. All of those women are so slim. Maybe they have a big investment in pharmaceuticals and get discounts on diet pills or something."

"You wish. See ya." I snatched my purse and headed out of the door.

My day at the library was pleasantly dull. Leonard Kydd had assumed his post in the magazine section and gave me a little wave. Terry agreed to let me have the afternoon off so I could meet with Heather. I spent the morning shelving books. Penny Sue tracked me down a little after eleven o'clock.

"I met the nicest lady at the investment meeting who invited me to lunch. Would you like to join us? She's skinny as a rail. I'm going to try to find out her secret."

"Penny Sue, we have to meet with Heather this afternoon. Besides, I want to go home and see what the alarm people are doing to my condo."

"Oh, yeah, I forgot about that. Well, if you're not going, we'll do an early lunch and I'll be home by one-thirty. Is that okay? I doubt Heather would come any earlier, since she pulled a double shift yesterday."

I sighed. My response really didn't make any difference. Penny Sue was going to do what she wanted to do, no matter what. "Sure, one-thirty's fine. How did the meeting go?"

"Everyone was real nice. I pledged to invest $100,000."

"A hundred thousand? You don't know anything about these people! Besides, you haven't gotten the settlement from your house yet, either. The papers haven't even been signed."

"Daddy said the sale was a sure thing and I can get that much money from my American Express card. I didn't want them to think I was a pauper and not let me in the club. Members have to be voted on, like in a sorority. I think that's the reason Susan invited me to lunch. She's the president, and I suspect she wants to feel me out. Anyway, they must be legit if they meet at the library."

"I don't believe the library does background checks on all of the groups. They're probably on the up and up. I've never heard anything negative, but you really should be careful. You need to check out the members like they're checking on you. Do you have a list of members?" I asked.

Penny Sue started twirling her hair with her index finger. It was a nervous habit I'd come to recognize. "I believe the membership is sorta secret, you know, like a twelve-step program."

"A secret investment club? Penny Sue, that doesn't make a grain of sense."

She untangled her finger. "Well, I may be wrong on that. Everyone seems to know everyone else. I suspect they're old New Smyrna." She patted my arm. "Don't worry, I'll be sensible like you and get the facts before I hand over any money." She glanced at a blonde lady standing by the front door, who was dressed in a tailored black dress and wearing a number of gold necklaces and bracelets. "That's Susan. Let me run, so I can get home in time to meet with Heather. You really don't need to worry. Thanks to Madoff, my poverty stint taught me a good lesson."

"Okay, but don't sign anything or give anyone money!"

Penny Sue smiled meekly. "Well, I signed a pledge card, but I'm sure it's not legally binding." She dashed off, clearly not wanting to discuss her stupidity any further.

I finished my shift at noon and drove to Wendy's for lunch. They were having a special on chicken sandwiches. I thought of calling Ruthie to see if she wanted one, but decided against it. First, Ruthie adamantly opposed fast food. "Full of preservatives and chemicals," she said. Maybe that's true, but those chicken sandwiches tasted good. Secondly, I was afraid an offer would turn into a big production involving Alice, Guthrie and maybe even the alarm crew. I was too tired to deal with it. So, I sat in the parking lot, eating a sandwich and drinking a chemical filled soda before going home.

A three-man crew was busy wiring my alarm system, while Ruthie sat at the counter reading the morning newspaper.

"How's it going?" I asked.

She canted her head toward the workmen. "I believe they're almost finished. But it has been one heck of a morning."

"Why, what happened?"

"Alice spoke with the lawyer, and Kevin isn't going to be released today," Ruthie replied.

"But the nicotine poisoning proves Kevin had nothing to do with it."

Ruthie folded the paper angrily. "Yes, but we're not supposed to know about that, and the lawyer didn't mention it. Alice couldn't tip her hand. The Medical Examiner apparently hasn't filed his report yet."

"So why is Kevin being held? I thought the New Jersey warrant wasn't going to be enforced."

Ruthie sucked in a breath and held her fingers like quotation marks. "That's unofficial." Frown lines formed between her eyes. "Kevin is still being held on the New Jersey warrant and is classified as a flight risk here. Needless to say, Alice is on the warpath and spent most of the morning calling her contacts up north. She may bring in another attorney."

"Oh, no. I hope it's not a mob lawyer," I moaned.

"My gut says it is."

I folded my arms on the counter, put my head down and spoke to the countertop. "That's all we need."

"I know."

Our pity party was interrupted by the crew supervisor. "We're finished. Let me show you what we did and how it works." Basically, we were alarmed to the hilt. Glass breaks on the windows in case of a smash and grab attack, sensors on all of the windows and doorframes, and a smoke alarm. The alarm panel was identical to Penny Sue's, with a panic button. They even wired the system into a call center that would report a break-in if we were away.

Ruthie gave the men a check and ushered them to the front door. "I dare anyone to try to break in tonight," Ruthie said when she returned.

I glanced at the boxes of books. "What in the world were the burglars looking for? I suppose they think one of the books is valuable. But, to risk breaking in two nights in a row? That's pretty gutsy."

"That's for sure," Ruthie replied. "As soon as Heather leaves, I think we should work on the book inventory. At least see if any of the books Kevin and I logged are missing. I was going to do it this morning, but there was too much commotion with all of the workmen."

There was a loud bang on the door. Alice let herself in and stomped down the hall, mad as a hornet. She was holding the manila folder she'd lifted the night before. "Leigh, you have to go with me to the Medical Examiner's office and return this folder.

I think this is why the cops are still holding Kevin."

"What?" I asked.

"Guthrie's not here. Besides, neither of us can do it because we'd be recognized," Alice said. "This must be the only copy of the information, and since they can't find it, the Examiner hasn't issued his report. Kevin will never be released until we take it back."

"What am I supposed to do? Waltz in and say 'here's a folder that someone stole yesterday?' And, why me? Why not Ruthie?"

"Because you look more like a tough reporter. Ruthie appears much too sweet."

Aunt Alice says I look like a tough reporter after Penny Sue said my condo didn't have anything valuable? That family was pushing their luck! "Just how am I supposed to pull this off?" I asked tersely.

Alice rolled her eyes. "You're going to walk in with a stack of folders and pretend you're doing a story on the Medical Examiner's office and ask to make an appointment. When the receptionist isn't watching, you'll put this folder on her desk. There was a red-headed receptionist working yesterday. I'll watch from my car and call your cell after you get rid of the folder. That will give you an excuse to leave quickly."

"I guess it could work," I said slowly. "Why not Penny Sue? She'll be here any minute."

"She couldn't pull it off. Penny Sue doesn't look like she knows diddly-squat," Alice replied.

Ruthie's eyes widened, as Penny Sue appeared directly behind Alice.

"Thanks, Auntie, dear," Penny Sue boomed.

Alice swung around to face her niece. "Do you know anything about news reporting?"

"No, but—"

Alice did a palms-up. "See, I didn't think you knew diddly about it. Don't get your panties in a wad. I was talking about newspaper reporters."

"Oh." Penny Sue stalked past Alice to the bathroom. I suspected Penny Sue was banging her head against the wall and muttering every cuss word she knew.

"Alice, we can't go anywhere until Heather interviews us about last night," Ruthie spoke for the first time.

"Well, where is she? And, what's to tell? The place was burglarized, the thieves got away and they couldn't lift any prints. End of story."

"Wait a minute," I said. "I wonder if Lu Nee 2 keeps a recording. Maybe Carl can retrieve pictures of the thieves. I was supposed to call him earlier to see if he could crack the code to Abby's computer, but forgot it in all of the commotion."

Penny Sue must have been listening at the bathroom door, because she came out talking. "Yes, Lu Nee has a recording function!"

"Well, for godsakes, call Carl and get on with it," Alice said curtly. "We need to get to the Examiner's office before the shift changes."

Thankfully, Heather arrived at that moment. True to Alice's prediction, there wasn't much to tell, except that we planned to call Carl about retrieving Lu Nee 2's video.

"Excellent," Heather commented, giving the robot an appreciative pat. "If Carl can get the recording, it may be the break we need to solve a number of robberies on the beach."

"What about the handprint?" Ruthie asked.

"It'll be a while before we have those results. Our lab isn't as fast as the one on *CSI*." Heather flipped her notebook closed. "Please call me as soon as you get the video. If Carl can't retrieve it, our technicians may be able to help."

I grinned. "Doubtful. Carl's a genius from MIT. If he can't get it, no one can."

"Probably so, but we still have to try. Call me as soon as you learn anything."

"Will do." I walked Heather to the front door with Alice breathing down my neck. Honestly, Penny Sue was right. Alice was one pushy broad!

To make me appear like a reporter, we rummaged through Abby's boxes and came up with about a half dozen file folders. I stuffed the stolen folder upside down in the center so I could find it easily, and Alice and I took off in her Caddy. I thought we were cutting it close until Alice hit the interstate. She drove like a NASCAR tire tester! A good thing, because we arrived only about ten minutes before the shift ended, which turned out to be fortunate since the red-headed receptionist, whose nametag read Harriet, was packing up for the day. She told me the Chief Examiner was out of the office and continued stuffing her brief-case. I slid the folder out of my stack, bent over, and straightened up holding it out to her. "This was under your desk. Is it yours?"

Harriet snatched the folder with an annoyed expression until she opened it. "My God, we've been looking for this all day! It was under my desk?"

My cell phone rang. I made a show of glancing at the readout and backed toward the door. "Yes. Sorry, I need to take this call."

"Sure." As I scurried to the car I heard Harriet mutter, "Under my desk the whole time!"

Chapter 13

Alice called a New Jersey attorney on the way home. I gathered he had already been in touch with the New Smyrna Beach officials and the local attorney. It also became clear that he knew Alice had stolen the file, and he instructed her to return it. She was surprisingly contrite.

"Can you get Kevin out tonight?" she asked. The response obviously didn't please her, given the muscle clench in her jaw. Hmm, another family trait, exactly like Penny Sue. "Tomorrow morning?" The smile told me that answer pleased her. "Are you coming down? You can share the room with Kevin. Sorry, single beds, but it's not my condo. I'd like to have you close in case anything comes up."

Wow! She was taking charge of the Judge's condo, too. If he knew a mob lawyer was staying in his place, he'd have a fit.

Alice chatted a few more minutes about travel arrangements to the Daytona Airport and hung up just as we reached our parking lot. As usual, she slammed on the brakes, spewing a massive cloud of sand. "Thanks, Leigh, I knew you could pull it off. Pretending you found the folder under the desk was a stroke of genius. Penny Sue would never have thought of that."

I gathered my purse and the files and prepared to get out. "I don't know. Penny Sue can be very resourceful. She learned a lot in all of those anti-terrorist courses she's taken."

"Anti-terrorist courses?" Alice asked incredulously.

"Sure, Penny Sue's a prime target for revenge with all the criminals her father has locked up. She's taken a number of courses on self-defense and terrorist avoidance."

Alice slammed her car door. "I'll be damned, I had no idea. She always struck me as a man chasing ditz, considering she's been married three times. Guess I was wrong."

"Yes, there's a lot more to Penny Sue than meets the eye."

"Seems so. Well, I need to hit the john. Thanks again." Alice headed into the Judge's condo while I went to mine. I found Penny Sue and Ruthie sitting on the floor, sorting through the books.

"How'd it go?" Ruthie asked anxiously.

I dumped my load of files on the kitchen counter and pulled up a chair beside them. "Amazingly well." I told them about the-file-under-the-desk ploy and how the receptionist was so happy to find it, she never suspected a thing. "Alice phoned an attorney from the car. He believes Kevin will probably be released tomorrow." Ruthie's eyes lit up at the news. "Only thing—the attorney is flying down tomorrow and will share the room in your condo with Kevin," I said to Penny Sue.

Penny Sue's jaw started to twitch. "That lady has the nerve of a bad tooth! She waltzes in and just takes over." Penny Sue straightened her shoulders defiantly. "Well, the old biddy can stay alone tonight. The place is alarmed, she'll be safe, and I've had enough of her for one day. I'm staying here."

"We'll all stay here," I said. "We can probably get Guthrie to come down and play cards with her. Alice looks real tired, anyway."

Ruthie stood and stretched. "I'll call Guthrie. If he'll come down and Auntie-sit, why don't the three of us go out to dinner? I need to get out of the house."

"Good plan. There's a new seafood restaurant near Flagler." I motioned at the books. "By the way, is anything missing?"

"No," Ruthie replied. "All of the books Kevin and I catalogued are present and accounted for."

"Did you hear from Carl while I was gone?"

"Yes, he's tied up on a project today, but will come over tomorrow. Carl is certain he can download the recording and enhance the photos." Penny Sue grabbed the edge of my dining room table and hoisted herself up. "I've got to take off some weight." She leaned backward and stretched. "I might get some help on that. The lunch with Susan went well. I'm a shoo-in for the investment club. I asked her how she stayed so slim. She alluded to a secret potion, a homeopathic concoction, I think. Anyway, an old lady she knew came in the restaurant and interrupted her story. I'll see if I can get the details at the meeting next week. Leigh, you want some if Susan sells it?" Penny Sue turned and gave Ruthie a disgusted look. "I know skinny minnie isn't interested."

Boy, Penny Sue was skating on thin ice. First she said my condo was cheap, then Alice said I look tough, and now Penny Sue implied that I was fat. One more insult, and Penny Sue would sleep with Alice. "I'll wait to see how it works for you. I really don't need to lose much weight." So there! I suppressed the urge to flash a rude finger salute.

Ruthie saw the look in my eye and dashed to the phone in the kitchen. "I'll call Guthrie right now. I'd love a grouper sandwich, wouldn't you?"

"Mmm-m," Penny Sue said. "Grouper with hush puppies and cole slaw. I can taste it now."

Guthrie had cooked a pot roast and brownies and was more than happy to keep Alice company. She also seemed pleased, Guthrie clearly amused her, not to mention he offered to bring the food. So, Ruthie, Penny Sue, and I retrieved our clothes and toiletries from next door, then piled into Ruthie's Jaguar and headed for Flagler Avenue, the center of New Smyrna Beach nightlife. I knew about the new restaurant and was surprised Ruthie didn't keep straight up Atlantic Avenue. Instead she stayed on A1A and took a right at Heath's Health Food Store.

"Didn't you miss the turn?" I asked Ruthie.

"I want to show you something."

"Well, I hope it won't take long. I'm starving," Penny Sue said. "I only had a small salad for lunch because Susan made me so self-conscious about my weight. I sure hope she really has some sort of diet potion. This extra weight makes me look old, and I don't want to have liposuction. They say it's painful, you'll be bruised for weeks."

"It's a short detour," Ruthie replied. "Another way to the restaurant." A moment later, she pulled into a parking space on Flagler Avenue across the street from a vacant lot. "What do you think?"

"Think about what?" Penny Sue asked. "It's a vacant lot and I'm ravenous."

"Don't you think New Smyrna Beach needs a beachside bookstore?" Ruthie asked.

"Yeah, I'm surprised there isn't one already," Penny Sue shot back.

"Well, there will be soon. I bought the lot yesterday." Ruthie pulled out of the parking space and drove to the restaurant, a couple of blocks away. Since Penny Sue was on the verge of starvation, nothing else was said until we'd been seated at the restaurant and ordered our drinks, grouper, slaw, and hush puppies. The wine came right away. Penny Sue downed hers like a person who'd stumbled in from the Sahara. She held up her glass for a refill.

"You're going to build a bookstore?" Penny Sue asked, as she waited for more wine. "Does that mean you're planning on moving down here?"

"Yep," Ruthie said with a grin. "I've found an architect, and the zoning will allow me to build an apartment upstairs. Actually, it will be about two thousand square feet, enough for two guestrooms and a studio for my art. I'm going to call the store *Hungry for Knowledge*. I want something fun to do. After all, I have a degree in library science, and I love books."

So does Kevin, I thought.

Penny Sue's wine arrived, and she took a big gulp. "You'll need some help, won't you? I have experience at the library, so I could sell books. I won't need a full time job, just something part time to satisfy Daddy."

Ruthie did a big eye roll. "Yes, Penny Sue, you can have a job." Ruthie cut her eyes at me. "Leigh, I was hoping you would agree to be the office manager. With all of your experience in Atlanta at the car dealership, you'd be perfect. What do you think?"

Her offer took me completely by surprise. I knew Ruthie was thinking of a bookstore, but never considered myself as part of the deal. I'd also envisioned a smaller store that Ruthie would handle herself. "That's really tempting. I'd love to work with you, but I need health insurance and retirement benefits like the library provides. At my age, I have to build a nest egg for the future."

Ruthie waved away my objection. "Oh, you'd get health insurance and a retirement plan. I'm not going to stiff my best friend."

Penny Sue's bottom lip stuck out. "How about me?"

Ruthie's lips screwed up into an are-you-kidding expression. "Yes, of course you'll get benefits, too. I wouldn't leave you out."

The food arrived, and Penny Sue's eyes shone like beacons. She took a big bite of grouper, chewed, swallowed, and shouted, "Yahoo! I've hit the jackpot. My stars must be in alignment." She shoveled down some slaw. "Ruthie, let's check my astrological chart when we get home. I must have something really good going." Penny Sue took a bite of a hush puppy and chased it with wine. "Leigh, don't take offense, but I think I'll resign from the library. I really don't like it, and my feet hurt all of the time. I know you and Guthrie were trying to help, but it's just not for me. Besides, it makes me look bad in the eyes of the investment club. I don't believe any of them are volunteers."

To be completely honest, Penny Sue's quitting the library was music to my ears. Since I'd recommended her, I knew it was just a matter of time before she screwed up and I got blamed. Of course, I couldn't say that. "I understand. There is a long list of lonely widows who are waiting for a spot. You're actually doing them a favor."

She shoveled down some more slaw. "You're right. With the money I have coming from the sale of my property, it's actually cruel of me to take a spot from a lonely widow."

Ruthie did a fabulous job of stifling a grin. "That's kind of you, Penny Sue. You're doing the right thing."

Penny Sue nodded. "I shouldn't put it off. I'll go in tomorrow and explain things to Terry. Are you going to quit, too?" she asked me.

"This caught me by surprise. I enjoy working at the library. When do you expect to start construction?" I asked Ruthie.

"As soon as they can pull the permits. But I'll need your expertise before then to keep track of the expenses and everything. Accounting is way beyond my ability, and I know I can trust you. Besides, with Penny Sue's windfall, she can hold off for a few months, right?"

"Yes, I actually need some time off to buy a new car and some clothes. I can wait until the bookstore is finished."

I took a hefty bite of grouper and chewed slowly, thinking. "It will take at least six months to build the store. "How about I continue working at the library and help you nights and weekends? There shouldn't be much to do until you're ready to buy fixtures and inventory. I'll quit my job then and work for you full time."

"Good, then it's settled? I don't want to push y'all into anything, but I can't think of two people I'd rather work with." Ruthie turned to me. "Do you mind sharing your condo with me until mine is finished? I'll pay all of the expenses."

"That's not necessary. You've already installed an expensive alarm system for me."

"I insist. It's the least I can do if you'll help with the accounting. Of course, when you start full time, we'll work out a compensation package."

No housing expenses for six months? Boy, I could save a lot of money. "Okay, it's a deal."

"We'll be together again. The DAFFODILS will take New Smyrna Beach by storm," Penny Sue said loudly. "We'll put this place on the map!" She held up her hand and we did our usual sloppy high five.

The lights were on in Penny Sue's condo when we got home. Figuring Alice was watching television, we knocked on the door to check on her. Guthrie answered, holding a scotch and wearing a shirt, black socks, and his "tighty whities."

Penny Sue drew back with her hand over her heart. "Where's my aunt? What are you doing?" Penny Sue screamed.

Alice appeared at the end of the hall wearing her bra and slacks. Judging from her gentle sway, she'd had a few belts of scotch, too. "Keep it down! You'll wake up the whole neighborhood." She snatched her blouse from the arm of the sofa and struggled into it. "We're playing strip poker and I'm winning."

Ruthie and I were dumbstruck. Penny Sue's eyes almost popped out of her head. "This is my condo, and there will be no strip poker here."

Guthrie staggered back. "Man, it was her idea. Alice said it was her only chance, since she's old and Kevin will be home tomorrow."

"Chance for what?" Penny Sue demanded in her School Marm voice.

Guthrie flashed a silly grin. "We were playing rummy when

Alice suddenly decided she wanted to see my wiener. She said my cooking was so good, she couldn't believe I had one. I told her it was private, so she challenged me to strip poker."

"Alice," Penny Sue bellowed, "Guthrie's wiener is off limits. He's just a good cook."

Alice smirked at Penny Sue while she finished buttoning her shirt. "Man, you are one uptight lady. A lot like your mother— no yearning for adventure."

"Leave my mother out of this. I've had plenty of adventure, and strip poker with Guthrie isn't one of them. I show you hospitality, try to help your son, and you take advantage of my neighbor who was kind enough to bring dinner."

"The food was good," Alice said. "And I didn't force him to play poker—he was willing."

Guthrie leaned toward Penny Sue and stage whispered. His breath was close to a hundred proof. "Don't worry, I would have gone only so far. You know my sexual persuasion, and I don't show the Big Boy to just anybody. Besides, I'm still engaged to Timothy."

Penny Sue unclenched her fists, but gave Alice a contemptuous look. "Don't you ever do that in my house again. Guthrie, I think you should get your clothes and go home now."

"No-o problemo." He did a little stutter step. "It will only take me a minute to gather my things."

Ruthie squeezed by us and took Guthrie's arm. "Here, I'll help you."

Chapter 14

Penny Sue and I were getting dressed when Carl arrived to examine Lu Nee 2. I threw a robe on and let him in.

"Sorry to come so early, but I'm working on a big project for an aerospace company. Navigation." He rolled Lu Nee to the dining room table and dug a laptop and a bunch of cords from his satchel. "Do you have the instruction book?"

I snatched it from the kitchen counter. I'd anticipated that he might need it. Carl checked the index, turned to a page, and quickly ran his finger down it. He was apparently a speed reader, because a moment later he powered up the robot and connected a cord to his computer.

"Would you like some coffee?" I asked.

"No, thank you. I'm finished."

Good Lord! He'd done it in less than five minutes. Genius wasn't an adequate description of Carl. "Do you think you can get pictures of the burglars?"

"I'm fairly sure I can. It appears the recording starts when the alarm sounds. Until then, Lu Nee's little more than a remote camera. I have a meeting to attend now, but I'll get on this right after lunch and bring you the pictures."

I gestured to the kitchen counter, where I'd put Abby's computer. "I apologize for being a pill, but do you think you can find the password for this computer? It belonged to Abby, the lady who died, and we think it might hold a clue to her death. It was willed to Kevin, and he's tried everything he can think of for a password. They were engaged in graduate school, but she broke it off. I guess she felt guilty because she published their joint research under her name alone and won the Register Award. Willing all of her books and notes to Kevin was probably her way of saying she was sorry."

Kevin stowed Abby's laptop in his satchel. "None of this should be a problem. I'll drop everything off here as soon as I'm finished. I'll call your cell phone if I have any trouble. Will Ruthie be here if you're not?"

"She should." I saw him to the door, once again amazed by his brilliance. The three of us could never have figured any of it out.

Penny Sue followed me to the library in her Mercedes. As soon as she turned in her resignation, she intended to drive to the dealership and buy a new car. She'd always driven a big yellow Mercedes, but said she'd consider a Jaguar if there was going to be a long wait. She couldn't stand the transmission clunk, or my tiny car, another minute.

Ruthie was up and dressed when we left, no doubt in anticipation of Kevin's release from jail. Although she tried to play it down, Ruthie was truly smitten with Kevin. Something told me that Kevin might end up living in that two thousand square foot apartment over her bookstore.

Ruthie had offered to pick Kevin up from jail, but it was questionable whether Alice would remember the offer this morning. So, Ruthie planned to call next door at about nine-thirty. Ruthie was also waiting by her computer to print some documents that the Judge was sending Penny Sue for the property sale. If they arrived in time to be express mailed today, she might have her money in a week or so. It was that early morning phone call from Judge Daddy that inspired Penny Sue's car shopping spree.

We parked at the back, far right side of the library lot and headed toward the front door. We'd just reached the outdoor, enclosed lunch area next to the book drop, when Leonard Kydd pulled in. One look at Penny Sue, and he drove straight through the lot and parked in a corner furthest from us.

"You intimidated him," I said.

"Me? Why do you say that?"

I couldn't tell her the truth, that she'd come on to him like a pushy streetwalker and scared the daylights out of the proper English gentleman. Yet that might not have been the problem, considering the shenanigans attributed to British Royalty by the tabloids. Leonard could be a happily married man, or gay, for all I knew. "You can be intimidating. You're tall and very direct, which many find overwhelming."

"The curse of beauty and height." She hooked her finger at a swirl of smoke rising from the fenced enclosure. "Someone's sneaking a cigarette. Isn't that against the rules?"

"Yeah, but I think it's pretty common, especially this early in the morning. Smokers can peek though the spaces between the slats and snuff the cigarette out if Terry shows up."

"I miss smoking. I could use one right now to calm my nerves. I like Terry and hate to disappoint her by resigning. She's been very nice to me. Of course, smoking in the bathroom is probably what did Abby in. Tragic. Just tragic. It's a nasty habit, but take it from me, it's a hard one to give up."

"I know. I've heard it's as addictive as heroin," I said.

"I believe it." Penny Sue picked up her pace. "Hey, that's Susan going into the library. The blond young man must be her son. She told me she had one son who was a champion surfer." Penny Sue broke into a slow jog. "Susan! Wait up."

I lagged behind, not wanting to get in the middle of Penny Sue's impressiveness. She visited with Susan and her son for a moment, then headed in to find Terry. Once Penny Sue was out of sight, Leonard parked and headed for the front door. We arrived at the same time.

"Good morning," he said stiffly.

"Here for surveillance, I presume."

"Yes. Have you learned anything about the cause of Duffy's death?" he asked.

Of course I had, but couldn't say anything, since the official reports hadn't been released. "No, do you have any leads?"

"I've been interviewing some surfers and have a suspicion, but nothing I want to talk about. It's still too speculative. I'm a journalist, after all."

"I understand. Penny Sue has come into some money and is going to resign from the library today," I said.

"She is?!" The relief in his voice was unmistakable.

"Yes, she has a few new things in the works," I said casually.

"I'm very happy for her." There was a definite lilt in his stride as he went inside and made a beeline for the magazine section.

I stored my purse under the counter and took a station at the checkout desk. A few minutes later, Penny Sue stopped by.

"Terry was very gracious. She said she hated to lose me, but understood that my dear friend Ruthie needed me more."

"Ruthie?" I blurted. "What did you tell Terry?"

Penny Sue started twirling a strand of hair around her finger. "The truth. Ruthie's father passed away and she needed my help." I slumped in disbelief. Was there nothing sacred? "Well, I need to run," Penny Sue said. "I hope Ruthie has received the documents from Daddy so I can mail them before I start car shopping. See you! I'll let you know if I hear anything about Kevin."

No sooner had Penny Sue left, than Susan and her son entered. I noticed that Leonard sat up straight and lowered his magazine to watch them. Why was he watching? She was an attractive woman, but there was something curious about it. I watched Susan and her son go down the biography aisle. They stopped midway and pulled out a book. Meanwhile, Leonard left his post and went to the same aisle, running his finger over the books as if looking for a particular call number. Susan put her book back on the shelf and left. As soon as she was out of sight, Leonard rushed to the spot she'd been in and started flipping through the pages of books in the vicinity. A couple of times he even turned the books upside down and shook them as if he expected to find something hidden inside. He apparently came up with nothing and sullenly went back to his seat.

The day was slow, and I kept my eye on Leonard most of the morning. He said he'd been interviewing surfers and had a suspicion, but didn't want to talk about it. Susan's son was a surfer, and Penny Sue was about to give this woman and her group $100,000! The situation smelled bad, like a week-old fish, and I did not want Penny Sue to be conned again.

Leonard left at noon, as he usually did. I'd already traded shifts with a colleague to take my lunch at that time. I hoped to find out what was going on before Penny Sue was taken for a ride. When Leonard left the library, I grabbed my purse and followed.

"Leonard, I need to talk with you," I called.

He stopped, clearly surprised.

I strode up to him, within inches of his face. "What's going on with the blonde lady and her son? Why are you watching her? Penny Sue is about to invest a sizeable amount of money with Susan Marzano's club."

"The New Smyrna Beach Ladies' Investment Club?" he asked.

"Yes. What do you know? Are they legitimate?"

He motioned to his car. "Let's talk over there." Leonard started his car and turned on the air conditioner. I got in the passenger side. He hung his head, thinking, before he spoke. "I pride myself on being a good journalist. That means I don't write or print stories that haven't been at least double-sourced. *Vainglory* is not a tabloid rag, and I take great pleasure in its reputation for honest, comprehensive reporting. William Duffy was an old school journalist, which is why I funded his project so long, even though I didn't know what he'd stumbled on to." He gave me a piercing stare. "I must have your word that you won't reveal the source of the information I'm about to tell you. I'm only sharing this to save your friend from a bad investment and hopefully solve the mystery of Duffy's death. I owe it to him. He was a good man."

The seriousness in his voice took me aback. He was an honorable man, one the Judge would like. "You have my promise."

Leonard cleared his throat. "I had some notes from Duffy when he first started the surfer story, before he ran into the bigger piece. He mentioned a surfer named Andy Marzano. He's the son of the blonde lady, Susan Marzano, who is President of the Ladies' Investment Club. I interviewed a couple of surfers the other day. Some are very upset about Duffy's death, and one knew there was a snake involved. He commented that the Marzanos were the real snakes."

"Heavens. What does that mean?"

"I haven't pieced it together, but suspect it somehow involves drugs. A couple of the surfers mentioned dexies, and their body language told me it was somehow related to Andy Marzano. Duffy also made a cryptic reference to the book drops at the library. I think that's why he was in the drop room the night he died."

Lord have mercy! Marzano was an Italian name, and Alice was flying a mob attorney down today. Actually, I didn't know which mob the man represented, and all Italians are certainly not connected to the Mafia. I was jumping to conclusions, still ... what had we gotten into? I suddenly felt like throwing up. "Leonard, this is distressing news. In fact, I feel sick. You have my cell number. Call me later, and we'll arrange a meeting so I can fill you in. I may be wrong, but this whole situation could be worse than we thought. Be careful." I bolted from the car and raced to mine at the other side of the parking lot. The air conditioning ran full blast on my face for several minutes before my

wits returned. I had to talk to Alice. I sat for a few minutes before I
drove to a side street. I'd been away from the library for about 45
minutes. Could food poisoning strike that fast? I didn't know but
took a chance. I called Terry on my cell phone and told her I'd
developed a terrible case of diarrhea. I wasn't sure if it was breakfast or lunch, but I needed to go home. Considering Penny Sue
had just quit, I suspected Terry didn't believe my story, yet she
didn't argue. I put the pedal to the metal of my VW Bug and
headed home to talk to Alice.

Our parking lot was almost full when I arrived. The Cadillac,
Jaguar, and a strange Honda were parked in front of our units. I
feared the Honda was a rental that belonged to Alice's attorney.
I glanced at my watch. The man must have taken a very early
flight, since it was only one o'clock. I decided to check with
Ruthie before I spoke to Alice, which I certainly didn't want to
do in the presence of an attorney.

Ruthie was sitting in the living room with Dr. Willows. He
stood when I entered, and we traded pleasantries. "I came to
check on Kevin," Willows said. "I didn't realize he was under
suspicion for Abby's death."

Ruthie's cheeks flamed. "That's not what I said. Kevin should
be released today. It's a big misunderstanding."

"Without a doubt," Willows agreed. "There is no way Kevin
would harm a hair on Abby's head, even though she did walk out
on him in college."

I crossed my arms and gave Willows a stern look. That was
an unnecessarily low blow.

"I won't keep you. Please ask Kevin to call me when he gets
home. I am interested in Abby's books, especially if some are
duplicates of books in Kevin's collection. I suspect she owned
some fairly rare volumes. Central Florida is my field of interest,
you know."

"Yes, we know that." I took his arm and guided him to the
door. "We'll give Kevin your message, but I suspect it will take

quite a while for him to compare Abby's books to his collection at home." I held the front door open for Willows. "Have a nice day."

"You do the same."

"That guy has some nerve," I said. "I'm sure he knew that Kevin is in jail. The jerk probably thought we were dimwits that he could bamboozle."

"My thought, exactly," Ruthie agreed. "He asked to look through Abby's books. Can you believe it? That man is truly a snake."

Snake. It reminded me of Duffy and why I'd come home. "What's the situation with the New Jersey attorney?"

Ruthie went to the kitchen for a bottle of water. "Can I get you anything?" I shook my head. "There's been a change of plans. The lawyer has an associate in Miami who's going to fly up here in his private plane and arrange for Kevin's release. Kevin may be confined to the condo with an electronic monitoring bracelet, until the Medical Examiner finishes his report. Alice's friend is going to stay in New Jersey and have that warrant quashed. Since you returned the missing file, I thought the medical report would have been released by now, but I guess there are several reviews that must take place first."

I slumped onto the sofa. "Well, at least he'll be home. Did Penny Sue get her documents?"

Ruthie joined me on the couch. "Yes, she snatched them up as soon as they came off the printer and headed to the bank to have her signature notarized. I suspect she'll have a new car when we see her again. Hey," Ruthie hauled back and looked at me. "What are you doing here?"

I told her about the Marzanos and Leonard Kydd's suspicion that there was a drug connection. He also thought the library's book drops were somehow involved. "I came home to talk to Alice. I know I'm probably being paranoid, but I'm afraid there could be a connection with the mob."

"Hmm, I think you are stretching things a bit. Al's group was a major supplier. Their shipments were so large they had to be buried on the beach," Ruthie reminded me.

"You're right, transactions like his couldn't possibly go through the library. I suppose I'm just on edge after the two break-ins." I'd put my purse on the coffee table, and it suddenly started to jiggle, taking us both by surprise. It took a minute for me to realize that it was my cell phone that was set to the silent/vibrate mode. I dug out the phone and recognized the number was Leonard Kydd's.

"Hello. Yes, I'm feeling better now, thank you. I'm sorry if I worried you. After some thought, I believe my imagination got away from me. I had a run in with the Italian mafia a few years ago, so when you mentioned drugs and Marzano in the same sentence, I panicked. Now that I've calmed down, I don't believe there could possibly be a connection. ... Sure, I'll keep you informed if we find out anything. I'm sorry to have caused a stir. ... You too."

No sooner had I clicked off the phone than Penny Sue bounded through the door. "Come see my new car! I'll get Alice."

"I wouldn't do that," Ruthie advised with a grin. "Alice's little escapade last night seems to have taken a toll on the old girl. I believe her one night drunk and gambling spree felt like a three-day binge this morning. She planned to take a nap before Kevin got home."

Penny Sue chuckled. "I suspected she was pretty looped to play strip poker. Has anyone seen Guthrie today? He was tanked, too." We shook our heads.

Penny Sue spread her arms apart to block the doorway. "Okay, this is going to be a big surprise, so brace yourselves." Ruthie and I both took a deep breath. Penny Sue had slipped into her Drama Queen mode. "Close your eyes." We obliged and allowed her to lead us into the parking lot. "Ta da!" she shouted.

"It's red," I mumbled.

"And a Jaguar," Ruthie exclaimed.

"I told y'all I was going to turn over a new leaf. It's an XJ model, just like Ruthie's, and the color is Claret. Isn't that perfect for me? I love Bordeaux wine. That's French, you know."

"Yes, I'm aware of that," Ruthie replied flatly. "Does this mean you'll start drinking red wine?"

"Couldn't hurt. I hear it's better for your heart. Want to go for a ride?" She sounded like a kid with a new toy.

"Sure, I just need to talk to you first. Come in the house and we'll toast your new car."

We took our usual spots at the counter and clicked together stemmed glasses of wine. "Mm-m, this Chardonnay is good," Penny Sue said. "I'm not sure I can give it up completely. So, what do we need to talk about? I want to take you for a ride. The car is fast and has that new car smell. Best of all, it shifts gears like they're made of Teflon. No more clunking."

I repeated the story Leonard Kydd told me about Susan and Andy Marzano, as well as their strange behavior in the biography section of the library. "You said Susan had a secret diet potion. Did you find out anything about that this morning?"

Penny Sue's brows knitted. "No. We didn't talk very long, because another member of the investment club wanted to speak with her in private. I waited for a moment, then left to meet with Terry before I lost my nerve. I did hear Susan say something about meeting tonight at ten-thirty."

"That's pretty late for cocktails or dinner." I stroked my arm, thinking. "You know, Duffy told Leonard there was something strange about the library's book drops. He thinks that's why Duffy was hiding out there. One of the surfers also referred to Andy Marzano as a snake."

"No way," Penny Sue said, refilling her glass. "You don't think Susan Marzano put a snake down the chute to kill Duffy, do you? She's a wealthy, classy woman—she wouldn't do that!"

"Yes, but her son might," Ruthie declared. "And what about that diet potion she supposedly has? Maybe it's not a homeopathic remedy like we thought."

"Well, I'm not sure she makes it herself," Penny Sue conceded. "I may have overstated things a tad on that point. I only know Susan has access to something." She turned to Ruthie. "Heck, it could be one of your flower remedies."

"How many times have you commented on how skinny all the women in the club are?" I asked.

Penny Sue scowled at me. "That doesn't mean anything. They all probably have personal trainers. And I think I'm going to get one, as soon as we clear up this mess with Kevin."

"Good Lord, Penny Sue. You have a whole basket of vitamins, and I haven't seen you take a single one," Ruthie said.

Penny Sue's bottom lip inched forward. "Well, I've been under stress, and my routine is completely off with Alice being here and all."

I put my hands in a T-formation to signal timeout. "We're getting off the subject. It seems to me that we need to follow this Duffy lead if we're going to clear Kevin and send Aunt Alice back to New Jersey. Are we in agreement on that?"

Penny Sue nodded vigorously. "Heavens yes, I'll do anything to send Alice packing."

"Okay, I think the three of us should follow up on the ten-thirty comment. If my suspicion is correct, someone will show up at the library tonight at ten-thirty. Maybe people meet in the parking lot to do drug deals."

"Yes, but how can we stake out the library without being detected?" Ruthie asked.

I grinned. "The fenced lunch enclosure on the side of the building. We'd get a good view of the parking lot by peering through the gaps between the slats, and we'd be hidden from everyone else. We'd park on a side street so no one would recognize our cars." I stared at Penny Sue. "We certainly can't take your new car."

"No way I'm leaving my new baby parked on a street," she agreed. "Ruthie's Jaguar would be a standout, too, and a lot of people know you drive a yellow Bug. We need something that fits in with the neighborhood."

At once our eyes met. "Guthrie," we said in unison.

Chapter 15

Carl pulled into the parking lot, and Guthrie appeared, as soon as we returned from our test drive in Penny Sue's new car. It was spiffy and made me long for the olden days of being married to a successful attorney and driving a BMW. But, my little Beetle would do. The car and my condo were paid for, and I still had some money left over from the divorce settlement. If I was frugal, or cheap, as Penny Sue put it, I could make it on my own. Having married right out of college, I went directly from my parents' care to my husband's, so this was a new experience for me. Since I was closing in on fifty, it was about time I learned to stand on my own two feet. Penny Sue was apparently getting the same lesson now, even though six million dollars isn't exactly poor!

Carl strode to Penny Sue's Jaguar and examined it appreciatively. "Hot car," he said to Penny Sue, as he passed a manila envelope and the laptop computer to me. "It fits you better than the Mercedes," he said. "Sportier." Penny Sue beamed.

Carl turned to me, "I got what you need from Lu Nee and printed it out. I made two copies so you can give one to the police. I also enclosed a disc of the entire recording, in case the still photos need to be authenticated. In the meantime, don't turn on Lu Nee 2. If there happened to be an alarm, it would record over these pictures. Keep Lu Nee off, at least until the authorities are satisfied. And that's Abby's laptop computer. The password is *Kevin*."

Ruthie's cheeks flamed.

"Carl," I started, hoping to divert attention from Ruthie's anger, "I can't tell you how much we appreciate this. May we pay you for your work?"

He grinned. "You can't afford me."

"I can," Ruthie said sternly. "You deserve to be compensated for your time."

Carl put his arm around Ruthie's shoulder. "Forget it, *Mom*. This was a no brainer for me. If you paid for my effort, it would be minimum wage. I wouldn't dream of taking a cent from you. Besides, I had fun the other night at the Medical Examiner's. It was a different kind of role playing. The gang and I are working on some new games now."

"You can't give up the Federation," Guthrie said, a hint of terror in his eyes. "Who'll save the universe?"

Carl smiled. Nice teeth. Why couldn't my Ann be attracted to him? So what if he liked to pretend he was a *Star Trek* Klingon? Everyone has a quirk or two. Carl was brilliant, handsome, a millionaire, kind to his mother and me. What more could a woman want? If Carl was planning to design other role playing games besides *Star Trek*, perhaps I should give the pairing another shot. I could have Ann down for Christmas or Spring Break. At least this time, she'd have already broken up with the old (my age!) State Department guy.

"Gotta run. Let me know if you need anything else. I'm happy to meet with the police to answer questions and explain my methodology."

"Thank you, Carl. Is your mother still in Boston with her sister?"

"Yes, my aunt isn't doing well. I'm not sure when Mom will get back."

"Give her our best, and let me know if there's anything we can do for her or you."

"I suspect doing for you will be more fun than your doing for me," Carl said with a grin. "You're always into something. You're magnets for trouble. But it's fun trouble, like a war game."

Magnets for trouble. I'd heard that description before. I was happy he thought it was fun. Carl was a great guy to have watching your back!

Guthrie gave Carl the arm-across-chest salute. "Live long and prosper."

Carl laughed as he slid into his SUV. "Guthrie, that's the Vulcan salutation."

"That's right, it is." As Carl backed out of the parking lot, Guthrie turned to Penny Sue's new car. "Wow, this is gnarly," he said. "I love the color. Have you taken it to the interstate and floored her yet?"

"Not yet," Penny Sue replied. "We have a lot planned for tonight, so we only took a short drive. The Jag does drive like a dream."

"The color's fabulous." That was all Guthrie seemed to notice.

"Claret, like the wine," Penny Sue replied. "By the way, how are you feeling today?"

Guthrie hung his head. "I wanted to talk to you about that. Alice and I killed my full bottle of twenty-five year old scotch. I think we got a little tipsy."

"Little?!" Ruthie replied. "I could hardly get you up the hill to your condo last night."

"Yeah, we were over-served. I want you to know, nothing would ever have happened between Alice and me. She was baiting me, and I couldn't back down."

Penny Sue patted his shoulder. "I can imagine. If you had a bad hangover, I think Alice paid twice the price, if it's any consolation. Do you know if Kevin's home yet?"

"He is. I was sitting on my balcony nursing my headache, when he pulled in with a slick looking Latino guy."

"That must be the Miami attorney," Ruthie said.

"Man, they arrived in a big limo. I didn't know New Smyrna Beach had limos."

"The lawyer supposedly flew in on his private plane to spring Kevin," Penny Sue said.

"It worked." Guthrie rubbed his temples, as if he were still feeling the aftereffects of his wild night. "I was going to go down there, but figured I should let Alice and Kevin have some time alone."

The expression on his face said he was really afraid Alice might have mentioned the strip poker, and Kevin would have decked him.

"Come in," I said. "Have a Coke. We have a favor to ask."

Since it was close to six o'clock, and Guthrie hadn't eaten, we passed out Cokes and ordered pizza. The mission we had in mind required unimpaired senses. While we waited for the delivery, Ruthie called next door and spoke to Kevin. After his days in jail, the one thing he wanted was solitude and a Philly cheese steak sandwich, which they'd ordered from Manny's. He said he was fine and apologized for not feeling sociable, but couldn't wait to eat and go to bed. His mother felt the same way. Ruthie guessed Alice didn't tell him why.

We outlined our plan to Guthrie while we ate. We figured his Lemon Aid VW bus would fit in with the neighborhood around the library. It was up to him. He could lend us the bus if he felt too bad, or tag along.

"Are you kidding? I wouldn't miss this for the world. You guys really spice things up, and the caffeine in this Coke helps."

We piled into Guthrie's van at nine-thirty, figuring that would give us plenty of time to park and hide out in the fenced lunch enclosure before anyone arrived. A full moon and cloudless sky made flashlights unnecessary, yet Penny Sue insisted that we take them, anyway, in case we had to bash someone over the head. I hoped it didn't come to that, but didn't argue. We took our positions in the enclosure at about ten o'clock. Each of us picked a spot and peered through the plastic slats at the book drop and library parking lot. At about ten minutes after ten, a big Cadillac pulled into the book drop lane. An older woman got out of her car, carrying a book.

"That's the lady who spoke with Susan this morning," Penny Sue whispered.

The woman opened the book drop but seemed to have a hard time getting the book in the slot. In any event, she fumbled around for a few minutes before returning to her car and driving away.

"She must have bad eyes," Guthrie said.

"Or just be dumb. How hard can a book drop be to operate?" I asked.

"Well, this is the beach and things corrode in the salt air," Ruthie came to the older woman's defense.

I checked my Minnie Mouse watch in the moonlight. "Yes, but it's not ten-thirty."

"Maybe she dropped off the book and is on her way to meet Susan."

Guthrie shushed us. "Here comes someone else." A black Lexus pulled into the lane beside the drop. This time Susan Marzano slid out of the car, carrying two books. She opened the door to the drop and tried to stuff the two books in. They apparently wouldn't fit, so she inserted them one at a time, then got back in her car and drove off.

"That's strange," I said. "Both women happened to return books, and it's not ten-thirty yet."

"Maybe your watch is wrong," Guthrie said.

"She's right." Penny Sue turned the face of her Rolex so we could see the lighted dial. The time was ten twenty-five. "There's something screwy going on with that book drop. Guthrie, why don't you sneak over there and check it out?"

"No, no, no. Man, I don't do snakes."

"Neither of them had a snake. We saw them return books," Penny Sue said.

"Hey it's, like, your idea—you do it."

"Well, I will." Penny Sue started out the back of the enclosure.

"Wait," Ruthie hissed. "It's ten-thirty."

We all took our positions at the breaks in the fence slats. The parking lot was empty and there wasn't a person in sight. After several minutes, an old green Volvo blasted into the lot, taking the turn on two wheels, and screeched to a halt at the book drop. Two young men were in the car. One had shaggy, blond hair, the other a close-cropped haircut on top with a brown pigtail. The brown-haired one jumped out of the passenger side and put a book in the slot. He, too, fumbled with the drop door for a moment before they sped off.

"Alert," Guthrie muttered. "Check out the side street on the right. I think that's the old woman's Cadillac." We stared out the openings on the right. A few minutes passed before the Cadillac slowly made its way back to the book drop. The old lady got out and seemed to be searching the ground around her car for something. Hunched over, she made her way to the drop, opened it, peered in and felt around. One hand went in the pocket of her skirt as she returned to her car, still bent over as if searching for something she'd lost. Once in the car, she rummaged around her large purse and finally drove away.

Ruthie checked her watch. "Ten forty-five," she whispered. "What do you think we just witnessed?"

"That's a drug deal," Guthrie said with certainty. "We should sit tight for a few minutes, in case this place is under surveillance by narcs, then get the shit out of Dodge!"

"Drug deal?" Penny Sue asked incredulously. "That old lady must be in her sixties."

Guthrie stared at us in the moonlight. "Ladies, this is the beach. You'd be surprised at how many upstanding citizens never gave up their teenaged habits."

I cut my eyes at him. "Are you speaking from personal experience?"

"Not any more. Your charity race got the last of my stash, and I promised Timothy I'd give up grass for good. I've kept my vow. I just wish they'd figure out the space program and send him home from Houston." Guthrie shook his head as if shaking off a bad memory. "Okay, let's stoop like the old lady and hightail it to my bus." And we did.

Penny Sue's condo was dark when we got home. True to his word, Kevin and Alice had apparently eaten their sandwiches and gone to bed. "Want to come in for a nightcap?" I asked Guthrie. He took a pass, saying his system needed to clear out before he put his toe back in the grand ocean of scotch.

"It's not your toe that was the problem," Penny Sue said.

He flashed a weak grin. "Man, everything was involved, from my head to my toe. See, we'd polished off a bottle of wine before we ever got to the scotch."

Penny Sue cackled. "Understood."

"Thanks for helping us out," I called as he inched the Lemon Aid bus up the hill to his condo.

Like zombies from an old B-rated movie, we mindlessly migrated to our usual stools, everyone except Penny Sue. She mindlessly migrated to the refrigerator. "How about a little of that cheap Irish cream on the rocks?" Penny Sue asked. We nodded. It had been a hard day's night as the old Beatles song went. "I'm going to ABC Liquor tomorrow and buying real Baileys. While I'm there, I'll consult Jerry on good brands of Claret. I really should stock up on it, now that I have the Jag. While Ruthie talked to Kevin earlier, I snuck in a call to Daddy. The papers should arrive tomorrow, and Daddy thought I'd get a check next week. Whew! It will be such a relief to pay off my credit card bills and buy some new clothes."

"Don't forget the car," I said.

"That, too."

"Will you buy a new house in Georgia, or stay down here? Have you given it any thought?" Ruthie asked.

Penny Sue lined a basket with a paper napkin, dumped in some chips, and passed out the drinks. "Considering Ruthie's bookstore and Daddy's insistence that I get a job and stop acting like a spoiled kid, I'm planning to stay here. I think he'll let me live in his condo. After all, he plans to will it to me, anyway. If he'll allow it, I may do some renovations. I'd like a larger, updated bathroom."

Why didn't that surprise me? Her master suite was considerably larger than mine, but it still wasn't big enough. If she had her druthers, I'm sure she'd build a second story master suite the size of the condo. But that was strictly forbidden by the condo association covenants. The whole point of building one-story beachfront duplexes, two-story duplexes staggered behind them, with a single three-story unit at the back of the cluster was to give everyone an ocean view. So, no matter how much money she had, she'd never pull off a second story.

Ruthie turned to me suddenly. "Hey, did you look at the pictures Carl brought over? I was so concerned about Kevin, I completely forgot them."

"No, I was too busy trying to find some Aleve for Guthrie." I hopped down from my stool and snatched the manila envelope from the coffee table where I'd dropped it. The package was sealed with one of those butterfly clasps that I twisted open. Inside was a computer CD and a stack of eight by twelve-inch glossy prints. The moment I saw the picture on top, I ran to my utility room, checking to make sure Lu Nee 2 was turned off and unplugged. The first picture told me Lu Nee was exhibit one.

"What's up?" Penny Sue demanded.

"Take a look at this!" I put the first photo on the counter between Ruthie and Penny Sue.

Both of Penny Sue's hands went to her throat. "Lord, have mercy! The blond guy is Andy Marzano!"

"Yeah, and the other boy looks a lot like the pigtail guy we saw tonight."

"Oh, Lord, Lordy, Lord. I almost gave Susan Marzano $100,000, and her son's a thief and drug dealer! Daddy will die. My new leaf is getting off to a rocky start."

I put my hand on her shoulder. "Now, calm down. You haven't invested anything yet, have you?" She shook her head. "So you haven't lost anything. How could you know? This is not your fault."

"What should we do?" Penny Sue asked.

The three of us sat at the counter, looking a lot like the see, hear, and speak no evil monkeys. I was rubbing my forehead, Penny Sue had her hands over her ears, and Ruthie was stroking her lips.

I found my voice first. "We should call Woody tomorrow and give him a set of the pictures. He'll tell us what to do."

Penny Sue glared at me like I'd lost my mind. "Woody? Are you crazy? He hates us."

"I don't think he really hates us—" Ruthie started.

"It doesn't matter," I interrupted. "It would be a big feather in his cap if he were responsible for solving the beach robberies."

Penny Sue sputtered her drink. "That's rich. Feather in his cap! Woody Woodhead, the Indian, whose mother thinks she's an Indian Princess."

"That's mean," Ruthie said. "His mother has dementia. You know that."

"I don't care, it's still rich. Woody is part American Indian." Penny Sue blew out a long breath. "But I think you're right, Leigh. Better to have Woody on our side than against us. Maybe this will help Kevin's situation. The sooner he's in the clear, the sooner Aunt Alice goes home."

"Right. I'll call in sick tomorrow, and we'll contact Woody first thing in the morning. I think we should also call Leonard and fill him in on the situation. Perhaps he can verify our suspicions about the book drop and drug deal. Guthrie said it was a drug deal, and I'm inclined to believe him, but another opinion couldn't hurt. Remember, Guthrie is the guy who played strip poker with Aunt Alice last night. His old habits may have scrambled a few neurons over the years."

"True," Ruthie said. "But there's no mistaking the fact that these guys, one of whom is Andy Marzano, broke into this condo." A terrified look crossed Ruthie's face, and she bolted to set my new alarm. "Heavens, until all of this is sorted out, we need to be extra careful." She drained her Irish cream. "You know, one thing I can't figure out is why a drug dealer, if that's what he is, would be interested in Abby's books. Do you think she hid drugs in her books or something?"

"That's it." Penny Sue reached across the counter and grabbed the bottle of Irish cream by its neck. "Abby was skinny. I'll bet those guys are dealing amphetamines. You know, there's been a big crackdown on prescriptions for diet pills. My doctor won't prescribe them for me because he says I'm not fat enough. The people I know back in Georgia who take them say the pills can only be prescribed for a short time, like a couple of months, because they are addictive." She munched on a handful of chips, thinking, and came up as Jessica Fletcher. "And," Penny Sue almost shouted, "Florida recently adopted a tracking system to catch people who doctor shop for painkillers and other controlled drugs." She hopped off her stool and started to pace. "So, let's say some ladies have taken diet pills, gotten addicted, and had their prescriptions cut off. Let's also suppose that a woman in that situation has a surfer son with access to drugs. Well, the surfer son offers to help his mother, and word gets out to her investment club. Case solved."

I nodded. "But what does that have to do with the books?"

Penny Sue sipped her drink. The wheels in her head were in high gear. "Abby was skinny. She probably bought the drugs from Susan."

"Abby was only here for two weeks," I objected. "How could she have gained Susan's trust in such a short time? Besides, judging from the cartons of books, she spent a lot of her time scouting old books in Deland. Heck, there's at least a dozen from The Muse Book Shop."

Penny Sue's eyes narrowed, and she ate another handful of chips. "I need to think about it," she allowed.

Ruthie snatched a chip. "I'm tired. We don't have to solve the case tonight, but I agree that we should call Woody first thing in the morning. If we helped him solve the burglaries, it would put us back on Woody's good list and might even help Kevin."

I smiled. I knew Kevin was foremost on her mind, but I didn't care. I was tired, too.

Chapter 16

I called Woody at eight o'clock, hoping to catch him before he left for work. As much as I hated to bother someone that early in the morning, I figured it would save us a lot of time because he lived in our complex, just a few clusters north. He hadn't left. Initially annoyed by my phone call, his tone changed dramatically when I told him I had pictures of the young men who'd burglarized my condo. Dressed in a brown suit, brown tie, white shirt, with black shoes and socks, Woody was on our doorstep fifteen minutes later.

I led him into the living room. Penny Sue was sitting at the counter reading the newspaper. Her eyes caught sight of his shoes as he strode by. Thankfully, he didn't notice her grimace at his mismatched outfit. Penny Sue was a real snob when it came to clothes, always carping at me if my shoes and purse didn't match. What difference does it make, if you're wearing sandals and you live at the beach? If Penny Sue were going to live down here, she'd have to loosen up. Matching outfits didn't make much difference in a place full of tourists who didn't know anyone, didn't care, or had simply forgotten to pack every item of an ensemble.

Woody took one look at the photo on top, with the clear view of Andy Marzano, and slouched onto the sofa with a loud grunt. He quickly paged through the rest of the photos, one showing the boys exiting my backdoor. Woody let out a loud breath. "This is not good. Antonio Marzano, Andy's father, is a local criminal attorney." Woody turned to me. "I'll need an affidavit from Carl Annina, and our crime technicians will have to verify his methodology. We may need to borrow your robot for a few days."

"I'd prefer you do it here," Penny Sue said. "We'll make it available to your staff, but little Lu Nee could easily be broken in transport. I'm sure Carl can arrange a time to meet your people."

"Fair enough," Woody replied. "Leigh, would you see when Carl is available, and I'll check with my staff?" He carefully put the pictures in his briefcase. "Ladies, for your own safety, please don't mention this to anyone. I'll be in touch."

I'd been careful not to mention that we'd staked out the library the night before and saw the brown-haired guy in the picture doing what appeared to be a drug deal. "We need to see what's up with that book drop," I said, as soon as Woody closed the door. "It's almost nine. Do you suppose Guthrie would check it out for us?"

Penny Sue reached for her cell phone. "Only one way to see." She hit speed dial and put her phone in speaker mode. Guthrie answered on the second ring. Penny Sue explained what she wanted.

"I've been wondering about that myself. I have a job in Edgewater and thought I'd stop by the library. I don't have any library books to return, but figured I could take an old telephone book in case anyone watches me. I'll call you when I get the scoop."

Penny Sue clicked off. "Now what?"

I reached across the counter and picked up the receiver for my home phone. "I need to call Terry. I'm not going to lie. I decided to tell the truth, that we needed to be here to meet with the police over the break-in. She'll probably be suspicious since I claimed I was sick yesterday, but so be it. I don't like telling lies." Terry's response was extremely chilly, and I had a bad feeling I'd jeopardized my job, since I was still in the probationary period when the library didn't need an excuse to fire a person.

Damn. I'd hoped to keep the job until Ruthie's shop was built. Oh, well, not much I could do about it. I poured another cup of coffee and fished Leonard Kydd's card from the recipe box I kept on the kitchen counter. "I'm going to text Leonard; he's probably at the library by now." I sent a text message asking him to call me at my home number. A few minutes later the telephone rang. It was Leonard. I explained the strange behavior we'd witnessed the night before and the fact that our neighbor, Guthrie, was going to stop by to check out the book drop.

"Does he drive an old yellow Volkswagen?"

"Yes."

"He's here now. I'll ring you back." Leonard hung up.

"That was short," Ruthie observed.

"Guthrie just arrived. Leonard's going to see if Guthrie discovers anything and call us back."

The phone rang two seconds later. I answered excitedly with, "What did you find? ... Oh, Ruthie, it's for you. It's Kevin."

Penny Sue and I moseyed to the living area to give the lovebirds a little space. They didn't talk long. "Alice told Kevin about the break-in, and he doesn't like the idea that the books may put us in danger. He's coming over to get them. We'll catalog them at Penny Sue's place."

Penny Sue and I exchanged a glance and a grin. Ten bucks said he was more worried about Ruthie being in danger than us. He showed up on the deck at our back door a few minutes later. The poor man looked awful. He clearly hadn't shaved and had dark circles under his eyes. A single night sleeping in his own bed was not enough to make up for his jailhouse ordeal.

He also had a thick bracelet on his wrist. Kevin held it up with a guilty smile. "I'm being monitored, so be careful around me. I hope this thing doesn't short out in the shower. I don't know how much latitude I have, so let's hurry. He hefted a box of books and crossed the deck back to his condo. I picked up a half-filled carton and followed. However, the rest of the boxes were too heavy for us to handle. When he finally lifted the last carton, he winked at Ruthie. "I'll call later. From now on you'll have to visit me. I'm confined next door."

Ruthie stood on her tiptoes and kissed him on the cheek. "No problem. Let me know if you need anything. I have some exciting news to tell you."

Kevin flashed a real smile for the first time. "Then I'll be sure to clean up fast, assuming I don't get electrocuted."

"No, those things are low volt—" Penny Sue started. I poked her with my elbow and she shut up. Honestly, sometimes that lady didn't know when to quit.

As Kevin crossed the deck, Ruthie's eyes brimmed with tears. "It's not fair," she said angrily. "How could anyone believe such a kind man would commit murder?"

"Don't worry," Penny Sue jumped in. "As soon as everyone digests the Medical Examiner's report, they'll know he's innocent. Abby was wearing a nicotine patch and smoked a couple of cigarettes in the bathroom. It's as clear as the nose on your face. Her death was an accident—an accident Abby caused herself. She got nervous during the debate and overcompensated, that's all there is to it." Penny Sue accentuated her statement with an air chop.

"I'm putting on another pot of coffee. I'm already exhausted. Anyone want some?" I asked.

"I'll have a cup with the rest of the Irish cream," Penny Sue said. "Might as well finish it off. I'm going to ABC Liquors to buy Baileys today."

We were sipping coffee and eating toast when the doorbell rang. "Now what?" I moaned.

"I'll get it." Penny Sue hopped down from her stool and pounded to the front door. "Guthrie," I heard her say. Then, "Gross, is that a big booger?!"

"No," came the unmistakable British accent of Leonard Kydd. "May we come in?"

"Only if that's not a booger on Guthrie's finger."

"I'm not familiar with the term, but we don't believe it's a substance of bodily origin."

By this time, curiosity had gotten the best of us, and Ruthie and I peered down the hall. Penny Sue was plastered against the wall as Guthrie paraded toward us with his right arm and index finger extended. There was a big brown glob on his finger. Leonard waited for Penny Sue, and we all crowded around Guthrie's finger.

"Ewww, what is that?" Ruthie asked.

"I think it's rubber cement. I found it on the upper part of the book drop." Guthrie rolled it between his fingers into a ball. "See, it will hold paper or something, but the item can be peeled off easily. Back in the day, I used it to hide my ... well, I used it to hide stuff."

"You see, there's a space between the top of the rounded drop door and its housing. I believe people are hiding items in that space," Leonard said.

"Which is why everyone was fumbling with the drop. They were actually sticking or peeling off money or drugs," Penny Sue said, in full Jessica Fletcher mode. She grinned at us. "Gee, that's smart. Who would think of that?"

Guthrie's brows knitted. "Man, that's not much smarter than alcoholics hiding their vodka in toilet tanks."

"Oh, Gawd." Penny Sue grimaced. "People drink it after it's been in the toilet?"

Guthrie rolled his eyes. "It's in the tank, the place where clean water is stored before the flush."

"That's still disgusting." Ruthie looked like she might lose her breakfast.

After we all got over the toilet trick, we headed to the living room. "We need to make this quick," I said. "The police could show up on another matter at any minute." Leonard's eyes shifted from side to side, and he looked as if he might bolt out the back door. "Sorry, I can't explain it all at the present time. So, where should we go from here? Should we tell Deputy Heather about our suspicions?"

"No," Leonard said firmly. "Give me a couple of days to see what I can dig up from the surfers. I'll stake out the drop tonight. We want to be careful and coordinate our efforts. In the meantime, Leigh, please keep your eye out for Susan and Andy Marzano. Make notes, if you can, on the times and dates of their comings and goings."

"And, I'll officially join the investment club," Penny Sue exclaimed. As usual, she didn't want to be upstaged. "I'll take Susan to lunch and try to find out about her diet potion and if I can buy some from her. I can be cagey when I need to be."

My eyes rolled to the ceiling. Leo! It was the Leo in her astrology chart, as Ruthie said. She just couldn't be outdone.

I was getting antsy about a possible call from Woody and wanted to keep the drugs and burglaries separate for now, even though they appeared to be linked. We hadn't discovered the connection yet, and frankly, I wanted to find it. I needed a tad of Leo in me. "Okay, it's settled. Leonard will take the shift tonight and we'll reconnoiter tomorrow morning, depending on his findings. I have to be at work at nine, so why don't you call tomorrow at seven. Is that too early?"

"No," Leonard said.

"Based on what you find, we'll plan our next move," I said to Leonard. "I'll watch for Susan and the other investment people tomorrow, so you don't have to come to the library if you'd rather sniff around the surfers."

"Very good," Leonard said. "That will speed our investigation considerably."

"Okay. Now let's scatter before the police arrive."

Guthrie and Leonard left through the back door. If the police happened to be in the parking lot, they would seem like men strolling up the public boardwalk from the beach. The ploy wasn't necessary; the two men made a clean get away. Except for Leonard's rental, there were no strange cars in the driveway.

"All of this commotion is giving me a headache." Penny Sue went to the kitchen's medicine shelf and helped herself to three ibuprofens. "We'd better call Carl," she said to me.

How come *we* usually meant *me*? I reached for the telephone and hit the speed dial button for his apartment in the basement of his mother's spacious home on the intracoastal waterway. The answering machine picked up, and I left a message asking when it would be convenient for Carl to meet with the police. "He checks his messages several times a day, so I'm sure he'll return the call soon."

At that moment the doorbell rang, followed by a couple of wall shaking bangs on the door. "What the—?" Penny Sue said as she stomped down the hall. Loud knocks always made her crazy. She flung the door open to reveal Aunt Alice flanked by two county deputies. Alice was dressed in her velour robe, and a brush had plainly not touched her hair. She was frantically waving a piece of paper. "This is a search warrant for your condo, Penny Sue," she screamed.

Penny Sue snatched the document and scanned it quickly, her lips pressed together so tightly they were white. "Good God," she exclaimed. "You want to confiscate all tobacco products, breath mints, strips, or any other item that can possibly contain nicotine." She shoved it at the older of the two officers, a stocky guy with a buzz cut. "This warrant is incorrect. You may not enter the premises. I don't own the condominium next door; it belongs to my father, Judge Warren Parker. Did you hear me? That's *Judge* Parker."

The other officer, younger and in much better shape, read from another document. "We also have a warrant to search the premises owned by Rebecca Leigh Stratton. Is Ms. Stratton here?"

I maneuvered around Alice, who had hidden behind Penny Sue, and grabbed the warrant. "You want my breath mints and tobacco products, too? This is insane. Is Woody Woodhead aware of this? He was here this morning. We're cooperating with your department on an important investigation."

The young officer shrugged. "Ma'am, we don't know what this is about. We're only following orders."

"Come in. You may sit on the sofa, but before you start searching, I want to make a phone call," I said.

Buzz interrupted. "We must secure both premises to ensure that evidence is not destroyed. My partner Frank will remain here while I go next door until the ownership issue is resolved."

"Well, I'm going with you." Penny Sue wagged her finger in his face. "Stay right there. I'm only going for my cell phone."

The telephone lines were burning bright that morning. Penny Sue was calling the Judge, Buzz was calling the office to correct the ownership mistake, and I called Woody. He swore he knew nothing about the warrants, but would see what he could find out. Woody called back a few minutes later.

"The warrants were issued at the request of the Medical Examiner, which is pretty unusual. However, they're legitimate, so you must not interfere with the search. Penny Sue's warrant will have to be amended, but I understand it's being done now and will be delivered shortly. Let the officers do their job and don't make any trouble. I'll be in touch with you on the other matter later this afternoon."

I turned to the young deputy. "Have at it, Frank. But, Ruthie and I are going to watch you."

Frank nodded. "No problem, as long as you don't get in my way."

"Ruthie, I'm going next door to tell Penny Sue what Woody said. I'll only be a minute."

Deputy Heather Brooks and I arrived at Penny Sue's front door simultaneously. She gave me a "sorry" shrug and frowned at the new warrant she was holding. "Hey, I'm the delivery person and don't know anything about this. By the way, I spoke with

Woody earlier, and he said you had pictures of the young men who broke into your condo. That's a huge breakthrough for all of the beach burglaries." She waved the warrant. "For that reason alone, Woody will try to help you out on whatever this is."

Unfortunately, as screwy as it probably seemed to Heather, I knew what it was about. Abby died of nicotine poisoning and they were trying to pin it on Kevin. "We realize you're only doing your job, but steer clear of Penny Sue and Aunt Alice. Penny Sue's wound up tighter than a tick and Alice is in pit bull mode."

"I'm going to hand this over and get away as fast as I can."

"Smart lady," I said.

Judge Parker informed Penny Sue that she could not deny access to the premises as soon as the document was corrected, so she gave Heather a sour glance when she passed the paper to Buzz, who Heather addressed as Miller. Duty done, Heather haul assed out of the condo and Miller wasted no time. He opened a large plastic bag filled with smaller bags and wrote the date and time on the large bag with a Sharpie permanent pen. Alice, Penny Sue, and Kevin peered over Miller's shoulder.

The big man stood. "I don't mind if you follow me around; just give me space. I don't know what this is about. I'm only doing my duty. The faster I search the condo, the faster we'll all get back to normal."

The search at both condos took over three hours and involved an examination of the contents of our purses, where Frank found several containers of Tic Tacs, some peppermint breath strips, and two tampons. His face turned red at the tampons and he graciously left them alone, since the paper seals had not been broken. Then there was an examination of all of the drawers and closets. Penny Sue's underwear drawer was probably the most embarrassing; thankfully, she was next door and didn't witness Frank handling her lacy thongs. However, he did find a pack of cigarettes in Penny Sue's purse, which he confiscated. All in all,

Frank found very little, so he went next door to help Buzz Cut Miller. We locked up the condo, set the alarm, and tagged along.

Penny Sue met us at the door and whispered, "Miller found a dildo in Alice's underwear drawer. It was a big one! Maybe she wasn't kidding around with Guthrie over the strip poker."

"Don't tell Guthrie!" I said. "He'd be so freaked out he'll never come down here again. Has the cop found anything else?"

"He found several packs of breath mint strips in Kevin's room and an old pack of my cigarettes in the master suite. I think he's almost finished once he goes through the boxes of books. He saved them until last."

We sauntered into the living room where Alice stood like a sentry. Buzz was going through the freezer as Frank started unloading the books.

"Please be careful," Kevin said to Frank. "Some of those books are very old and are one-of-a-kind. Would you like me to help you?"

"Not necessary," Frank responded. "That could be construed as contaminating evidence."

"Oh," Kevin said. "I was just thinking about handling the fragile books. Anyway, some of those books—particularly the boxes on top that are still sealed—were shipped down from Abby's apartment in New Jersey. I haven't even touched them."

"Miller," Frank called suddenly, as he lifted a small brown container from the bottom of a box. Frank dropped it in a clear plastic bag and showed it to his partner.

Miller checked his watch. "Mark it, two-thirty-three."

Frank wrote on the envelope and deposited the find in the large plastic bag.

"What is it? A pack of breath strips?" Alice asked.

"Can't say," Miller responded in an all-business tone.

Whatever it was, the find focused both men on the boxes. It was as if the deputies suddenly become jet-propelled.

"Hey," Kevin objected, "be careful. Those are valuable books!"

The admonishment slowed them down but didn't stop the frenzied search. They finally examined the last box, which had been sealed, and found nothing."

As Miller was about to toss the books haphazardly into the empty carton, Kevin stepped forward. "I'll do that if you don't mind." Miller shrugged and stepped aside.

"Well, I think we have all we need," Frank said with a forced smile. "Thank you for your cooperation."

"Wait, what did you find?" Alice demanded.

"Sorry ma'am, we're not at liberty to say."

Kevin stepped forward. "The box you found that container in came from the library. Ruthie and I started cataloguing the books but never got to that one."

"We really can't discuss it," Frank said. "Thanks again for your cooperation." And they left with their big plastic bags.

"What did they find?" Alice asked. We shook our heads. None of us had a clue.

Chapter 17

Woody swung by my condo on his way home from work. For once, he seemed like a friend stopping by instead of the enemy. He ditched his briefcase on the floor and took a stool at the counter. He glanced around, obviously looking for Ruthie. "She's next door with Kevin," I said, anticipating his question.

Penny Sue held up her glass of scotch—it had been a hard day. Woody closed his eyes, shook his head, but said, "light, on the rocks. No fruit." Penny Sue's version of light and everyone else's were two different things. To her, light means three fingers of liquor. Woody took a sip and his eyes bulged. "Boy, when I said light, I didn't mean light my fire! I'd better wait a few minutes for the ice to melt." For the first time since his apology for his demented mother's shenanigans, Woody acted like a real person and not a persecutor, as Penny Sue typically called him. "It's been one heck of a day," Woody said. "We identified the guy with the brown hair and pigtail. His name's Stuart Cobb, and he's a student at Deland University. He has a record of breaking and entering. Petty stuff. He never did any time, and most of it happened when he was a juvenile. But we have his prints from an adult arrest and are waiting to see if they match the handprint on your door from the first attempted robbery.

"Andy Marzano is another matter. He's been implicated in petty crimes over the years, but as you can imagine, his father always got him off. All of the crimes were juvenile and the records are sealed, so it will take some doing to get a fingerprint. If we petition his records, we'll have one hell of a fight on our hands from his father, Antonio. Rumor has it Antonio is thinking of running for the State House of Representatives in the next election." Woody took a small sip of his scotch. "I'm sure you understand that I don't want to get mixed up with Marzano unless we have a foolproof case. It would be one big can of worms, and he has lots of connections.

"Have you heard from Carl yet?" Woody continued. "My crime techs will schedule around him. It seems Carl's something of a legend, and everyone begged to be assigned to the case. I think a few of the women only want to meet him. Anyway, the sooner we can verify his methodology and findings, the better. That provides the ammunition to seek Andy's juvie records. I don't doubt Carl's pictures, and neither do any of the crime techs since he's such an icon, but we have to have an independent evaluation."

I was surprised I hadn't heard from Carl, but he could have called while we were next door. I picked up the phone and heard the beep-beep-beep that indicated I had a voicemail. "There's a message. I'll bet it's him." I punched *98 and the message started to play. It was Carl, and I frowned.

"What, what?" Penny Sue asked.

"He has to leave first thing in the morning for an aerospace project in Seattle. The only time he can meet with Woody's staff is tonight."

Woody unpocketed his cell phone and hit a button. "See if Carl can come over now."

While Woody spoke with the crime tech department, I talked to Carl. I could tell by his voice that he was having dinner. "I'm eating some of Mom's lasagna, but could be there in about forty-five minutes. Is that okay? The procedure was straightforward; it won't take long."

"Hold on. Forty-five minutes?" I mouthed to Woody. He nodded. "That's good. Whenever you can make it will be fine."

Carl was clearly a techno rock star. Within a half hour, six techs, four of whom were female, arrived. Woody called home and told his wife that he was going to be late. To ensure the findings, Woody figured it would be best if he waited and recorded Carl's demonstration. A few minutes later, Carl arrived dressed in his Klingon garb, barbed toe boots and all, but thankfully without his Klingon forehead prosthesis. What a relief. A video of that definitely wouldn't go over well in court.

The Klingon outfit didn't faze the group. Apparently they were all Trekkies, and his garb only made the women swoon. What was wrong with my daughter, Ann? She hated the Klingon shtick that other women thought was a turn on. Different strokes for different folks, I guess. Maybe when Carl came up with new games she'd give him another chance. Honestly, I couldn't imagine a better son-in-law.

We went into the utility room, where I plugged in Lu Nee 2. While the unit powered up, take-charge Penny Sue gave her rendition of the robot's capabilities and all the times it had saved our lives. Now it was going to solve a major crime spree, she exuded. Carl waited patiently until she finished before he switched on the robot, connected his computer, and started explaining the robot's recording function and how he'd retrieved the pictures and recording. At the end of his demonstration, he ejected the CD from his computer and handed it to Woody. "Your tech staff will find the exact pictures on this disc. Is there anything else I can do for you?" He glanced down at his outfit. "As you might have guessed, I have a party to go to. A birthday party. Any questions?"

The female techs gaped at him as if God Himself had descended from the Heavens. The men, also impressed, merely shook their heads.

Carl packed up his computer. "Sorry to run, but I'm on a tight schedule. Leigh knows how to reach me if you have any questions."

Woody offered his hand with a big thank you. "Since I recorded your demonstration, I believe we have all of the bases covered."

"Leigh," Carl turned to me. "Keep Lu Nee 2 off and unplugged in case the actual unit is needed for court." He swung around to the adoring women. "I've been through a few similar cases."

Carl shouldered his computer and headed out the door. The women stood transfixed for a good minute. After all, they'd just encountered a Klingon Adonis.

Ruthie came home at nine o'clock, and we took our usual seats at the counter to discuss the day. Penny Sue and I had already eaten Stouffers Chicken Lasagna and salad from a bag. Ruthie had picked up take-out dinners from the local seafood restaurant for Alice, Kevin, and herself.

"How's Kevin holding up?" I asked.

"He's fine as long as he's doing something, like cataloguing the books, but he was really traumatized by the jailhouse experience. The search warrant didn't help matters because now he knows he's a real suspect. The thing that worries me is that this mess may ruin his chances for the chairmanship of Deland's History Department. Kevin's afraid they'll eliminate him simply because of the bad publicity."

"Umm," Penny Sue groaned. "That throws a wrench in your bookstore plans and my job, doesn't it?"

Ruthie turned on Penny Sue with her eyes flashing. "For godssakes, Penny Sue, can't you think of anyone but yourself? Kevin's freedom and whole future are at stake!"

"Sorry, I was merely thinking ahead. For goodness sake, I care about Kevin. He's my only cousin!"

A fight was brewing. I patted the air, hoping to calm the waters. "Hold it. We need to stick together to help Kevin. We're stressed to the hilt and need to take a deep, calming breath. We can't help Kevin—"

"—or get rid of Alice," Penny Sue interrupted.

I cut my eyes at her angrily. "Let's not go there and muddy the waters. We have to stay focused." I stared at her scotch. "A little decaf might help your focus."

Penny Sue's bottom lip inched forward. "You don't have to be snippy about it. I was about to fix myself a cup of coffee." Penny Sue stomped to the kitchen, poured a mug of black coffee, and put it beside her scotch.

"I apologize if I'm irritable," I said, "I'm exhausted and want to go to bed. Let's not get sidetracked. The focus is Kevin and why he's suspected of killing Abby."

"Don't forget the break-ins and Duffy," Penny Sue said, blowing on her coffee.

Honestly, I felt like giving her arm a good poke, but didn't. That would really start a catfight, a term I detest, but it was the most accurate description for the current situation, especially considering the length of Penny Sue's fingernails. "Let's do one thing at a time and concentrate on Kevin for now. If we solve that, I believe the other pieces of the puzzle will fall into place." I took a deep breath.

"Okay. One thing I keep wondering is why the police think Kevin's responsible for poisoning Abby with nicotine," Penny Sue led off. "The lady smoked some cigarettes in the children's bathroom to calm her nerves—end of story."

I studied my French vanilla decaf. "I've been thinking about that, too. The bathrooms in the library have smoke alarms. Abby couldn't have poisoned herself with cigarettes; the alarm would have gone off."

"Could she have disabled it?" Ruthie asked.

"I suppose it's possible, but why go to all that trouble? We were going to leave the building in a matter of minutes," I replied.

"Nicotine gum," Penny Sue stated emphatically. "You know, they even have nicotine pills nowadays."

"Yes, but the police would have found the package in her purse," I countered, "in which case Kevin wouldn't be under suspicion."

"Maybe she threw the package away and the cleaning crew dumped the trash," Ruthie suggested.

"No. Remember, Terry said she'd given the crew the night off."

"I know!" Penny Sue almost shouted as she headed for the kitchen. "Chocolate. We need chocolate to help us think." She pulled a bag of York Peppermint Patties from a cabinet, ripped open the cellophane and dumped its contents on the counter. We all took one. "Now," she continued, sucking down a good portion of the mint, "did either of you see what Frank found in the box of books? Whatever it was, it virtually ended the search. I got the feeling they'd found the smoking gun."

Ruthie nodded. "I had the same impression. It was a small plastic container, you know, the type breath strips come in. But, it wasn't green, it was brown."

"Whatever it was, it had to be related to nicotine. Either something that contained nicotine or enhanced its effect," I said.

Ruthie was already jogging to the bedroom for her laptop computer. It was booting up as she trotted back to the counter. A moment later she was on the Internet doing a search on nicotine. I leaned over to view the screen, while Penny Sue peered across Ruthie's shoulder sucking peppermint patties. The search on nicotine didn't yield anything. Next she tried *smoking cessation.* Bingo! A row of tiny pictures of products popped up. Apparently, stop-smoking aids had progressed considerably. There was everything from patches to gum to mints to *nicotine strips!* And, one brand of nicotine strip was in a brown container.

"That's it!" Ruthie nearly jumped out of her seat. "I'm not one hundred percent sure, but that one," she pointed at the computer screen, "looks like the container Officer Frank found that got them so worked up."

"Do you recall which box it came from?" I asked.

"It was one that had never been sealed, which meant it came from the library, or Alice and I brought it from Abby's condo. The ones her mother shipped were taped shut and had to be slit open."

I arched my brow and grinned mischievously. "It sure is taking y'all a long time to make a list of those books."

Ruthie's pale face flamed with embarrassment. "We're being careful to label each book's origin and compile an inventory of each box. Besides, Kevin keeps getting distracted and starts reading the books."

"I can see Kevin doing that," I said, deciding to let her off of the hook.

Penny Sue sipped her coffee and morphed into Jessica Fletcher. "Kevin thought the book came from the library, but it's possible it was one of Abby's."

"We were careful, but I guess it's possible," Ruthie admitted.

"So Abby, herself, could have dropped the container in the box." Ruthie and I nodded. Penny Sue exchanged the coffee mug for her scotch and started to pace. "As bad as it may look, I think this will clear Kevin." She took a sip of her drink. "Suppose Abby initially used the strips to stop smoking, but they didn't work, so she switched to the patch?" Penny Sue stopped dramatically and twirled around, sloshing scotch on the floor. "For whatever reason, Abby agreed to debate Kevin, maybe to give him a final, old lover's dig. Yet, the more she thought about it, the more nervous she became, so Abby had a couple of strips of the nicotine, in addition to the patch, before she left her condo for the debate. That could explain how she overdosed and there was no container in her purse. She dropped the empty container in the box. Hell, maybe those were books she planned to throw away."

"True, but there was a good while between the time Abby left her condo and when the debate started. It seems it would have hit her sooner," I said.

Ruthie jumped in. "Remember the argument she had with Willows in the library, before the debate? Maybe she was irritable because of the drugs. She was hyped up, on edge."

"Yes. She was sweating like a pig during the debate," Penny Sue added.

"So we think Abby accidentally overdosed?" I asked

Penny Sue nodded. Ruthie stared into space. "Maybe the container was planted in the box from the library," Ruthie mused.

"Are you getting a psychic hit or something?" Penny Sue asked. "If so, it would be hard to fathom. The area was roped off and under guard at all times. The chances of someone getting to the box while it was in the library are pretty slim."

Ruthie stroked her arm, thinking. "You know how they always talk about the chain of custody on *CSI*? Well, what was the chain of custody for that box?"

"It was in the library with tight security, then Woody took it and gave it to me," Penny Sue said. "You don't think Woody planted the container to get back at me, do you?"

Ruthie shook her head vigorously. "No, Woody wouldn't frame Kevin. What about Peter O'Brien? He carried the box for you, didn't he?"

Penny Sue's eyes narrowed. "He did, but what motive would Peter have to frame Kevin for Abby's death?"

Ruthie jumped in. "He's Willows' old friend, and he's trying to buy part of the Canaveral Park for a big real estate development."

"I can see that the real estate deal might be a motive for wanting to kill Abby, since she was so hot on St. Augustine, but what does he have against Kevin? Besides, how do you know he's Willows' old friend?" Penny Sue asked.

"Willows told us when he and Abby entered the library for the debate. O'Brien was with them," I said. "With Abby's unfortunate death, Kevin is one of the few historians with knowledge of Central Florida that rivals Willows'. Maybe O'Brien wanted to help his friend get the chairmanship to lend prestige to their Canaveral development deal. Or better yet, O'Brien wanted to incriminate, thus eliminate, Kevin, the one person with credentials that rivaled Willows."

"That's a stretch," Penny Sue scoffed. "In fact, the whole buying up part of the park sounds fishy to me."

Ruthie shook her head. "It's not as far-fetched as you might think. Wyoming is looking to sell part of the Grand Teton Park to fund their education budget."

"You're joking," I said.

"No, it was on the news the other day. It could be the beginning of a trend with state budgets in such bad shape."

"Hmm, maybe I should think of investing in Peter's deal," Penny Sue said.

"No!" Ruthie and I shouted in unison. "Put your money in a CD or a good solid mutual fund. Stay away from risky real estate ventures."

"Kidding!" Penny Sue assured us. "I've truly learned my lesson with Madoff. Besides, I don't think Peter will pull it off, and we certainly shouldn't mention it to Guthrie. He's upset enough about the shuttle program being canceled. He'd go berserk if he thought the whole Kennedy Space Center is going to be closed and Timothy will never come back from Houston."

"Yes, let's banish that thought for good. It's an extreme long shot, and if we keep talking about it, we might let something slip out in front of Guthrie," I agreed. "So, where does that leave us? Did anyone else have access to the box?"

"Willows looked in it when he stopped by supposedly to visit Kevin. I turned my back for a mere second, and he was already pawing through the books," Ruthie said. "He had enough time to drop something in there."

"Wait a minute," I held up my hands. "Did you ever think that Marzano and his buddy might have intended to leave something instead of take? Maybe they put in the container in the box."

Penny Sue took a long drink of her now watered-down scotch. "Damn, Leigh. I'm getting a headache. There are too many possibilities." She glanced at the clock. "It's almost midnight and I'm tired. Why don't we think about this tomorrow?"

No one argued.

The next four days were blissfully uneventful. Ruthie spent most of her time with Kevin, since he was confined to Penny Sue's condo. They were supposedly going through Abby's computer and cataloguing books. Wink, wink. There was no way there were that many books, but they did find interesting information on Abby's computer. They discovered several letters about the Deland U. chairmanship, and a couple of emails to Willows saying she was coming down for a visit and hoped they could meet for dinner. There was also an encrypted folder marked SWD. It would have to wait for Carl's return from the West Coast. None of us had any idea how to crack the code.

Alice played cards at Guthrie's place several times and even tagged along on a couple of his repair calls. I believe Alice's absences for repair calls and card games explained why it was taking Kevin and Ruthie so long to inventory the books. Of course, Kevin was also helping Ruthie with the plans for her new bookstore and apartment.

Penny Sue was hot on the trail of a new wardrobe, as well as Susan Marzano, which conveniently fit together. Susan did all of her shopping at The Mall at Millenia in Orlando, which housed upscale shops like Neiman Marcus, Chanel, Louis Vuitton, and Cartier, so Penny Sue was able to talk Susan into a couple of shopping sprees. Along the way Penny Sue bemoaned the fact that she had put on weight, and she pumped Susan for tips. Whenever Penny Sue asked Susan for her weight loss remedy,

Susan changed the subject, apparently not trusting Penny Sue enough to reveal her secret.

When Penny Sue wasn't shopping, she was focused on Peter O'Brien, who came down from St. Augustine for the library's Wii bowling tournament. Of course, Penny Sue made a point of being there to cheer him on. The local champ was in the game, and the tournament came down to a roll off between the two men. It was close, but Peter was ultimately victorious, which provided the perfect excuse for Penny Sue to take him out for a celebration. Their little party was a big success, evidenced by Penny Sue's smudged lipstick and the news that Peter was driving down to take her to dinner the following night. Penny Sue had obviously ruled him out as a suspect.

I worked at the library, doing my best to go the extra mile since Terry was noticeably cool after my day and a half absence, though she thawed slightly each day. I also volunteered for the checkout desk at every opportunity, to keep an eye out for Susan and Andy Marzano. On one occasion, Susan met a member of the investment club in the library, and they chatted briefly on a deserted aisle.

Leonard Kydd staked out the library that same night and saw a repeat of the merry-go-round of cars and book drops. He also trolled surfers by day and found out that Andy Marzano's nickname was Speedo. Although the moniker might refer to a bathing suit, Leonard believed it meant that Andy either used or supplied speed. Once he overheard a surfer say, "Speedo had dexies."

The day after Leonard witnessed the library drug deal, he called and asked to speak with us. I invited him over to my place. "I think it's time to report this to the authorities," he said. "My magazine won't allow me to stay much longer, and I won't rest until the people responsible for Duffy's death are arrested. I owe the man that much."

The weather was pleasantly warm and Penny Sue, Leonard and I were sitting on my deck sipping sweet tea. He stared out over the water for a few minutes. "The police haven't released Duffy's autopsy report, but it's clear the rattlesnake was the cause, one way or another. I feel certain Marzano and his drug buddies got wise to Duffy and put the snake down the book chute. Poor Duffy may have asked too many questions."

"We'll need irrefutable evidence," I said. "The Marzano family is very prominent in New Smyrna Beach. I know the prosecutor won't touch it without solid proof." I stared at three small children chasing birds on the beach and considered whether I should tell Leonard that Cobb and Marzano were linked to the attempted robberies at my condo, and the police were checking fingerprints. I hadn't told him before, because I was certain the burglaries were linked to Abby's death, and I didn't want to confuse the issue or get Kevin involved. Perhaps it was time to tell Leonard the whole story, which I did.

When I finished, Leonard drained his tea and motioned to the pitcher on my circular deck table. I told him to help himself. He took a long drink before he spoke. "I heard about the burglaries and suspected they were related to the death of the lady scholar. I figured you'd tell me in due time."

Unusually quiet until now, Penny Sue said, "There's only one thing to do. We need to set up a sting!"

"Pardon?" Leonard said.

"A sting. You know, arrange a drug drop so the cops can catch them red-handed. That's the only way Woody would go after Andy Marzano and his mother."

"How do you propose to do that?" I asked.

Penny Sue reared back. "While Susan and I were shopping, I mentioned Rich and how desperate I was to lose weight before his return."

"Who's Rich?" Leonard asked.

"An old boyfriend," I replied, before Penny Sue could confuse Leonard with the details of Bike Week and the police protection program. "Have you really heard from Rich?" I asked Penny Sue.

"No," she said with a hint of sadness. "I told Susan that as an excuse. I can read people fairly well, and I believe she's on the verge of divulging her diet secret."

"You mean the dexies," Leonard said.

"Yes. I'll call her right now and see if I can buy some of her secret potion. I'll tell her Rich is due in a week and I'll pay anything to lose ten pounds. If she agrees, we'll call Woody and arrange for a police sting."

"That could be risky if she suspects a trap," Leonard cautioned.

"I'll be okay if Leigh brings the liquid taser, and the police have the place staked out."

"Liquid taser?"

"Don't ask," I replied. "It's a long story." I turned to Penny Sue. "Are you sure?"

She picked up her BlackBerry and stood. "Nothing ventured, nothing gained."

Leonard and I made awkward small talk as we watched Penny Sue pace and talk in the great room. Children scampered up the boardwalk, chasing a cat. A fisherman rambled by, pulling a wagon laden with a chair, pole and other gear. The minutes dragged on, and still Penny Sue talked. Leonard and I both poured another glass of tea. Finally, Penny Sue turned our way and gave us the thumbs up. She made a few more quick comments before she hung up and joined us.

"Tonight at eleven o'clock. Five hundred dollars for twenty pills. It's the real stuff, not something cooked up in a garage," Penny Sue said. "I'm to come alone with the $100 bills in a zip lock bag. She said I should buy rubber cement at the drug store and spread a thick layer on one side of the bag. When I open the door for the book drop, there's a flat space above the curved door where I should stick the money. I need to return a library book at the same time. Then I'm to drive around for a half hour and park on a side street. A green Volvo will deposit a book and a few minutes after it leaves, I'll find the pills in the same place I put the money." She took a long drink of her tea. "It was a tough sell. Susan only agreed when I told her I wanted to wear Rich's favorite dress, a Versace, and I couldn't zip it up."

"Well done," Leonard said. "You proved our suspicions were correct." He turned to me. "Will you call the authorities, or should I?"

"I'll call. We're already working with the prosecutor on the break-ins."

Wonder of wonders, I reached Woody on my first try and gave him a quick outline of our plan. There was a long pause before Woody said he'd prefer to discuss it in person and would be right over. About a half hour later, Woody and a very muscular man dressed in black arrived at our front door. Woody introduced his partner as David Yates of the Drug Task Force. Penny Sue's eyes lit up at the sight of David. Good grief! A few minutes later, Ruthie wandered in from next door.

I ushered them into the living room, served sweet tea, and we hatched a plan. David and his men would stake out the area with sound equipment and cameras situated around the nearby gymnasium. If Penny Sue felt she was in danger at any time, she was to flash her headlights. They were going to focus on Stuart Cobb and Andy Marzano, not Susan, since the boys were suspects in two crimes. They would set up their equipment and be in place by ten o'clock, in case the druggies were casing the scene. David thought that was plenty of time, since this seemed to be a penny ante deal that he hoped would lead them to bigger fish and the source of the drugs and beach burglaries.

David, a taller version of Guthrie's hunky Timothy, put his arm around Penny Sue's waist and asked if she was up to the task. If not, they could have a female detective make the drop.

She gave David the big grin that showed her gums. "Thanks so much for your concern," she replied with honey dripping out of her mouth, "but I'll be fine. I've taken a number of self-defense courses. My father's a judge, you know."

David backed away after a stern look from Woody. "Don't worry, Penny Sue, I'll be there, too," Woody said. "With the Marzanos involved, I don't want anything to go wrong. Let's synchronize our watches," he said, which came out like a line from *Dick Tracy.* In any event, we did as told. "Call me if you have any problem."

"Don't worry, Woody, I've handled tougher stuff than this," Penny Sue said.

"Yes, I know you have."

We saw them to the door and once it was closed, Ruthie turned on us with a panicked look. "What in Heaven's name are you doing?"

Kydd spoke up. "I witnessed another drug drop at the library—" he started.

"And we're sure the druggies are linked to Abby's death," I added. "So, if we nab them, we can clear Kevin." Ruthie was mollified by that response.

"Just one more thing," Penny Sue said, leading us into the great room. "Leigh, I want you there in the enclosure by the library with the taser. It's charged, isn't it?

"Yes, and I received additional saline," Ruthie shot back.

Penny Sue turned to Leonard. "I think you should go with Leigh and take your car. Everyone knows she drives a yellow VW Beetle." Leonard had obviously become acquainted with her take-charge persona, so he agreed without hesitation. "If the cops are going to be set up by ten, you need to be in the enclosure next to the book drop by nine-thirty," Penny Sue continued. "You should park at the movie theater; it won't draw attention so late at night. I have to drive my car. Otherwise I'll look suspicious."

We nodded. Penny Sue was on a roll.

"I'll dress normally. I think y'all should wear dark clothes."

We nodded again.

Penny Sue glanced at Ruthie. "Your job is to keep Alice and Kevin in check. They don't need to know anything about this."

"Understood," Ruthie agreed. "Maybe I'll invite Guthrie down as a diversion."

"Good idea. It keeps him out of the way, too." Penny Sue turned to Leonard. "If you and Leigh are going to be in place by nine-thirty, you should here no later than nine." He winked. Finally finished with her instructions, Penny Sue held up her hand, and we did another one of our high-fives that Leonard definitely didn't understand.

Leonard and I followed our directions to the letter. We parked at the theater and walked the few blocks to the library. I carried the taser in a gym bag. We were sitting at the table by the library at nine-thirty, as Penny Sue instructed. We peeked through the spaces between the slats in the fence and saw motion over by the gym. David and Woody were getting in place. Since we had an hour plus to wait, Leonard brought a deck of cards, and we played gin rummy by the dim glow of a streetlight. I'd never have thought of that, but he'd obviously done a lot of waiting in his line of work and knew how to pass the time. He was a good player; I wasn't. Thank goodness we were playing for pennies, or I would have gone broke. We were in the middle of a hand where I had good cards for a change, when Leonard whispered, "Here she comes."

I grabbed the taser, he grabbed his night lens camera, and we both peeked through the fence. If anyone went after Penny Sue, I was going to fire, and he was going to get a picture. It went like clockwork. Penny Sue got out of the car with a book, went to the drop, pretended she had a hard time getting the book into the slot (I think it was my phonebook!), and left. Just as before, another car, this time a Caddy, pulled in shortly afterward. At first I feared it was Alice, but soon realized it was Susan. She must have switched cars with her husband. Susan went to the book drop, fiddled around, probably stripping off the money, and left. In about the time it took her to drive several blocks and call her son, the green Volvo sped in. The pigtail guy got out with a book, exactly as he'd done before, and was returning to the car, when a helicopter appeared with a spotlight. Floodlights flashed on from the gym. A hoard of men in dark outfits headed their way.

Before pigtailed Cobb could get into the car, I put the tip of the taser in a gap between the fence and the building, and fired off a round that downed him. With Cobb half in and half out of the car, Marzano hesitated long enough for the police to shoot out his tires. No tires, a helicopter overhead, and a spastically twitching friend were enough to bring Andy Marzano out of the car with his hands up.

As this went down, Leonard ran out of the enclosure to snap photos and noticed Susan's Cadillac parked on a side street. Bless his heart, he took a half dozen pictures of the car that included its license plate. Yep, 'ol Leonard knew his business.

A moment before the Drug Task Force arrived, Leonard and I dashed into the darkness, hoping to stay out of the fray. However, I'm sure Woody recognized the taser's effect on Cobb and knew we'd been there. Leonard and I jogged back to the theater, where Penny Sue's Jag was parked next to his car.

"Did they get them?" Penny Sue asked.

"Yep, the cops got them, and Leonard has pictures of Susan Marzano."

"That's fabulous. But, damn, I never got any pills," Penny Sue moaned.

"You don't need pills! You're perfect the way you are. How about we go home and have a drink?" I asked.

Penny Sue grinned. "No argument from me."

Chapter 18

Yes, it was a good four days, which was Alice's limit. We were sitting in Penny Sue's living room, having early afternoon cocktails and congratulating ourselves over the sting, when Alice exploded. "Why is Kevin still under suspicion and wearing that stupid bracelet?" she screeched. "What's wrong with those dimwits? Why do they want to frame Kevin? He had no motive for killing Abby, and we know she died of nicotine poisoning. Why hasn't the autopsy report been released? I called Myrna Johnston today, and she said the people down here told her they hadn't ruled on the cause of death. It's time to light a fire under these local hicks!" Alice reached in her pocket and pulled out her cell phone. Kevin lurched and snatched it out of her hand.

Brave man. I wouldn't have done it! I believe a move like that could lead to a bullet between the eyes. Penny Sue wasn't kidding: Alice had a mean streak a mile wide.

"Mom," Kevin said, holding the phone behind his back. "Let's talk about this first. There's no sense calling in the heavy artillery until it's the last resort."

Alice stared at him with her hands on her hips. "Okay, son, I'll try it your way. Talk."

"I'm a candidate for the chairmanship of the History Department of Deland University, one of the most prestigious private institutions in the South. This is the chance of a lifetime and I don't want to blow it, if it's still a possibility after this mess. I fear that your friends could ruin my chances while they're trying to help."

Alice tilted her head back and looked down her nose at all of us. "All right. I want to know everything you know. Don't leave out a single detail. I have years of experience dealing with complicated situations. You think managing a sewer department is easy? You can't imagine how complicated *waste* disposal is in New Jersey, especially with all of the rival factions. I'm still alive, so I must be good." She gave us a searing glare and handed her empty glass to Penny Sue, who got her a refill. Alice was sitting in the wicker throne chair, and the rest of us sat across from her like grinning fools. No one wanted to admit we'd withheld information from Alice. She was already angry that we'd kept her out of the loop about the drug sting.

I was the first to find my voice. "Why don't you tell us what you already know," I said to Alice, "and we'll pick up from there."

"Abby died of nicotine poisoning and the cops think Kevin was responsible. I surmise the little container they found in the box was for nicotine and they're probably checking it for fingerprints now. I'd bet money the container's been wiped clean, if the perps are pros. I know my son is innocent, so who would want to frame him? I believe we need to concentrate on a motive first, and the suspects second."

Damn, the old girl was sharp. We'd been following suspects and hadn't focused on the big question: why?

"Why would someone want to kill Abby?" Alice asked.

"Revenge," Penny Sue blurted, and then realized what she'd said. "Of course, I didn't mean Kevin. Their affair was over years ago."

"Money," I said. "It's truly the root of all evil and the motive for most crimes."

"Add to that power and prestige," Ruthie said. "Money, power, and prestige are all tied up in the chairmanship, and we know from her emails that Abby had dinner with Willows while

she was here. Maybe they thought Kevin was the strongest candidate, so they wanted to discredit him."

"Discredit him in the debate, discredit him with Abby's death,
or both?" I asked with a smirk. "There's only one person I can
think of who would really gain from her murder—Willows! He
eliminates all of his competition and kills two birds with one stone."

"You're right," Penny Sue said. "Someone has been feeding
information to Woody. Remember when Woody came over for
the first interview with Kevin? He already knew Kevin and Abby
had been engaged. How did he know? Who told him that? Their
old college friend, Willows."

"And, did you notice the look on Officer Miller's face when
they found the brown container?" Ruthie added. "He looked as
if it was exactly what he was after. Miller didn't even examine it
closely."

Kevin's face lit up like a light bulb. "The liquor! Abby took
a swig of Jack Black, and I gave her some of my breath strips.
Willows was there. I'll bet he insinuated that I gave her nicotine
strips. That's why they believe I killed her!"

"You're right," Ruthie said. "But I know they were breath
strips, because you gave me one earlier."

Alice wiped her lips and raised her empty glass. Penny Sue
gave her aunt a hateful look, but took the glass and refilled it.
Alice nodded a thank you, took a swallow, and thought for a
moment. "My gut says you're right about Willows. Now, why
would he want to kill Abby?"

"To eliminate her as a candidate for the chairmanship and to
frame Kevin. Money, power, and prestige," Ruthie said.

Alice leaned back in the throne and laced her fingers around
her glass. The muscles in her jaw were twitching. "Not enough.
If this were Atlantic City, I'd say it was a possibility." She shook
her head so hard her curly, gray hair blossomed out like a poodle's.
I stifled a grin. "No," she continued, "there must be more at
stake than the chairmanship."

"Abby was the person who suggested dinner in the email," Ruthie said. "Maybe Abby was snide to Willows over dinner, like she was to Kevin. We all saw her argue with Willows at the library."

Alice blew off the argument with a flick of her wrist. "Still not enough. When's that weird computer guy coming home from the West Coast? I believe the answer is in the encrypted folder."

"Mom," Kevin objected, "that could be something as simple as Abby's tax returns."

"Or, maybe not." Alice was not one to give in.

"I have Carl's cell phone number. I'll give him a call." I went to the guestroom, and Carl picked up on the fifth ring. "Are you in a meeting?"

"No, I'm headed home on the corporate jet."

"When will you arrive?"

"I'll get into Daytona Beach at about ten o'clock tonight. I'll call you when I land. Got to go—have to turn my phone off now." The line went dead.

I've never been able to sleep on airplanes, so there was a good chance that Carl would be too tired to do anything until the next morning, at the earliest. I hated to even ask for such a favor, but Alice was not one I wanted to trifle with. I went to the kitchen and refilled my wine glass for courage before I delivered the news. Penny Sue saw me and signaled me to bring the whole bottle, which I did. As they poured wine for themselves, I delivered the news that Carl wouldn't return until late and probably would be too worn out to work on the computer until the next day. He was already on the plane, and I didn't have time to tell him why I was calling, but I felt certain he could decode the message.

Alice graced us with a slight nod.

"Okay, now for the attempted robberies. What were they after? And how are Cobb and Marzano involved with Willows, if he is the culprit?" I asked.

"Woody should be able to tell us that," Penny Sue replied. "He has them in custody and is probably questioning them now. Besides, he has the green Volvo. A Volvo like the one seen driving on the beach after the first break-in attempt, so he surely knows who owns it by now. Leigh, give Woody a call. You have better luck with him than I do."

I stared at my fingernails and bit my lip. I was not anxious to speak to Woody, because I was afraid he'd confront me about my shooting Cobb with the taser. I knew he wouldn't suspect Ruthie; she was far too timid for that maneuver. I glanced up and locked eyes with Alice. It was a scary sight. Well, I'd have to face one of them. Woody or Alice? I chose Woody.

"I'll call from the bedroom," I said, as I paged through my cell for Woody's number. My call went to his voicemail, and I left a message. Then I tried his office number and got his assistant. She said he was questioning suspects, and there was no telling when he'd be available. I asked her to have him call me when he got a chance. She said she would. I supposed the suspects were Stuart Cobb and Andy Marzano. Then I thought of Leonard Kydd, and wondered if he'd given copies of the photos he'd taken of Susan's car to Woody. I found his cell phone number and dialed. He answered on the first ring.

"Yes, Leigh," he said, sounding weary.

"I'm sorry to bother you, but I wanted to thank you for your help last night."

"On the contrary, I should be thanking you. I believe we have Duffy's killers, so I can rest in peace." He paused a moment, then quickly added. "Not literally, of course. I didn't mean for all time."

I chuckled. "I know what you meant. The reason I'm calling—did you give copies of your photos of Susan Marzano's car to Woody?"

"Yes, I downloaded the pictures to my computer and put them on a flash drive for him last night. I delivered it first thing this morning. I also emailed the pictures to my office in New York for safekeeping. If the Marzanos are as influential as you say, I'm not taking any chances."

"Very smart. I wouldn't have thought of doing that."

"It's fairly standard in the news business. Everything must be backed up. After last night, I slept most of the day once I delivered the pictures. I'll probably stay for another day or two to tie up the loose ends on Duffy's autopsy and the drug ring. I hope we can get together before I leave."

"To be sure. You must come over for a congratulatory toast. We couldn't have gotten this far without your help. We hope last night's sting will clear Kevin of Abby's murder."

"You think those punks killed her?" Leonard asked.

"No, but we suspect they know who did and hope they'll spill the beans when questioned."

"Well, if I can assist, don't hesitate to ask. I'd say 'cheers,' but I'm not feeling particularly cheery right now. You know, Duffy and all. He was a fine reporter and a good friend."

"I understand. Please keep me posted on anything you find out, and I'll do the same."

"Absolutely. Best to all."

I sat on the end of the bed and thought about the sad tone in Leonard's voice. All this time I'd focused on drugs and books, but he'd lost a valued friend and colleague. Why didn't I see that? The man was in mourning. I took a deep breath and shook off my feeling of sadness. I had to go face Alice.

"Woody's tied up questioning suspects," I announced to the group in as light a tone as I could manage. "I left a message for him to call me." I snatched my wine and took a self-medicating sip. "I also called Leonard Kydd, the editor for *Vainglory*. He took a flash drive of the pictures he snappd of Susan's car to Woody this morning. So there's concrete proof she's involved."

Penny Sue piped up. "Well, you and Kydd saw her drive up to the book drop, right?"

Oh Lord, I hadn't thought of that. I might be a witness in another drug deal involving one of the most prestigious local families. Sweat started to bead on my forehead. "Yes, we did."

Penny Sue did an air karate chop. "Case closed. She and her son are headed to the slammer."

"Please don't say that," I pleaded. "I like New Smyrna Beach and would hate to move."

Alice gave me a big eye roll. "Don't be silly—you won't have to move. If they're as influential as you think they are, they'll work a deal, especially if the father is a criminal attorney. Now, the other guy with the pigtail may be in deep shit, but I'll lay money that mom skates and junior does minimal time, if any. If the deal includes the break-ins and how they knew about the books in the first place, junior may get off scot-free. The books are the key to Abby's murder."

"Well, they were after the books, and maybe Abby's computer," Penny Sue said. "You could see that from the video. Something in those boxes was valuable enough to attempt a break-in two nights in a row." Penny Sue glanced at the stack of boxes next to the credenza in her dining area. The books shipped down from Abby's apartment were still in their original cartons.

"Stuart Cobb went to Deland University, and Willows knew the books were at my place," I said. "He probably found that out from Woody while he was snitching on Kevin. If Cobb and Andy Marzano didn't want them for themselves, they were probably sent by Willows. It would be interesting to find out if they were Willows' students. Maybe Willows knew about Cobb's criminal past and hired them to steal Abby's research."

Alice gave Kevin a stern look. "Have you finished the inventory yet?"

His face went red. "No, ma'am."

"I know you've been reading the stuff on Abby's computer, but my gut says there's something in the books and encrypted file. We can't do anything about the file now, since the alien won't be home until late tonight. But you can damned sure finish the book inventory."

Kevin took a deep breath and puffed out his chest. "Yes, we're close to finishing, anyway."

"Then get to work," Alice said. "I'm going to bed.

Kevin divided the boxes into three groups—the ones already inventoried and two sections of corrugated cartons that needed attention. After we thoroughly washed our hands at Kevin's insistence, we broke into two teams. Penny Sue and I formed one team while Kevin and Ruthie made up the other.

Penny Sue and Ruthie listed the books that Kevin and I carefully unpacked. Many of the books were fairly new, but a few were so old the paper had turned brown and crumbled to the touch. We'd worked for about an hour, when Kevin suddenly stopped to examine a faded green book entitled *The History of Enterprise and Orange County, Florida.*

"I think this book is a duplicate." He turned to Ruthie. "Didn't we already inventory this book in another box?"

Ruthie crawled to the boxes they'd finished. In a few seconds she found the carton and the book. "Here it is. It was in one of the boxes taken from Abby's condo down here." She held it out to Kevin, but I snatched it first.

"Wait, I know that book! It's the one Abby bought from the book sale room at the library. I remember it because I thought it might be part of our rare book collection that ended up in the sale room by mistake."

Kevin took the book from me and compared the two copies. He checked the copyright pages, but given their age, it was nothing more than the name and address of a printer in England. "Why would Abby buy a book that she already owned?" he asked.

"Well, she only paid five dollars for it," I said. "Considering its age, she certainly knew she could sell it to another scholar for a nice profit."

My cell phone rang at that moment. It was Carl calling from Daytona Beach. He had his computer with him. Did we want him to swing by the condo on his way home? I briefly told him about the problem with the encrypted file. He responded, "Piece of cake."

"Yes, if you're not too tired, please come to Penny Sue's condo."

"I'll probably be there at about eleven o'clock. This way I can sleep tomorrow."

"That's terrific. We'll be here."

I quickly relayed our conversation to the group.

"Should we wake your mother up?" Ruthie asked Kevin. "You know how she hates to be left out."

Kevin shook his head vigorously. "No. If Carl can decrypt the file we'll wake her up; otherwise, she'll just be in the way. I love my mother, but she can be a pill."

No one said anything, because we all agreed.

As Penny Sue and I returned to our inventory, Kevin was intrigued by the two identical books. "You know, for all of my research, I don't recall ever encountering this book. There isn't even a date. And to think Abby had two copies." He stopped, suddenly, on the third page of the library-bought version. There, in black letters, was a stamp—*Property of Stanley Willows*. The blood drained from Kevin's face. "That's why Abby bought the book! It used to belong to Willows. But why would he donate such a rare book to the library?"

"Tax deduction?" Penny Sue offered.

"No scholar would give away a book this old that involved their own field," Kevin countered.

"Wait," Ruthie said loudly. "When Willows came over the other day and asked to look through Abby's books, he told me he'd recently moved to an oceanfront condo in New Smyrna Beach. He said there were so many desperate people who'd bought condos to flip, that ended up flopping, that he got a great deal. Maybe, in the course of the move, this book got mixed up with others he intended to donate to the library. Once he realized it was missing, he was desperate to find it."

"Why would he be so desperate?" I asked.

"Because it was rare and valuable?" Ruthie suggested.

"Abby also had a copy, so it can't be that rare," Kevin said. "At least not rare enough to kill someone."

"Well, what else could it be?' Penny Sue asked.

"I don't know, but I think we should complete the inventory," Kevin said. "For once, I believe Mom's right. The answer lies in the encrypted file."

"Well, we have an hour before we find out what it says."

Chapter 19

We finished the inventory and were sitting in the great room, waiting for Carl. The Weather Channel played in the background, but no one paid attention. We were all thinking about the duplicate books and their possible implication.

A little after eleven, there was a soft knock on the door. Kevin ran to let Carl in. Ah, youth! Carl looked fresh as a daisy, and we all looked like we'd been ridden hard and put up wet.

Despite his appearance, Carl was obviously tired and not into wasting time. "Where's the computer?" he asked. His own super-duper laptop and a few cables were stuffed under his arm. Kevin led him to the great room and pointed to the laptop computer on the coffee table.

"Can I get you something to drink?" Ruthie asked.

"A Pepsi would be great if you have one, but anything with caffeine will do. It's been a long day."

Before Ruthie returned with the drink, Carl had hooked his computer into Abby's and was scanning the folder. Honestly, the guy was a genius. He took one sip of the soda and decoded the file. "I figured it was one of the standard algorithms. I've saved the decrypted folder on the hard drive as *Folder Two*." He took another swallow of Pepsi. "I'll leave it to you to review the files and figure out what they mean. I'm tired and need to go home."

"Carl," I said, following him out, "we're so grateful."

"No big deal. This is child's play."

Child's play! I knew I needed to hire a ten-year-old to teach me about the new technology.

Carl left, and we all stood around looking at the computer and the book with Willows' name in it. Thankfully, Penny Sue said what we were thinking. "I'm too tired to mess with this. Let's get together early tomorrow, say eight, and review it." Everyone nodded, though I noticed Kevin's eyes were glued to the computer.

When Ruthie, Penny Sue, and I arrived the next morning, Alice was in her velour robe and Kevin had already read the decrypted files. He'd apparently stayed up all night. Of course, he had the most to lose.

We brought a pot of coffee and tray of freshly baked sweet rolls with us—Ruthie's idea. As we served up the food, Kevin explained his findings.

"The major file was Willows' dissertation. The other files in the folder compared his work to *The History of Enterprise and Orange County, Florida*. I'll skip through a lot, but Willows plagiarized his dissertation. I remember now that Abby critiqued a draft of Willows' dissertation and apparently recognized some of his passages, after she found the old book in New Jersey. I discovered a letter in the folder to a boyfriend or colleague at Yale. Abby said she planned to meet Willows for dinner and confront him about the plagiarism. Knowing Abby, I suspect she threatened to expose Willows to force him to drop out of the chairmanship competition. He was really the strongest candidate, considering he'd already worked there. I'm speculating, but that's probably the reason for the argument she had with Willows at the library. She had his copy of the book with her, because it came out of the box that was returned by Woody."

Kevin ran his hand across the stubble on his chin. "I know from experience that Abby would stop at nothing to get what she wanted.

"She also kept a diary on the computer, and there was an entry after she discovered Willows' book at the library. She wrote that it proved her theory and guaranteed that Willows would drop out of the competition. She also planned to blackmail Willows into raising questions about my credentials."

"So, Willows plagiarized his dissertation. Big deal," Penny Sue said.

Kevin gazed at her like she'd lost her mind. "Penny Sue, plagiarism would not only disqualify his dissertation, but his Ph.D. would have been rescinded! No Ph.D., no job, tenure, or chance for the chairmanship. Don't you see—the book with Willows' name was concrete proof that he cheated, and his career would be ruined."

"Oh."

As Kevin spoke, Ruthie paged through Willows' copy of the book. Suddenly she gasped, staring at the inside of the back cover. "Oh my God, look at this!" She pointed to a square patch, like a nicotine patch, that was riddled with pinpricks."

"Don't touch it," Penny Sue screamed. "There may be fingerprints."

"Right," Alice chimed in. "Remember the drawing of the marks on Abby's body? There was a square on her upper arm filled with dots. It said something about irregular concentrations of nicotine." She slapped her knee. "Darn, I wish we'd thought to make a copy of that report."

"I wonder if the pinpricks could have caused the irregular concentrations," Penny Sue mused. "Does anyone know a pharmacist?"

"I do, at Publix." I called my friend Beth, and asked her if pinpricks could compromise a nicotine patch.

"Are you kidding? Of course it would. Transdermal patches have a complex matrix designed to release the medicine in a constant dosage over time. Disrupt the matrix—like with pinpricks or cutting a patch in half—and the medicine would be delivered unevenly. Messing with a nicotine patch could easily cause too little or too much nicotine to get in a person's system."

"Could a big dose of nicotine cause a heart attack?" I asked.

"Absolutely. Leigh, you aren't trying to quit smoking, are you?"

"No, this isn't about me."

"Thank God. Whatever it's about, don't ever alter a transdermal patch, especially not one for blood pressure medicine, a painkiller, or nicotine. You could easily kill yourself."

"Kill yourself," I repeated. "Wow, I had no idea."

"If you know someone who's altered a patch, take it off, and get them to a hospital," Beth said seriously.

"No, you confirmed my suspicion and averted a disaster," I lied. "Thanks for your time. I'll see you soon." I hung up the phone and turned to face four gaping mouths. "An altered nicotine patch could cause a heart attack!"

"Especially if the person already had a patch on. Remember, the drawing indicated that Abby was wearing a patch on her shoulder blade," Kevin said.

"Why would she put on another patch?" Penny Sue asked.

"She didn't," Ruthie said excitedly. "Willows did it. He grabbed her arm when they argued in the library, remember? I'll bet he had the altered patch in the palm of his hand and just slapped it on her." Ruthie massaged her temples. "Let's see, how did it go?"

"Abby started to stomp away from Willows, but he snatched her arm and swung her around to face him. That's when he noticed we were watching them, so he walked away. Abby started to follow, but tripped, dropping her books. That's it! I know what happened. That's why she stayed in the bathroom so long," I shouted.

"What? What?" Penny Sue demanded.

I was so excited I couldn't stand still. "She faked the fall so she could hide the book in the stacks. Willows probably threatened her, and she was afraid he might try to steal the book. So, she waited until we left and went back to get it. Don't you remember that her right hand was clenched as if she'd been holding something? But, by that time, there was so much nicotine in her system that her heart gave out, and her hand relaxed enough for Willows' book to fall to the floor along with everything else."

"Yes, but how did the patch get inside the book?" Alice asked.

Penny Sue answered. "Abby was sweating like a pig. I'll bet she wiped perspiration from her arm, and she discovered the patch, or it came off in her hand. Abby realized that Willows slapped it on her, so she held on to it to prove he tried to kill her. It was probably in her hand when she pulled the book off the shelf. In fact, she may have put it in the book for safekeeping. Only her heart gave out!"

I reached in my pocket and pulled out my cell phone. "I'm calling Woody. That patch is the murder weapon, and the book proves Willows did it."

Woody said he'd send someone over for the book and Abby's computer. He also told me he'd put out an All Points Bulletin (APB) to have Willows picked up by the police. Alice brought out her gun to protect the evidence, and Penny Sue wrapped the book in plastic wrap with the patch still stuck inside. Kevin nervously channel surfed, Ruthie loaded the dishwasher, and I sat in stunned silence. Plagiarism and a nicotine patch. Who would have thought?

After what seemed like an eternity, but in reality was only about forty minutes, there was a knock on the door. We all bounced up to answer it, but Penny Sue beat us to the punch, followed by Kevin. It was Deputy Heather Brooks.

"I hear you people had an eventful morning," she said. "Woody sent me to make a pick up."

Kevin handed over the book and computer.

Heather grinned. "I've had a busy morning, too." She canted her head toward the patrol car. Her partner, Tommy, was riding shotgun, and there were two men in the backseat. "Guess who I found on the way over?"

By this time we'd all gathered in the hallway. "Willows?" Penny Sue exclaimed. "But who's the other guy?"

"Peter O'Brien. They claim they were on their way to survey some real estate."

"Peter?!"

"Yep, the men were right in front of us, in the drive-thru lane of Dunkin' Donuts, when I got a call from Woody and the APB came though. Poor guys. Their coffee cost a bundle, in more ways than one. Just as the coffee was passed over to them, I turned on my lights and gave the siren a couple of whoops. Both men were so startled they dumped the steaming coffee in their laps and jumped out of the car. By then Tommy and I were standing beside them and merely had to slap on the cuffs."

"Oh, my Lord!" Penny Sue was laughing so hard tears were streaming down her face. "What happened then?"

"Tommy put them in the backseat of our car and drove Willows' Honda to a parking spot. I pulled up and got our coffees." Heather suppressed a grin. "I didn't want to hold up the line, you know."

"That's unbelievable," Kevin said, cracking a smile.

Heather grinned widely. "Yeah, but it's not so clear cut anymore. Willows claims that O'Brien killed Abby with the nicotine patch over a real estate deal."

My hand went to my throat, as I recalled the scene of O'Brien and Abby entering the library for the debate. O'Brien did have his arm around Abby to shield her from the crowd. It was her left arm, the one with the square patch, and not a round one like all of the others. My gosh, we were right about *how*, but might be wrong about *who*. "I saw O'Brien with his hand on Abby's arm at the library. Willows may be telling the truth. Is that why you're taking O'Brien in?"

"For now, he's under arrest for assaulting an officer. The old guy kneed Tommy in the crotch for trying to cuff him. That's excuse enough to get fingerprints and confirm Willows' story one way or another, assuming there are fingerprints on this patch. Don't worry," Heather said, shifting the computer to her other hand. "I'm sure Woody will report back to you. After all, you guys probably saved the county a ton of money. In fact, Woody's probably so happy that he might even be pleasant for a few days."

"One quick question," Penny Sue said. "Do you think the Marzanos will do time?"

"Probably not. I heard the two boys sang like birds on the drug/burglary operation. Your break-in had nothing to do with drugs, though Papa convinced Andy to give that up in a deal to avoid jail. It seems Andy and his friend were Willows' students that he hired to help him move into a new condo in New Smyrna Beach. The dumbbells accidentally switched the boxes of books intended for donation with the ones headed for Willows' condo. They donated the valuable books to the library and took the rejects to Willows' place. He didn't realize anything was wrong, until Abby confronted him with the fact that she'd purchased his copy of the book from the library, and that it proved he'd plagiarized his dissertation. According to Andy Marzano, Willows threatened everything short of murder if the boys didn't get the book back. That's why they kept trying to break into your condo."

"What about Susan?" Penny Sue asked.

"Momma Marzano claimed she was only following her son to see what he was up to. But the c-notes found in her possession were marked by the Drug Task Force, so she could be charged. It's iffy. I doubt they'll pursue it if they nab the ringleaders of the drug gang. I give her credit, though. The lady played it smart. If not for your sting and the marked bills, there's no way Susan could have been tied to the drugs."

Heather left, and we dragged ourselves back to the living room still laughing at the thought of Willows' and O'Brien's steaming crouches. We had barely snuggled into our usual seats when there was another knock on the door.

"Dammit, you know it's Guthrie!" Penny Sue said as she stomped down the hall. "He saw the police car and just had to find out what happened." She jerked the door open and shrieked.

Then a deep male voice said, "Long time no see, Honey Bunny. How about lunch at the Riverview?"

Epilogue

We were sitting at my dining table, going over the blueprints for Ruthie's new bookstore and apartment. The "we" in question were Ruthie, Penny Sue, me, Kevin, and Rich. Although the DAFFODILS reunion began on a down note, it turned out okay. Kevin was chosen for the History Department Chair of Deland University, and was staying with Ruthie in my master suite until her apartment was finished. I'd moved into one of my guestrooms, which was all I needed. Penny Sue and Rich were staying next door. Alice had gone home. (Praise the Lord!) Guthrie still dropped in from time to time, lonely without his partner, Timothy.

At nine a.m. the phone rang. It was Woody. "We finally have the fingerprint results," Woody said. "The prints on both the nicotine patch and strip container match O'Brien. He killed Abby and tried to implicate Kevin by slipping the container in the box when I gave it to Penny Sue. That was a stroke of luck. He'd planned to put the container in another box, but when I gave Abby's materials to Penny Sue, it provided the perfect opportunity. Stupidity on my part."

Woody was growing up. At least he acknowledged a mistake.

"After intensive interrogation, O'Brien admitted that Willows was hired to trump up a reason for the government to sell part of the Canaveral Seashore Park. Willows was regarded as one of their most convincing experts because of his book on Central

Florida. When Abby came forward threatening Willows' credentials, O'Brien told him to take care of Abby, or he would do it himself. Millions were at stake! Willows knew Abby was trying to quit smoking and told O'Brien that a second patch would kill her, but Willows couldn't bring himself to do it. So, O'Brien arranged to meet Willows in the library parking lot before the debate, and he slapped the patch on Abby's arm as they struggled through the crowd at the front door."

"Heavens! Does Willows get off scot-free?"

"Hardly," Woody replied. "He's being charged with conspiracy to commit murder, as well as your burglaries."

"Does this clear up all of the beachfront break-ins?" I asked.

"No, but we're making real progress with some of the new information."

"Does that mean we don't have to hold our breath each time there's a knock on the front door?" I quipped.

I could almost see Woody smile. "Maybe, for a while."